DOWN IN FLAMES

DONNY'S Inferno

DOWN IN FLAMES

· 2 ·

P. W. CATANESE

ALADDIN

NEW YORK   LONDON   TORONTO   SYDNEY   NEW DELHI

ALADDIN

An imprint of Simon & Schuster Children's Publishing Division
1230 Avenue of the Americas, New York, New York 10020
First Aladdin hardcover edition April 2017
Text copyright © 2017 by P. W. Catanese
Jacket illustration copyright © 2017 by Jeff Nentrup
All rights reserved, including the right of reproduction
in whole or in part in any form.
ALADDIN and related logo are registered trademarks of Simon & Schuster, Inc.
For information about special discounts for bulk purchases,
please contact Simon & Schuster Special Sales at 1-866-506-1949
or business@simonandschuster.com.
The Simon & Schuster Speakers Bureau can bring authors to your live event.
For more information or to book an event contact the Simon & Schuster Speakers
Bureau at 1-866-248-3049 or visit our website at www.simonspeakers.com.
Jacket designed by Jessica Handelman
Interior designed by Nina Simoneaux
The text of this book was set in Perpetua.
Manufactured in the United States of America 0317 FFG
2 4 6 8 10 9 7 5 3 1
This book has been cataloged with the Library of Congress.
ISBN 978-1-4814-3803-2 (hc)
ISBN 978-1-4814-3805-6 (eBook)

For my sequels:
Kristina, Michael, and Andrew

CHAPTER 1

What if you were hit by a train?" asked Donny. "Could you survive that?"

Angela Obscura, beast of the underworld, traveler to the mortal realm, member of the Infernal Council, and friend of Donny Taylor, popped another cheese curd into her mouth and chewed it while considering the question. "You mean," she said after a gulp, "hit and bounced off, or run over and scraped underneath?"

"Both," Donny said. "I mean, either."

"Bounced off, I'd probably be okay. Run over, not so much. I'm not completely impervious, you know. If an infernal being's wounds are bad enough, all the heat and steam leaks out. Then you're gone, good-bye."

Donny nodded and grabbed another curd. "But fire doesn't hurt you, right?"

"Don't talk with your mouth full," she scolded, one of

her own cheeks puffed with food. "And no, I thought that was obvious. I'm fireproof, right down to the hair."

"Oh yeah, that makes sense," Donny said. Angela's hair, which returned in a different length and color every time she switched from her monstrous to human forms, was currently long, auburn, and abundant with curls. She'd also been remade with a cinnamon sprinkle of freckles across the bridge of her nose.

Donny pointed with a curd. "What if you were electrocuted?"

"This one time, when electricity was kind of new, I didn't know about the no-appliances-near-the-bathtub thing, and I got a pretty good shock. It would have killed you, but I was fine."

"How about hit by lightning?"

"Happened once, when I climbed a tree for a better look at a storm. Apparently you're not supposed to do that, either. That hurt like crazy, and I'm pretty sure I saw my skeleton for a second."

"Wow." Donny thought for a while. "What if you fell a long way, like out of an airplane?"

She brushed her hands with a napkin and dropped it onto her empty plate. "Donny Taylor, are you trying to figure out how to kill me?"

He laughed. "No. It's just . . . It's just cool. I'm curious."

"No doubt you are," she said. "So, the verdict on cheese curds?"

"Pretty great," he said. They were sitting at a sidewalk table under a blue umbrella on a street in Milwaukee. Across the street and a block over, he could see where the Milwaukee River flowed toward Lake Michigan, barely a mile away. Back in Brooklyn or Manhattan, where he'd spent his first twelve years, the streets would have been bustling with crowds and crackling with the weird, grimy energy of that frantic metropolis. This town was sleepy in comparison and sparsely peopled, but perfectly pleasant, especially on a crisp fall day.

Speaking of pretty great, he thought to himself, looking at his friend across the table. A person might possibly think Angela Obscura was anywhere from fifteen to nineteen, but they would *certainly* think that she was beautiful in a way that was different from all the other beautiful people. The truth was that she was approximately one hundred and fifty years old, and wasn't human at all. Angela's left hand, currently clad in an elbow-length red glove, was always covered with reptilian scales. There was an ancient gold bracelet on that wrist, and if she were to take it off, the rest of her body would quickly transform.

Just a few months before, Angela had saved Donny from a fiery death. In return, he'd promised to assist her on her missions in the mortal world. That was the deal, anyway. Most of the time it felt like she just dragged him along because she wanted the company.

"Not a bad little town, eh?" she said. "It all smells like bratwurst and beer, don't ya know?"

Donny laughed. "Kind of."

"And, golly, look at all the sandy-haired, earnest Midwesterners. Bless their hearts." She put a fist to her mouth and burped. "Well, I guess we should go. Now that my craving for cheese curds has been vanquished." She pushed her chair back and stood up.

"We didn't pay for the food," Donny said.

She reached into her handbag, pulled out a hundred-dollar bill, and looked questioningly at Donny. "That'll cover it, right?"

"With, like, an eighty-dollar tip," Donny observed. But Angela was already on the move and five paces away. Donny anchored the bill to the table with a saltshaker, grabbed the empty backpack Angela had given him, and followed.

Before Donny could catch up, a car slowed beside her. It was filled with guys who looked like college students. The driver, a brawny blond quarterback type, put his elbow out the window and patted his horn so that it gave a little squeak. He grinned at Angela. "Hey, girl. You're pretty sweet, you know that?"

Angela gave him a sideways glance and rolled her eyes.

"C'mon—don't be that way," the driver said. "Why can't you be friendly? Hey! I'm talking to you!" He kept the car rolling at the same pace that Angela was walking. His friends inside the car laughed.

4

Donny kept a few paces back. Part of him was twitchy and nervous, but part of him wondered how this would play out. This guy had no idea what he was dealing with.

"Hey, how about a smile, girl? I bet you have a pretty smile."

Angela stopped. She pivoted on her feet, turning to face the car. The driver slowed to a stop and grinned at her. Inside the car, the friends nudged one another and stared.

Angela's mouth spread into a broad, toothy smile, but Donny recognized a fiery look in her eyes. *Uh-oh,* he thought. She stepped off the sidewalk, right next to the car. Before the driver could say another word, she put two hands on his side-view mirror, tugged, and snapped it off. There were wires inside, and she pulled it sharply back to break them free. Then she turned the mirror to herself, looked into it, and announced: "Look, I'm smiling now!"

The driver stared back, his mouth open. His friends burst into laughter, and the one behind the driver reached forward and slapped him on the shoulder.

Angela tossed the mirror through the window and onto the driver's lap. "Now you can use that to take a good look at yourself." She blew him a kiss and walked away.

Donny heard the clunk of the car being thrown into park. The driver's door swung open and the driver shot out, the broken mirror in one hand. "Hey!" he shouted.

Angela turned, and Donny took two steps to the side. He knew from the look on her face that she was about to hit the driver with a telepathic beam of sheer terror, and he didn't want to be anywhere in the line of fire. Even from where he stood, he felt the tiny hairs on his arms tingling. The driver opened his mouth again, almost certainly to bark something truly unpleasant, but instead of speaking, he moaned with fear as his eyes bugged from his face. Inside the car, his friends sensed it too. Donny heard their manic, high-pitched shrieks: "Get back in the car! Let's get out of here!"

The driver staggered backward, stumbling over the curb. The mirror slipped from his hand and clattered onto the pavement. He fumbled his way back into the car, tugging the door shut behind him. The tires squealed, spitting blue smoke, and the car accelerated away, driving straight through a red light. Cars that were crossing the intersection slammed on their brakes to avoid a collision. The driver's bad day got even worse, because a police car appeared from around the corner, firing up its siren and flashing its lights.

Angela rolled her shoulders and cracked her knuckles as Donny jogged up beside her. "You really need to be careful," he said. "I mean, that guy was a jerk, but he could have hurt someone just now."

She giggled. "What do you suppose he'll tell the officer?"

"That there's a crazy girl down the street with gorilla muscles," Donny said. "We shouldn't attract police attention, you know."

"Why not?"

"Because I'm still a missing kid. Remember?"

"Oh, ha-ha, yeah," Angela said. "Well, we only came for the curds. And something almost as good. Come on— it'll be dark soon. Time to get to the marina."

CHAPTER 2

Long after sunset, they waited in the shadows of the building beside the marina. The slips were filled with sailing ships, cabin cruisers, and other powerboats. The water was calm, protected inside a long stone seawall. Beyond that barrier, the vast waters of Lake Michigan glittered with fractured light under a crescent moon.

Nobody was in sight, though a few of the boats had lights on, as if the owners might be spending the night inside.

"Are you sure this is safe?" Donny asked.

"Courage, Cricket," she replied. She pointed to one of the biggest of the boats, an expensive-looking cabin cruiser. "That's the one." It was as big as a small house, nearly three stories high with a tower perched on top. A floodlight was trained on its stern. Donny read the name in curving letters above the waterline: BEAN COUNTER.

"*Bean Counter*," Angela said, and snorted. "He should've

just called it *Embezzler*. Come on—let's check it out." With a final look left and right, she walked casually out from the shadows and onto the dock.

"Hey," Donny whispered. "Security cameras? Witnesses? Hello?"

"Land's sakes, you worry too much. Just walk like you belong here. Who'd be suspicious of an adorable girl and her little brother?"

Donny frowned at that characterization as he sped up to her side. Something about her referring to him as her brother, even as a cover story, irked him in a way he couldn't quite define. "Nobody says 'land's sakes' anymore," he grumbled. His heartbeat accelerated as she hopped onto the boat. He jumped on after her and followed her to the open deck on the stern. She headed straight for the door that led inside.

"Not even locked," she said, swinging it open. "Thought for sure I'd have to rip it off the hinges."

Donny was going to mention that an unlocked door didn't seem like a good sign, but it was too late. She had already slipped inside. He followed her into the dark interior.

"Must be a light switch in here somewhere," she said. He heard her hand slide along the wall until she found the switch and flicked it up.

Donny was about to remark on how luxurious and roomy the boat was, until a more important detail became apparent. Someone had been here and made a mess of the place. Cushions had been pulled off the furniture and sliced open. Cabinet doors had been flung wide. Panels on the walls and floor had been torn out, exposing the spaces behind and below.

"Aw, for crying out loud," Angela said, putting her fists on her hips. "Well, he warned us about this."

Before Donny could ask who had warned them or what the warning was about, a narrow door opened and a man stepped out. It was bad enough that someone had caught them, but even worse, the man had a gun in his hand.

"Who are you?" he said, nearly growling the words. He didn't look like the violent type—he looked more like a businessman, with thinning close-cropped hair and glasses. He was dressed in a black turtleneck shirt and dark pants.

"Eww, were you in the bathroom?" Angela asked, wrinkling her nose. She edged sideways until she'd put herself between Donny and the man with the gun.

"What? Yes, but—never mind that!" the man snapped.

"You're Francis, aren't you?" Angela said. "Walter said you might get here first."

"Walter s-said . . ." the man sputtered, and then recovered. "What do you mean? Walter's dead! How do you know my name?"

Francis was using the gun to gesture, pointing it at Angela and Donny to emphasize his words. Angela put her hands over her face, and her knees began to tremble. "Please, mister, don't hurt us," she whined. "We're just a couple of kids. You're scaring me with that gun!" Donny didn't find the display convincing, but Francis lowered the gun for a moment, looking bewildered.

Angela must have been peeking between her fingers. Her arm was a blur as it shot out and snatched the gun. Francis stared at his empty hand as if a magic trick had been performed.

"So you didn't find it?" she said, holding the gun the way someone might hold a rotting banana.

Francis raised his hands halfway, unsure if he should be surrendering. "Find what? I wasn't looking for anything."

Angela shook her head with disdain as she looked at the trashed interior of the boat. Then she rushed at him, using the palm of her hand to shove him into the tiny bathroom. "Get back in there, Francis," she said with a final push that sent him staggering into the far wall. She tugged the door closed. "And flush it, you pig!"

She handed the gun to Donny. "Shoot him if he comes out," she said loudly.

Donny shook his head and whispered back angrily. "I'm not shooting anyone! I hate guns!" He laid the gun on the kitchen counter.

Angela jabbed her thumb at the bathroom door. "*He* doesn't know that!" From the other side of the door, they heard a flush, and Angela clapped a hand across her mouth to stifle a laugh. The laugh turned into a snort, and she kept chuckling as she opened the freezer door in the galley and pulled out what appeared to be a frozen fish wrapped in aluminum foil.

"Fish? That's what we came here for?" Donny asked.

Angela smirked and tore the foil open. Inside were stacks of hundred-dollar bills arranged in the shape of a fish. She reached into the freezer and pulled out five more just like it.

Donny nodded, finally understanding. This was how Angela got her endless supply of cash. A man named Walter, the owner of the boat, had died and, like the evil soul he was, ended up in the underworld, which was currently known to its denizens as Sulfur. The dead were encouraged to reveal any hidden money they'd stashed away—and Walter had hidden these bills here before he'd died.

Angela twirled her finger, gesturing for Donny to turn around. She shoved the bundles of foil-wrapped money into the empty backpack that Donny had worn all day. "You should have checked the freezer, Francis!" she shouted at the door. "The money you two stole was wrapped in foil, just like Walter said!"

"Are you *serious*?" came the muffled reply. "In the *freezer*? I looked everywhere! Wait, how did you know about the money? Who are you anyway?"

"I'm a hundred-and-fifty-year-old archdemon of the

underworld, and my little buddy is the runaway son of a hit man." She grinned at Donny, who shook his head grimly at her.

"Oh yeah? You think that's funny? Well, you know where you can go, miss!"

Angela guffawed. "Yeah, look me up when you get there."

On the way off the boat, she took the gun from Donny and tossed it into the lake.

"So this is where the money comes from, huh?" he said as they left the marina and walked along a footpath in the park nearby. "People hide it like this?"

"Sometimes it's in banks or safe-deposit boxes, and we have people who are good at retrieving it," she answered. "I don't usually go after the cash myself, but this one looked like fun. Plus, I had a craving for cheese curds."

"So that guy Francis, and Walter—they stole the money from some company?"

"Uh-huh. Embezzled it."

"Shouldn't we give the money back to the company instead of keeping it?"

She gave his shoulder a gentle push. "You're hilarious."

"That wasn't a joke."

"Chortle," she replied.

CHAPTER 3

They caught a cab a few blocks from the marina. A ten-minute drive brought them to a stately home built with cream-colored brick, in a well-to-do neighborhood only a few blocks from the lake. A grandmotherly woman answered the doorbell, opening the door a crack. She nodded when she saw Angela. "Leaving already?"

"Yes, but we had a splendid time," Angela replied.

The woman opened the door wide. "Can I make you some tea?"

"Aren't you a darling?" Angela said as they stepped inside. "But no, thanks, we should be getting back. Don't mind us—we know the way."

She and Donny went through a door in the main hallway that led down an old set of creaky stairs. In the basement was a tall fireplace, empty except for pipes running across the bottom. When Angela turned the knob of a timer that was set into the wall, fire burst forth from the pipes. Donny caught a whiff of propane.

Angela cupped her hands beside her mouth and whispered into the flames. A moment later a space appeared inside the wall of fire, covered by a thin sheet of ash. The dark space expanded until it was wide enough to step through. Angela poked her finger into the ash, and the sheet crumbled into tiny flakes. On the other side, Donny saw the familiar passage carved from stone, and the strange little demon named Porta who controlled the fire-portal on the other side.

They stepped through the hole in the fire, leaving the mortal realm and entering the infernal world of Sulfur.

CHAPTER 4

Donny used to feel like he was losing his mind when he stepped into the underworld. But lately he was starting to believe that a person could get used to almost anything. They left the fire-portal behind and walked down the curving tunnel. As usual there was a hint of rotten-egg smell in the air. Next was the ominous door guarded by a tall, cordial monster in a suit of armor. Then came the short walk through another passage that ended with the mind-blowing vista of a vast, cavernous world with mile-high ceilings propped up by titanic pillars.

Clouds made of luminous vapor billowed overhead, bathing everything in reddish-golden light. There were towns and cities at the feet of some of the pillars, with architecture ranging from crude to exquisite and ancient to modern, some in pristine condition and some in ruins from the great war that had happened decades before. The rest was a strange, twisted wilderness with vast stretches of undulating stone, fissures and craters, eerie formations of rock, and forests of dark mushrooms and ferns. A river slithered through the midst of it all, glittering under the burning clouds. On it, Donny saw one of the ferries, crowded with the souls of the newly arrived dead.

But the most significant feature amid all this strangeness, more vast than any earthly canyon, was the Pit of Fire. Once the great pit had been filled with torturous flame and the howling, suffering dead, but since the reform, it had been extinguished and now only steamed with lingering heat. These days the dead were ferried to the vast Caverns of Woe instead, where they spent years spellbound, trapped in dreams woven from their own misdeeds. That fate was hard to bear, but not as cruel as the flames, of course. And, unlike the flames, a soul that entered the Caverns of Woe could someday be released and allowed to move on. It might take decades or centuries or even millennia, but redemption was possible.

Donny stared at the bizarre world in all its strange grandeur. It was fearsome. It was unimaginable. It was terrible.

It was home.

They were nearing the Pillar Obscura, Angela's ancestral home, when she said, "Brace yourself." Donny looked down the path and saw a blur coming at them.

"ARGL! ARGLBRGL!" the blur shouted.

"Easy, boy," Donny pleaded, holding out his arms. Fortunately, it was Angela that the imp plowed into at the speed of a car. She could handle the impact, but it still knocked her a dozen feet backward, where she landed in a giggly pile.

"Hello, Arglbrgl," she said, scratching the imp behind the ear. Arglbrgl looked at Donny and bounded over, knocking him down with only a fraction of the force.

"Thanks for taking it easy on me," Donny said as Arglbrgl's forked, raspy tongue scraped across his cheek. The imp was shaped like a huge horned toad and was covered in loose skin. When he was wary or angry, he could double in girth by puffing himself out with sharp spines protruding everywhere. Among friends, he kept himself deflated. His short tail, which ended in the shape of a spade, wagged furiously.

A few more minutes along the path brought them into the city that surrounded the pillar. They passed strange beings of all types. There were gargoylelike imps, scary demons, and imposing archdemons, along with others who looked human. That last group might have been archdemons in human form, or more likely one of the souls of the dead who had assumed physical shape upon arriving in Sulfur. It was less likely that they were plain old people. A living human being like Donny was the rarest creature of all in Sulfur.

When they arrived at Angela's home, carved into the

stone of the enormous Pillar Obscura, a familiar being opened the door for them. It was Zig-Zag, the archdemon who served as Angela's advisor. Donny had almost gotten used to the fact that Zig-Zag had two heads, each with one eye, one ear, and a sort of half nose with a single nostril.

"Welcome back," said the head on the left.

"Zig-Zag, you old so-and-so," Angela purred.

"Hi, Zig. Hi, Zag," Donny said, speaking to each head in turn. They nodded and smiled back.

"Did you have a successful trip, Angela?" asked Zag.

"Got the two things I wanted. Cash and curds," Angela said.

"And did you enjoy your return to the mortal world, Donny?" asked Zig.

Donny paused, thinking about that moment on the boat with a gun pointed his way, and how he'd stared into the black hole of its barrel, waiting for death to come flying out. "The cheese curds were good," he finally said. He looked around the room. "Is Tizzy asleep?" Tizzy was the seven-year-old bundle of effervescence who Angela had found as an abandoned baby.

"She is," said Zag.

Zig smiled at Angela. "We have news. I think we have identified the next candidate in line for one of the council seats. It should make you very happy."

Zag sighed. "Unfortunately, Zig is correct," he moaned. Donny grinned. As usual, Zig and Zag did not see eye-to-eye, especially when it came to the politics of Sulfur. Zig was all in favor of the great reform that resulted in the extinguishing of the Pit of Fire. Zag always thought the old ways were the best ways.

"I was going to hit the sack," Angela said, "but now you've got me curious."

Donny had been worn-out by his brush with danger. "I'm going to bed," he said. "I'll see you guys tomorrow." He went upstairs and down the stone hallway to his bedroom. He passed Tizzy's room, where Nanny sat in a chair outside the door.

Donny always had to stifle a laugh when he looked at Nanny. She was a plump reptilian imp dressed like someone's demented idea of a traditional British storybook nanny. At the moment she (if Nanny even was a she) wore brown tights, a dress with long sleeves and puffy shoulders, a white apron, and a flat hat with a plastic flower sticking up from one side.

He kept to the far side of the hall, because Nanny was baring her sharp, crooked teeth. Fortunately, Angela had given her strict orders not to attack or bite him anymore. "Hi, Nanny," he said with a wave.

"Nanny no bite," she muttered.

"Right. Nice to see you, too."

It wasn't long before he'd washed up, brushed his teeth, and flopped into his insanely comfortable canopy bed. *Princes must sleep in beds like this,* he thought. There were definitely perks to living with Angela Obscura.

He smiled. But as he dozed off, his mind turned back to that gun and the close call on the boat. His dreams were haunted by all the terrors he'd faced since arriving in a place that, only a few months before, he would have said didn't really exist.

CHAPTER 5

The next morning Donny's mood improved when Tizzy dragged him out of bed to play a board game. As soon as Angela came downstairs, they headed out the door and to the diner.

It still felt strange to find a classic diner tucked among buildings that looked hundreds or thousands of years old. But there it was, with its checkerboard floor, a long, shiny counter lined with stools, and a row of booths on the other side. The place felt like it came out of the 1940s or '50s, and so did its only employee, Cookie. Cookie was human, or at least she used to be. Now she was basically a solid ghost, because she was one of the souls who'd been useful enough to be spared punishment. She worked in the diner, cooking for archdemons with a craving for human food, and the occasional mortal. Considering that she'd done something bad enough to be sent to the underworld, Donny thought she was pretty nice. And she sure could cook.

Donny demolished a grilled blueberry muffin, a ham and cheese omelet, way too much bacon, and a glass of milk, then sat happily back with a full belly. Tizzy ran to the jukebox, fired up some old rock and roll songs from the fifties, and danced by herself at the other end of the diner.

"All righty, Cricket," Angela said to Donny, pouring herself another cup of tea. "We have a new assignment on our hands."

"Uh-oh," Donny said.

"Uh-oh what?" Angela shot back. "Where's the enthusiasm?"

"It's just that so far, whenever you tell me we have a mission, I end up nearly getting killed."

"Aw, c'mon. Name one time."

"In Brooklyn, when that demon thing knocked me off the fire escape and tried to claw me to death. And just now in Milwaukee, when that guy waved the gun at me. That's not all, but I'm just saying, I don't think you worry a lot about my safety."

She waved that thought away with the back of her hand. "Safety, shmafety. You'll be fine."

Donny frowned. He wasn't so sure. "Well, what's the assignment?"

She raised two fingers. "It's twofold. First, as you know, we're down a couple of members of the council. So we'll head to the Pillar Cataracta, almost at the far end of

Sulfur. Ungo Cataracta lives there. Since he appears to be in favor of keeping the Pit of Fire extinguished, I'm going to talk him into joining the council."

"That doesn't sound very dangerous," Donny said.

"Exactly! You worry too much. Now then: part two of our assignment is to help Ungo track down a mysterious beast that's on a murder spree."

Donny sighed. "That sounds *extremely* dangerous."

"You'll be fine," Angela cooed, patting him on the knee. "I could use all the help I can get on this, so you really need to come."

"I don't see how I can help—"

"Of course you can," she interrupted. "Listen, Donny, this is important. I need Ungo on the Infernal Council. Invitations are given based on the prestige of the pillar and the family. If Ungo Cataracta declines, the next invitee may not see things my way. If I can help Ungo catch this monster, maybe he's more likely to accept the invitation."

"Why wouldn't he accept anyway? Isn't it, like, a big honor to be on the council?"

"You've obviously never governed anything. It's an honor, but a crummy one. You sit around with a bunch of blowhards and argue about stuff for what feels like centuries." She leaned in to stare at Donny with those luminous eyes that were somewhere between black and purple. "But anyway, you understand that I need you, right? Don't forget: you promised to help me the first time we met, when

I saved you from the fire. And I also rescued you from Havoc's lair. . . ." She tilted her head and batted her lashes.

That much was true, Donny knew. If it weren't for Angela, he wouldn't be alive. "Yeah," he said. "Sure. Of course I'll go."

CHAPTER 6

They walked up the stone steps toward the exit from Sulfur. Donny wore a backpack with a few days' worth of stuff, as Angela had advised. She had a big leather satchel slung over one shoulder. At her side she wore a scabbard, and Donny saw the grip of a sword at the top. He knew that weapon well.

"You brought the flaming sword," he said.

"Yup. You can tell I mean business."

As usual, the monstrous creature named Grunyon was guarding the doorway that led to the fire-portal. He was easily eight feet tall and clad in armor from head to toe.

"Circus peanuts?" Grunyon asked. He was in the habit of requesting some earthly treat to devour each time Angela ventured to the mortal realm.

"Seriously, Grunyon, I didn't think anybody ate those nasty things," Angela said. "But I'm sorry to tell you that I won't be spending any time on Earth right now. We're just hitting a way station so we can get to the Pillar Cataracta. Maybe next time." Grunyon's head sagged at the news, but he opened the door for Angela and Donny to pass through.

"What do you mean, *way station*?" Donny asked as they walked down the curving tunnel.

"Ah, let me explain," Angela said. "We can't use fire-portals to go from point to point in Sulfur. Nobody knows why. It just doesn't work. So we'll go to a way station in the mortal realm, and from there we can jump to a different place in Sulfur."

"But we took a chariot a long way to the Caverns of Woe," Donny pointed out. "And to the refinery. Why don't we do that now?"

"Don't be dense. Those places were relatively close; plus, they don't have portals nearby. So the chariots were the quickest way to go. But the Pillar Cataracta is much, much farther. It would take us days by chariot."

The orange glow of the fire-portal grew stronger as they approached. They came around the final bend in the stone corridor, and there was the wall of brilliant ruby-red flame, flowing upward in an almost liquid style. It looked like a waterfall running in reverse.

Sitting beside the fire was the tiny hunched figure of Porta the keeper, cloaked in a dark, shabby robe. Anyone might have thought that it was a child inside that costume. Donny knew better. Porta always made him nervous—but that was probably because of the nasty weapon propped beside her chair, a club with vicious spikes jutting from its head like a steel flower. Her hand edged toward the weapon and her hooded head lifted by a fraction as they approached.

"Hello, Porta," Angela said with a wave of her hand. "We'll be traveling to the Pillar Cataracta. What way stations are available?"

Porta relaxed and took her hand from the shaft of the club. She turned slowly to the wall of flame. She reached out and made a broad circular gesture with her arms. A round bulge appeared in the flame and transformed into a fiery depiction of Earth. All of the globe, land and sea, was made of that deep-red fire, with the oceans darkest of all. Porta wiggled her fingers at the map, and points of light appeared across the land.

"There were a lot more lights the last time we did this," Donny said.

"We're only looking at way stations this time, and those are special. They're well hidden, and not so numerous." Angela hummed to herself as she watched the globe spin. Donny recognized the continents as they rotated past. North America rolled out of sight, and the dark Pacific passed by. In the middle of that darkness he saw a single point of light. *Hawaii,* he guessed. Then he saw Australia to the south, with just two spots of light. Next Asia came into view, and Angela pointed. "Oh, that one!" she cried. "That's the one."

Porta swept her hands as if drawing the scent of a flower to her nose, and that portion of the globe came into closer view. She reached out, her fingertips brushing the wall of flame, and made a diamond shape between her forefingers and thumbs. When she drew her hands apart again, the diamond shape grew. The flames within darkened to black and burnt out, leaving a layer of papery ash behind. Donny knew that an earthly destination was on the other side of that flimsy parchment. All they had to do was walk right through it.

"Here we go," Angela said. She took Donny by the wrist. The ash disintegrated as they stepped into another world.

CHAPTER 7

A temple, Donny thought as soon as they'd entered the beautiful stone-walled room. After the heat of Sulfur, a world that always felt like a Florida summer, the blast of cool air that greeted him was sweet relief.

"Hello, keeper," Angela said. Donny turned to see who she was talking to. Beside the fire was a creature the size and shape of Porta, dressed in a similar cloak and hood. Like Porta, this creature had weapons next to her chair. In this case, it was a row of foot-long daggers, sitting in a bucket like a bouquet of flowers. The keeper took one dagger by the blade and raised it over her shoulder, ready to launch it directly at Donny's torso.

"Wait!" Angela cried. "This mortal is with me. Donny, show her the mark on your palm."

Donny's hand shot up, displaying the symbol that Angela had embedded there when they'd first met: a winged *O* that stood for Obscura, her family name. The keeper's head angled to one side. Then she relaxed and set the blade back down inside the bucket.

"Yikes," Donny muttered. Sometimes he forgot that unauthorized mortals were not tolerated in Sulfur. And apparently not in its way stations, either. He took a second glance at his palm, because he'd noticed something peculiar. The symbol used to be distinct and almost pure white, as if his skin were bleached. But now it seemed to be fading. "Look," he said. "It's going away."

"Yeah, it'll do that over time. I'll freshen it up for you soon," she replied.

Donny rubbed the mark with his other thumb. Then he allowed himself to appreciate the beauty and antiquity of whatever this place was that they'd come to. He spun in a circle to take it all in. The high walls were natural rock, but almost completely etched with carvings. Some of them were words, with ancient characters that looked a little like stick figures. It was vaguely familiar, as if he'd seen it somewhere in history class or a museum. Not Egyptian hieroglyphics, or ancient Chinese, but not too different from either of those. The rest of the carvings were bold patterns or animal forms. At a glance he saw lion heads and elephants and two-headed birds and even faces that looked like the arch-demons of Sulfur.

Halfway through his turn, he once again faced the

fire-portal through which they had entered, and this time he took a closer look at the fire. The flames were coming out of a pile of rocks in a deep niche at the back of the chamber—blue at the edges, with a bright wave of orange in the middle. He hadn't seen anything like this in their travels so far. Typically the fires they passed through on Earth came from propane, or even an old-fashioned wood fire. But this came out of the ground itself, like the portal in the infernal world.

"Wait, are we still in Sulfur?"

"Nope," said Angela. "You're looking at a natural eternal flame. This one's been coming out of the ground here for thousands of years. These happen around the globe. People know about lots of them—but not all of them. We keep the best ones to ourselves."

Donny stared at the flame as it rippled like a pennant. "How does it work? I mean, why is there fire coming out of the ground?"

"Oh, natural gas leaking out of crevices, something like that," Angela told him. "It started burning a long time ago and won't stop until the gas runs out. These were probably our first doorways to the mortal world. But it's getting harder to keep them secret. You people keep sticking your noses into every corner of the planet."

Donny completed his circle, absorbing the sights of the temple. "The whole place is amazing," Donny said.

"Yeah, Indiana Jones would wet his pants if he saw this."

Donny chuckled. "Where exactly are we? It looked like we were going to India."

"This is Tibet. Thousands of feet up in the Himalayas, inside a lost temple."

"This is in the Himalayas? Like, Mount Everest? Those Himalayas? Seriously?"

Angela pointed toward the narrow cleft in the rock that led out of the temple. There was dim sunlight seeping through and a ghostly whistle of wind. "You doubt me? Go take a gander."

Donny walked to the opening. Frigid air rushed in as he approached, overpowering the warmth of the eternal flame. Before he stepped through, he looked up. A jumble of boulders was poised delicately above him, and the only thing that kept them from collapse was a thick steel beam supporting a wide stone at the bottom. Leaning against the stone wall, right near the beam, was something like a sledgehammer. It was easy to picture the keeper swinging the hammer, knocking the steel beam loose, and dropping a few tons of boulders into the gap. He looked back at Angela.

"Don't worry about that," Angela told him. "It's only there in case this place is about to be discovered. We'll seal it off completely if we have to."

Donny nodded. He took one more doubtful look up, hesitating.

"Oh, relax, will you? Come on—I'll join you," Angela said.

Donny let out a deep breath and stepped cautiously into the gap. The whistle of wind turned into a howl, and with every step he took, the temperature dropped a few more degrees. Just ahead, the walls were clad in ice. The ground was a rippling icy sheet as well, and he had to keep to the rocks that had been placed there like steps.

The passage widened, leading to a sudden broad vista, and his breath caught in his throat. He had seen mountains before, on Earth and in Sulfur. But here stood the mighty, massive Himalayas, an endless expanse of black stone and white snow. The air was so crisp and clear that he witnessed everything in astonishing detail. Below him, an avalanche had left miles of hostile terrain, all sharp-edged rubble and gleaming ice. Much farther down, where the bands of ice and snow fed twinkly streams, he saw the first hints of green valleys. There wasn't a village or road in sight.

Angela spoke softly behind him. "Once there was a path that led to this temple, but an earthquake destroyed it hundreds of years ago. The temple was lost and forgotten, but not by us."

Donny stared and a chill shook his body. He couldn't have said whether it was from the cold or from awe. "Wow."

"Wow, indeed. It really is quite a world that you miserable people occupy."

"Yeah," Donny answered. "I wish everyone could see this."

"That would be nice except it's exactly what we don't want. The remoteness is the whole point. Now, if you're done gazing at all this bleak magnificence, we need to move on to our final destination. We have people to see, monsters to catch, et cetera."

Donny's teeth chattered and his muscles ached in the biting cold. He took one last look, wondering which way the mighty Everest was, and then followed Angela back to the temple that no other human had seen for centuries.

"We're going to Pillar Cataracta," Angela told the keeper. The keeper nodded, and then worked her magic in the same way as Porta. A sweep of the hands transformed the eternal flame into what must have been a map of the entirety of Sulfur. Donny wished he could take his phone out and snap a picture to study later, but he had a feeling he might get a dagger through his heart if he tried. So he left his phone in his pocket and just tried to remember everything he could about the fiery map that appeared before him.

It reminded him of a time he and his father were on a plane, and the plane flew over the Grand Canyon. The pilot had even gently tilted the plane to one side and then the other to give the passengers a better look. Sulfur was a massive cavernous world, narrowing and bulging and narrowing again, with more caverns branching left and right and dropping out of sight. A black vein ran through the middle, and Donny knew that must be the River of Souls that brought the newly dead into the underworld.

With one palm raised and the other hand sweeping the air from right to left, the keeper scrolled across the world of Sulfur until she finally slowed on a specific place and waved it into closer view. Along the way, starlike points of light showed where portals could be opened. There were only a few of those points in Sulfur, compared to many thousands on Earth, but now the map had centered on one. The keeper formed the familiar door shape with her fingers, and drew her hands apart to open it wider. The ashen door appeared inside the wall of flame.

"Thanks a bunch," Angela told the keeper. She led Donny by the hand through the burning portal, out of a lost temple in Tibet, and back into Sulfur. But this was a far different corner than the one Donny now called home.

CHAPTER 8

The first thing Donny heard was a hiss directed at him. He was getting the hang of things now, and he immediately raised his hand and showed the mark on his palm to yet another one of those tiny long-armed keepers. This one was reaching for a short two-headed ax. But she relaxed when she saw the mark on Donny's palm and heard Angela speak. "No need for homicide; he's one of mine."

This portal occupied the back wall of a short tomblike space. Heavy iron bars blocked the exit. A pair of enormous guards in armor, almost as imposing as Grunyon, looked in from the other side. "It's me, guys," Angela said. "Angela Obscura of the Pillar Obscura. Member of the Infernal Council. I'm here by the invitation of Ungo Cataracta."

Metal squeaked as the guards looked at each other and nodded. One of them started to turn what looked like a ship's wheel. With a shudder and groan, the gate rose off the ground. Angela ducked under before it was fully raised, and Donny followed. "You guys rock," she called over her shoulder. "Toodles."

"Whoa," Donny said as he saw what lay before them.

The chamber they'd left was in a niche high on the cavern wall. A narrow ramp of stone built on a series of lofty arches led to the cavern floor a hundred feet below, curling as it descended in a nearly complete circle.

The roof of Sulfur was lower here than near Angela's pillar—less than a thousand feet, with the points of the giant stalactites much closer. It made everything feel more cramped and foreboding. The landscape was wilder, a labyrinth of natural pillars, mounds, and arches. More things grew here, especially some species of giant black fern as tall as telephone poles.

One feature set this place clearly apart from Angela's neighborhood. It didn't seem possible for such a thing to exist, but there it was, not a half mile away: a waterfall tumbled from a hole in the ceiling, shedding swirling sheets of vapor. It was so large, it looked like it was coming down in slow motion. The bottom of the falls was hidden behind a mass of weird rock formations, but Donny heard its roar, rolling across the terrain like thunder. It was astonishing—like seeing an Empire State Building made of water.

Angela knew why he had stopped to stare. "Yeah, I'm jealous of that," she grumbled. "Wish I had one of those."

Donny stared for a while, wondering how it could be. Was there a giant ocean or lake somewhere above the roof of Sulfur, either inside the crust or up on the surface of whatever world they were inside? He was still trying to puzzle it out, and had become dimly aware that everything seemed to be growing brighter, when Angela diverted his attention.

"Oh, look what's coming," she said.

Knowing that "what's coming" might mean any manner of amazing or horrifying thing, Donny whipped his head around. She was pointing at something to the right. When he saw what it was, and how close it was, he gulped a mouthful of air.

"You sure do gasp a lot," Angela said. "Seriously, I think you get most of your oxygen via gasping."

"We have to run," Donny croaked.

"Nah, we'll be fine," Angela said. She put her arm around his shoulders and held him in place.

A cloud was about to engulf them. On Earth, this would not be a problem. But in Sulfur, the clouds were made of fire.

"Let me go," Donny said. He struggled to move, but her grip was like steel.

"Nothing to worry about," she murmured.

"Angela, I'm a human! I'm not like you!" He jerked his shoulders, trying to break free, but she was too strong. The cloud of fire was almost upon them.

Panic swept through Donny's brain. He thrashed in place. Angela cradled his head with her other hand, putting her mouth to his ear. "Hush," she said as he screamed. "It'll be fine. You'll see."

Donny might have trusted her, if it hadn't been for what had happened to him not long before. Suddenly he was trapped in another moment, when an archdemon named Havoc had tied him to a chair and produced a jar filled with the Flames of Torment—the awful hellfire that had been used to punish human souls for eternity. That was pain like he'd never experienced before, and it had left a deep scar in his brain. He'd tried to put it behind him, but all the agony rushed back as vividly as yesterday. He screamed all the louder.

Angela shouted, trying to be heard. "Cricket! It won't hurt you! Quit freaking out!"

Then the cloud was there, sweeping all around him. It didn't hurt. Not at all. There was only light and warmth and a soft orange haze. It was like being inside a ray of sunlight.

"See? You're fine. I told you," she said. "We have all kinds of fire. The clouds give light, but they don't burn. Breathe, Cricket."

Donny managed to stop screaming, but then his breath caught in his throat. He concentrated and took a deep gulp of air and then another. He pulled up the bottom of his shirt to wipe the dampness off his cheeks. "You shouldn't have held me like that. I was scared, couldn't you tell?"

"Yes, I could tell, and the way you were acting, you might have run right off the edge." She didn't sound entirely sympathetic. "For crying out loud, try to enjoy this for a second, will you?"

Donny took another deep breath and straightened himself up, looking into the glowing mist all around him. Just when he started to relax and enjoy the sensation, it was over. The cloud floated past them, leaving a few curling strands behind. Donny swept his hand through one of the tendrils, and the light scattered and evaporated.

"That's good times, right?" she said. "Kid, you have to believe what I tell you. Now let's go find Ungo."

CHAPTER 9

They descended to ground level and followed a road made of wide slabs of stone. The tracks of chariot wheels had been grooved into the stone over the ages. The road was lined on both sides, those tall black ferns waving high overhead.

As they made their way toward the great pillar, Donny realized what else was different about this corner of Sulfur. It was cooler and the air was misty, both thanks to the towering waterfall that pounded down from above. He saw tiny drops collecting on the fine hairs of his arm, and he could smell the water when he took a deep breath.

"Dang, this humidity will make my hair curl like crazy," Angela said, patting her tumbling reddish-brown mane.

There weren't nearly as many buildings around the foot of the Pillar Cataracta as there were around Angela's pillar. This was more like a village than a metropolis, with humble dwellings amid a few impressive buildings. Donny spotted a steep pyramid that would have looked at home in some ancient Aztec city.

It didn't seem as densely populated here either. At first he just saw a few beings in the distance, harvesting ferns. Farther down the road, they passed a dozen imps gathered around another imp who was hitting himself on the head with a rock and staggering around, looking dazed, while the crowd howled with laughter.

"What's that all about?" asked Donny.

"Stand-up comedian," replied Angela.

The road led to the entrance of a mansion carved into the pillar. The front door was at the top of a long, wide staircase that flared down to the road. At the bottom of the stairs, a pair of imps squatted on pedestals on either side. Donny thought they were statues at first, because their skin was shiny and red and cracked like old china, and they sat perfectly still. As he and Angela drew closer, the illusion was shattered as they lifted trumpets and sounded a deep, sour note.

Angela smirked. "No need to ring the doorbell."

By the time they reached the bottom of the stairs, the tall door at the top swung open. "Heeeere's Ungo," Angela said.

Donny gulped. He was glad the archdemon was a reasonable distance away. From that far off, he hoped Ungo wouldn't notice his shocked expression.

The archdemon had a cruel, terrible face. His lower jaw was shoved far to one side, with a single nasty tooth jutting high. Glowing orange eyes were buried deep under his brow. Strangest of all, the top of his head was cratered and cracked with wisps of smoke rising from within like a simmering volcano.

"Ungo," Angela called up with gusto. "You look marvelous."

"Angela Obscura," Ungo said in a phlegmy, wheezy voice. "Join me inside, and we shall talk." Donny felt those burning eyes shift toward him, and he was sure the smoke rising from the cratered head turned darker and thicker. "Is that a living mortal?" Ungo said.

"It sure is," Angela replied. Donny raised his hand to show the symbol on his palm—better safe than sorry. Ungo squinted at the fading mark. A thick puff of smoke shot from his skull.

"It can wait there," Ungo said. "A mortal has never set foot inside the Pillar Cataracta. And never will."

Donny bit down on his bottom lip and reminded himself to breathe normally.

"It's a he, if you'd like to know," Angela clarified cheerfully. "Will he be safe by himself?"

"Watchmen!" Ungo shouted, and the two on the pedestals turned to look at their master. "See that no harm comes to the mortal." The imps nodded.

"Don't worry, Cricket. I won't be long," Angela said quietly.

"Didn't you say something about a monster on a murder spree?" Donny whispered back.

"Nothing will happen this close to the pillar," she assured him. "Come on—be a pal and just hang here for a while."

Donny clenched his teeth as a tide of anger rose inside him. "Okay, sure." If he'd known he wouldn't be welcome, he would have stayed back at the Pillar Obscura and played games with Tizzy.

He sat on the bottom step for two solid hours. "Won't be long," he muttered. Every time he fidgeted, the watchmen on the pedestals jerked their heads around to see what he was doing. Donny got a closer look at their red skin. It looked like it had been painted on and baked, like ceramic, long before. Now it had started to chip and crack. *Everything is so weird,* he thought. He took out his phone, which had no signal, of course, and played games until the battery was almost dead. Then he broke into the snacks he'd packed for the trip, gobbling down string cheese and a granola bar. "You guys want one?" he asked the red imps, holding out a granola bar. They just scowled back.

The door opened at last, and Angela and Ungo appeared at the top of the steps. They spoke quietly for a few more minutes. Smoke continued to leak from the fissures in Ungo's head. Finally he bowed to Angela, fired another unpleasant look at Donny, and went back inside.

Angela trotted down the steps with a puckish grin. "I think I reeled him in. But he said he won't leave until they catch this beast that's stirring up trouble. So tonight we'll join the hunting party. Should be fun, right?"

"Oh yeah," Donny said flatly. "Probably too much fun."

CHAPTER 10

A few hours later, when the fiery clouds withered away and gloom gathered, Ungo and a band of well-armed imps assembled at the foot of the stairs. Donny stared at the imps, trying to figure out what they called to mind. These had been glazed white, like a porcelain sink. He counted sixteen of them. Eight were tall and thick, and eight were half that size, barely as tall as Donny's shoulders.

They lined up for Ungo's inspection, the eight small ones in front of the eight tall ones. Donny noticed the black emblems that had been painted onto their chests, and it suddenly clicked. "They look like chess pieces," he said to Angela. The symbols represented the usual pieces: crowns for the king and queen, horses for the knights, and the usual designs for bishops, rooks, and pawns.

"He's got a whole set, both sides," Angela replied. "They get painted black or white, and then they sit in a fire and end up glazed and shiny. This is only half of them. Now, stay here for a minute, okay?" Donny waited by himself as she walked away and engaged Ungo in yet another lengthy conversation. Donny passed the time by taking a closer look at the monstrous platoon in front of him. In some places, the white glaze had cracked and fallen away, revealing a silvery reptilian hide beneath. The pawns were armed with crossbows. The big ones had long-shafted weapons with heads that were part ax and part spear, along with what looked like bullwhips slung from the belts at their waists. Donny realized they were all staring back at him, and he dropped his gaze toward his feet.

Ungo growled something that Donny couldn't hear, and the chessmen started to move. After they passed, Angela fell to the rear of the pack and waved for Donny to join her. It was the last thing Donny felt like doing. But he didn't have another option, so he stood and followed.

"You look grumpy," Angela said.

"I don't feel very welcome here," Donny told her under his breath. "What exactly are we looking for, by the way?"

"We don't know, now that you mention it," Angela said. "Except that it's large, strong, and overly fond of killing. Oh, and it attacks at night."

"That's awesome," Donny grumbled, looking at the darkening landscape. His nervous system was on full alert. As they followed Ungo and his chessmen, he kept glancing from side to side. He frowned when he saw the direction they were heading: straight into the maze of tall, dark stone formations.

Angela tapped Donny on the shoulder and pointed up. "See the tiny bits of clouds that are still out? Those were just released. So it won't get *too* dark." Donny nodded, looking at the wisps of fire. At least he wouldn't be stumbling around in total blackness.

They were getting close to that massive waterfall. It sounded like rain and rolling thunder, a booming hiss that rose and fell as the noise swept over the obstacle-ridden terrain. The air grew wetter. Sheets of mist floated down, putting a slick coating on everything.

The bottom of the falls was still hidden behind the strange rock formations, which looked like enormous wax figures that had melted beyond recognition. From a distance, Donny had thought those shapes were black, but now that he was closer, he could see that they were dark green. The green was a plush coat of moss that clung to every stony surface. Donny pushed his hand into the moss as they passed one formation, and his fingers sunk deep into the spongy growth. It made sense, he figured, in such a damp place. When he took his hand away, the moss sprang back into its original shape, leaving no trace of his touch.

The group stopped. Ungo gestured to a ledge of mossy rock that they'd come to, and muttered something to the others that Donny couldn't hear. But Donny saw what he was talking about. Across the face of the ledge, about six feet high, three long slashes had been cut through the moss, revealing the rock beneath.

When the group started moving again, Donny walked closer to Angela. "What was Ungo talking about? Did the monster do that?" he asked.

Angela nodded. "They found an imp there. Partially eaten. Well, technically, *mostly* eaten."

Donny's throat constricted. He coughed to loosen it. His head swiveled from right to left, and since he was at the end of the line, he turned to look back every few seconds in case something was creeping up from behind. "You know, maybe we should have brought a weapon for me," he said. "Like a machine gun or something."

Angela laughed. "Modern weapons aren't popular down here, you know. They're considered vulgar."

"Okay, but I'm feeling kind of vulnerable right now. Can I borrow something?"

"I just brought the sword, Cricket."

Great, Donny thought.

The sound of the falls grew to a deafening roar as they passed beneath an arch of stone. The water tumbled to the ground right in front of them, pounding into a deep pool. Plumes of mist shot into the air and collected into hundreds of puddles and ponds around the foot of the falls. The water that overflowed the pool spilled into a deep channel that disappeared into the maze of rocks.

"They've looked in every cave and every crevice, but they just can't find this monster," Angela said. "It must be hiding somewhere."

Donny's gaze swept over the formations again. "Could there be a cave where the opening is covered with moss, so you can't see it?"

"Interesting theory," Angela said. "Hold on. Ungo wants to talk."

Angela joined Ungo and his chessmen as they stepped behind a tall moss-clad rock to shield themselves from the noise of the falls. Donny kept turning in a circle to keep an eye on every direction. His teeth hurt. He realized he'd been grinding them together. He rubbed his jaw and shook his arms to loosen his nerves. *Whatever. Stay calm,* he told himself. He took a moment to glance straight up to where the waterfall emerged from the stone ceiling almost a thousand feet overhead. It was a stunning sight: a vast column of water dropping out of a black hole. He would have stared for hours, but he didn't dare to take his eyes off his surroundings for long. Not with a vicious monster in the vicinity.

Angela finally came back from their huddle. "I have a fabulous idea!" she shouted to be heard over the thundering falls.

"I hope it's 'Angela takes Donny home'!" he shouted back.

CHAPTER 11

We'll use you as a lookout!" Angela called into his ear. "You can stay in a safe spot and signal us if this beastie turns up!"

Donny looked around again. "There's a safe spot?" he shouted back. If there was, he didn't see it.

Angela pointed to a tall spire of rock close to the falls. "Right up there!"

Donny squinted at the formation. It was thirty feet high and shaped like a crooked traffic cone with a small flat top. "How am I supposed to get there?"

"Ungo said there was a way up. Around the other side, I guess. Come on. Let's see." She tugged him by the arm.

On the other side of the cone, opposite the falls, Donny saw what Ungo meant. There were narrow stairs etched into the side. Each step was maybe a hand's width across. It looked like treacherous footing.

"Here's what we're gonna do," Angela said. She dug into her satchel, pulled out a pair of bright yellow walkie-talkies, flipped them on, and handed one to Donny. "You go up there and keep a lookout. If you see anything, hit this button once. If you're in real trouble, hit the button twice."

Donny had an awful feeling about the plan. He frowned and hit the button twice. Angela's walkie-talkie beeped in reply.

"Funny, Cricket," she said. "Don't do that again unless you're really in trouble. I'll be nearby, and I'll get here quick if that thing shows up."

"This is a terrible idea. First off, I might break my neck climbing up there."

"Come on. Don't be such a poltroon."

"Did you say *poltroon*? There's no way anyone uses that word anymore. I don't even know what it means."

"It means fraidy-cat."

"And I haven't heard *fraidy-cat* since kindergarten."

She pointed to the peak. "Quit stalling. Start climbing."

Donny held both hands up. "Just a minute, okay? I'm feeling really weird about this. Can't I stay with you?"

Her eyebrows darted down, and the smile left her face. It was like a thundercloud blotting out the sun. "This is the plan, Donny. Up you go."

"But—"

"Listen, *Donald*," she snapped. "We're friends and all,

but remember how all this started. I saved you from a crispy death, and you said you'd do what I asked."

"But that didn't mean—"

She stepped closer, putting her nose an inch from his. *"Do. What. I. Asked."*

Every word was a hammer. Donny felt the hairs stand up on his neck. Shivers rushed down his arms. He staggered back and hugged himself, trying to catch the breath that had deserted his lungs. The pace of his heartbeat had suddenly doubled, and he felt it pulsing in his ears. "Did you . . . did you just use your fear-beam on *me*?"

He'd watched her use that psychological weapon on many others, from his own father to that obnoxious guy in Milwaukee. But now, for the first time, he was the target of one of her focused waves of terror.

Her expression shifted quickly. For a moment her bottom lip trembled, as if she'd regretted what she'd done. Then her eyes narrowed and her jaw jutted and she lowered her head. "Enough, already. Climb up there. *Right now.*"

Donny sniffed. He stuffed the walkie-talkie into his pocket and started up the stairs, glad at least that Angela wouldn't see his reddened face and watery eyes. Each step was covered with slick wet moss, making the ascent that much more dangerous. He turned his feet sideways for better traction, and sunk his fingers deep into the growth on either side. Gravity was the enemy, trying to tug his feet off the steps with every move.

When he was halfway to the top, he glanced down. Angela was right below, watching his progress. She was either waiting to catch him if he fell or checking to make sure he did what he was told. Step by step, moving slowly all the way, he made it to the flat peak, which was the size of a picnic table. He stood and peered down at Angela. She was already moving away, toward the others.

Donny looked at the gleaming white imps below. "Great plan. You guys stick out like sore thumbs," he said aloud. It's not like they could hear him. Ungo gave a signal and the group scattered, disappearing behind the tall moss-clad formations.

"The heck with all of you," Donny grumbled. He let out a deep breath and looked around. The thundering falls were right in front of him. It was a little dizzying to stand at the peak with no railing to keep him safe, so he sat and folded his legs underneath him. Then he dug the walkie-talkie out of his pocket and positioned his thumb over the button.

Every ten seconds or so, he turned to face a different direction. Once in a while he whirled to look another way, in case the monster was watching him and timing his movements. But there wasn't a living creature in sight except for the occasional small flying imp high overhead.

The first half hour was tense, and then it was tension mixed with boredom for the next hour. After that it got purely boring. His shirt and shorts were soaked from the mist of the falls. For the first time in Sulfur, he started to feel a chill.

He looked at the walkie-talkie in his hand. He'd seen ones like it before. Families used them to keep track of one another at amusement parks and cruise ships, and on hikes. He hoped Angela wasn't venturing too far away, because the range wasn't always great with those things. *Especially with all those weird stone things in the way,* he thought. Did she even know that? Her knowledge about human stuff tended to be spotty.

There was the button he could use to send a beep, like she'd instructed him. But there was also the main button. You used that one to have a conversation. He thought about it for a while, almost pushed it twice, and finally did. "Angela?"

Her voice crackled back a few seconds later, hard to hear over the roar of the falls. "No talking. Just the beeps, and only if you see something. Don't do that again."

Donny gritted his teeth and came very close to hurling the walkie-talkie as far as he could. He decided that the formation he'd climbed wasn't shaped like a traffic cone. It was shaped like a dunce cap, and he was an idiot for being here. "Stuck on Dunce Cap Hill," he muttered, giving the cursed formation a name.

Something moved to his right. A shape passed between two of the formations. Donny's heartbeat raced again, but then he took a deep breath to calm himself. It was a flash of white. *Probably just one of the pawns.*

Another half hour passed, and nothing else moved. It occurred to Donny that, if there was any more detail to this master plan to catch the beast, he was completely unaware of it. Would he be up here for hours? Days? He was starting to shiver. This was getting old.

The only upside to this adventure was the sight of the falls in front of him. He looked again at where it emerged from the cavern ceiling, and followed it all the way down until it slammed into the pool. The swirling sheets of mist at its foot were hypnotic.

Tatters of the clouds of illumination drifted by, not far overhead. They cast the blurry shadow of a stalactite over the falls for a moment. Then the shadow moved as the cloud passed.

Donny squinted at the falls. The shadow had moved, but some darkness had remained behind, where the falls hammered the pool. The darkness flowed toward him, just under the rippling, frothing surface of the pool. A pair of dark round spheres, big as softballs and a foot apart, rose from the water, dark and glistening. They moved toward him, trailing a long dark shape behind. Every muscle in Donny's body clenched at once.

The spheres were froggy eyes. They rose from the pool as the monster stood.

It was close to ten feet tall, with arms that dangled low to the ground. It turned right, revealing its profile, and Donny could make out a long wolfish snout, still dripping water. The snout rose and fell. Then the thing turned to the left, and the snout moved again. *Sniffing,* Donny realized. He sucked in a sharp breath as the monster turned toward him, hunched over, and walked out of the mist, coming into sharper focus with every step.

Donny jolted. He'd been so transfixed by the appearance that he'd forgotten the walkie-talkie. He found the button and pushed it once.

When he looked up again, he nearly screamed. The monster was coming directly toward him. It was *stalking* him, moving swiftly through the knee-deep water. Its skin was dark and sleek, like an eel's. And the teeth in those gaping jaws looked like a drawer full of steak knives.

CHAPTER 12

With his heart drumming madly, Donny hit the button twice, calling for help.

Those froggy eyes were looking right at him. As soon as the monster reached the edge of the pool, it burst into a sprint across the moss-covered stone, directly at Dunce Cap Hill.

Donny hit the button twice again. And again. "Come on, Angela; come on!" He saw a frothy tongue inside that awful mouth, and the webbing between the long toes and claws. *Water monster,* he thought.

The hill was thirty feet tall, but the long arms of this thing would reach halfway up. "Safe place, my butt!" Donny shouted. He nearly crushed the talk button with his thumb and screamed into the walkie-talkie. "Angela! It's here, it came from under the water, *and it's gonna kill me!*"

The monster bounded across the terrain, gaining yards

with every step. When it reached Dunce Cap Hill, it leaped and raked at the moss to get a grip. The moss tore into ribbons under its claws, and it slid back to the ground.

Donny didn't even bother with the walkie-talkie anymore. "Help!" he shouted. "Angela! Anybody! Chess guys! That thing is right here!"

The monster sprang again, and this time its claws found a crevice to hold under the moss. Its feet scratched at the hillside, and before Donny could even think of heading back down the treacherous stairs, the horrible face with its googly frog eyes rose in front of him. The mouth opened and the head reared back to strike. Its rotten breath washed over him. He stared into a nightmare of jagged teeth, frothy tongue, and quivering throat.

Barely aware of what he was doing, he flung the walkie-talkie into the jaws. It hit the roof of the mouth and tumbled into the throat.

The monster hacked and gagged and turned its head to the side, expelling the device like a spitball. Donny used that moment to lower himself over the edge, feeling for the top step with his foot. He found it, and sought the next one with his other foot, but he was moving too fast and shaking too much. Both feet slipped at once. He struck his chin on the edge and heard his teeth clack together. As he slid, he felt the top step brush past his stomach. He reached for it, gripping the moss with both hands. The moss peeled away from the rock with a sound like tearing fabric. He held on tight, because it was the only thing that kept him from a free fall. His feet stabbed at the hill as he dropped, searching blindly for the steps. He finally found one and came to an unsteady stop.

Something splattered on his shoulder. When he looked up, the monster was on top of the formation, staring down, drool pouring from its jaws. It leaped off the top and landed in a crouch on the stony ground. When it stood, Donny was within easy reach, and the terrible claws at the end of those long arms came for him.

A whorl of orange light swept between Donny and the beast. Angela was there, leaping through the air. She whipped her flaming sword in a circle so fast, it looked like a propeller. The monster took a step back and hissed at her. Its arms darted high and low, searching for a way to reach her, past that spinning blade.

Donny heard cracking sounds. Whips wrapped around one of the monster's arms, then another. There was a large chessman wielding each whip. The monster yanked one of the whips hard, tugging the white imp with it, and the imp smashed into one of the formations, sending bits of the white enamel flying. Two more whips wrapped around the same arm at the wrist and the elbow. The chessmen hauled the whips back, spreading the arms of the mon-ster wide. Arrows flew, piercing the monster's legs. More chessmen burst from the shadows, tackling the monster from behind and dropping it to its knees. A third whip wrapped around its neck, and they tugged the thing down. Ungo raced forward with a glass bottle and smashed it into the monster's jaw. A burst of vapor came from the broken bottle, and the monster made one more weak attempt to break free of the whips, before it fell senseless with a final twitch of its claws.

"Nighty-night," Angela said to the thing. She looked at Donny, still clinging to the hillside. "Come on down! You look like a kitten up a tree."

By the time Donny made it to the ground, the others had gathered around the creature in a circle, staring and prodding. Angela lifted the monster's enormous hand and examined the webbing that spanned from knuckle to knuckle. "What do you know? It was a great water imp," she said. "I thought the last of these died a while ago."

"I have never seen such a beast before," Ungo said.

"It c-came from under the f-falls," Donny said. He folded his trembling arms tight across his chest, his hands in the opposite armpits. He had been quaking from the cold, but now he shivered because his nerves were shot. "Th-that's why you couldn't find it. There must be a cave under the water, or something."

Ungo gave him a sour sideways glance. Then he nodded at Angela. A nasty smile bent his mouth. "Well done," Ungo said. "Thank you for bringing the boy."

Donny stiffened. Why would Ungo thank Angela for bringing him? It was pretty obvious that the craggy archdemon hated mortals. Donny stared at Angela, trying to read her expression, but she just smiled back at Ungo. "My pleasure," she told him.

The chessmen were busy tying ropes around the water imp's ankles and wrists. "Take the creature to the dungeon," Ungo told them. "Then we celebrate."

As they walked back toward the Pillar Cataracta, winding through the moss-clad formations, Donny jogged up beside Angela. "What was that about? Why did Ungo thank you for bringing me?"

"Not now," she told him.

"But—"

She wagged a finger close to his mouth. "Just cork it and hang back while I finish up here, okay? I'll talk to you later."

Donny waited outside the pillar, sitting on the bottom step, watched once again by the pair of red imps on the pedestals. *What are you guys, checkers pieces?* he wanted to say, but didn't dare. The more he thought about what had happened, the angrier he got. The celebratory sounds coming from inside the pillar, including Angela's raucous laugh, poisoned his mood even more. He thumped the step with his fist until it nearly started to bleed.

Angela finally emerged, laughing and grinning. She waved good-bye to Ungo and trotted lightly down the stairs, almost dancing. "Mission accomplished, Cricket! Let's go home."

She tousled his hair as she went by, humming to herself. Donny sighed and got to his feet and followed her.

"I was the bait, wasn't I?" he said as they walked toward the ramp that led to the fire-portal.

She stopped humming to say, "Sorry, what?"

"You brought me along because you wanted me to be the bait."

She hid a smile with her fingers. "Oh. You figured that out, huh?"

"Yeah. That's why Ungo thanked you for bringing me. You used me to lure that monster out."

She stopped and put both hands in the air. "Okay. You got me. See, a lot of these nasty giant imps have a craving for mortal flesh. They go crazy for the stuff, probably because it's so rare down here, and they can smell it a mile away. So I figured, if I brought you along, that might help us catch it, and if we caught it, Ungo might be grateful enough to join the council. And it worked!"

Donny's hands crunched into fists. "Don't you think you should have told me what I was there for?"

She snickered. "You were so nervous to begin with, I figured you'd never do it if I told you that part. Come on. That was a rousing success! It was boffo! Quit being such a wet blanket."

Donny's simmering anger finally erupted. He flung his arms wide, waving them in the air as he ranted. "I'm a wet blanket because you used me as bait and didn't even tell me, and because you were mean to me when I told you I didn't want to go up there, and because it took you forever to show up after I called for help, and because I almost got eaten by a monster!"

The good humor drained from Angela's face as she listened. She put her hands on her hips. "Well. That's a lot to respond to. First, I'm sorry you were such a chicken that I couldn't tell you the whole plan, but that's part of our deal. I saved your life, and you do whatever I ask."

Donny opened his mouth to respond, but she stuck two fingers near his face to silence him. "Second," she went on, "I was stern with you because you weren't obeying, and you were embarrassing me in front of the guy I needed to impress. A guy who, by the way, doesn't think humans should be talking back to archdemons. And third, I got there as fast as I could, because everyone had backed off to make the monster think it was safe to come out."

Donny's jaw trembled. "I could have died," he said hoarsely.

"You could have died in Brooklyn," she shot back. "You could have died in Havoc's lair. But someone keeps saving you, remember? Golly, I wonder who? Oh, that's right: it's Angela Obscura! And yet you're ungrateful and frankly kind of whiny about it, and now you've put a rotten ending on a great day. So I cordially invite you to stop talking for a while. Got it?"

Donny hung his head. "I thought we were friends," he said quietly.

He was staring at the ground but heard her coming toward him. She wrapped her arms around him and lifted him off the ground in a hug. "Aw, Cricket," she cooed into his ear. "Look at your sad little face. We *are* friends. The best of friends. I didn't mean to hurt your feelings. But sometimes you just have to do what I ask." She lowered him to the ground and put her hands on his cheeks. "Listen, buddy, I get a little overheated now and then. That's part of what I am. Don't take it personally, okay? Come on. Calm down. I can hear the breath whistling out of your nose; that can't be good."

Donny shut his eyes, waited a moment, and then opened them again. "Okay."

"Super! Now let's get out of this place before moss grows on *us*." She linked her arm in his, and they walked up the ramp, side by side. "It could have been a lot worse, you know," she said. "That could have been a titan imp instead of a water imp."

"A titan imp?"

"Oh yes. They were the biggest things in the pit. Absolutely massive. Insanely strong. Dark purple with yellow spots. Claws like garden spades. Teeth like—"

"Great," Donny interrupted. "Let's never hunt one of those."

They walked quietly for a while, until she gave his

elbow a tug and pulled him close to her side. "Cricket," she said into his ear. "Tell me it's all right between us. Are we good?"

A little snort of laughter shot out of Donny's nose. It wasn't that he found it funny. It was just so unnerving, so baffling, how she could turn his emotions upside down, inside out, and then back again with just a few words and gestures. There were buttons in his brain that only she could find and push. It was impossible to stay truly angry when she was smiling at him and holding him close by her side. In its way, her charm was every bit as powerful as her psychic beam of fear.

"We're good," he said quietly. But inside his skull, a little voice whispered a quiet warning.

Maybe not, though.

Just be careful.

CHAPTER 13

They were on the street near Angela's pillar when a chariot approached. It was pulled as usual by a pair of runner imps with long legs and horsey faces. Angela and Donny stepped aside to let the chariot pass. As it clattered by, the single rider inside shouted to the runners: "Whoa! Stop right here!"

Before the chariot even rolled to a halt, the rider leaped over the side and jogged back toward Donny and Angela, his arms flung wide. "Angela Obscura, the one and only!"

"Chimera, is that you?" cried Angela.

Chimera's face was divided by a line that snaked down the middle of his forehead, nose, mouth, chin, and neck. On the right side, he had the pale flesh of a human, and on the left, the scales of a demon. He wore a pinstriped vest and baggy high-waist pants that might have been in fashion in the 1920s. His shoes were shiny and black with gold buckles. The sleeves of his white shirt were rolled to his elbows, revealing a human arm on the right and a demon arm with clawed fingers on the left.

Chimera clapped his hands. "You remember! How long has it been?"

"Years and years!" Angela said. "I've barely seen you since the war. You're so far from home. What brings you to this neck of the underworld?"

Chimera rose on his tiptoes and tugged at the pockets of his vest with his thumbs. "An invitation to join the Infernal Council! I was apparently next in line for Havoc's seat. I'm not convinced that I'm worthy, but I suppose I will accept. Actually, I am on my way to meet Formido and tell him the news. It was out of my way, but I took the road past the Pillar Obscura, hoping I might see you. I was disappointed that you weren't home, but here you are!"

"Here I am," Angela said. Her gaze narrowed, and she crossed her arms. "So, you're joining the council. Might I inquire where you stand on the issue of the Pit of Fire?"

Chimera shook his head and chuckled. "I knew you'd ask." He raised his hands in a gesture of surrender. "Don't be angry at me, Angela. I'm the traditional type. In my humble opinion, the pit should return, and the souls should be marched into the flames once more."

Angela's face reddened. She wagged a finger, ready to rant, but Chimera spoke first. "Hold on a moment. I may favor the pit, but I'm nothing like Havoc. I believe in the rulings of the council. As long as it favors the current solution and the Caverns of Woe, I will abide by that decision. You have my word on that. But either way, I hope we can discuss this like reasonable beings."

"Humph," Angela said, pressing her lips tight together.

"Please, Angela. For just a moment try to see things through the other side's eyes," Chimera said. "Many of us feel that overseeing the suffering of the dead in the pit is our one true purpose. Even after all these years our hearts ache with longing when we remember the flames. You may not crave it, but we do." He patted her on the shoulder. "My point is, I think both sides can learn from each other, as long as we can talk with open minds."

"My mind might be more open if you weren't so completely wrong," she replied.

Chimera flashed a wide grin, with square white teeth on one side and yellow fangs on the other. "Ha! You're a tough one, Angela Obscura, but I'll soften you up yet. I have compromises in mind that I don't think have even been proposed until now."

Angela squinted so hard, her eyes practically disappeared. "Compromises?"

"Yes! What if we sorted the dead? The worst of the worst go to the pit, and the rest to the Caverns of Woe."

"No way," she said. "Not a soul."

Chimera nodded. "No? Try this on for size. We torment

the dead with fire only for the *first* hundred years. Then they can go to your caverns."

"Stop it."

"Fifty years."

"Not a chance."

"How about twenty-five?"

"How about zero?"

Chimera tilted his head back and laughed. "Oh, Angela. It may take a century, but I'll wear you down eventually! I'm a very patient archdemon." He turned his gaze toward Donny. "Now, who is this companion of yours?"

"This is Donny," Angela said. "My personal assistant or my aide-de-camp or something along those lines."

Donny had to clear his throat before he could speak. "Hello," he said.

"And a very good day to you," Chimera replied. He held out his human hand, and Donny shook it. Chimera's eyes widened, and he took Donny's hand between both of his. "Your hand is lukewarm. I took you for a dead soul, but that's not the case at all! You are a living mortal child. That's a rare sight down here. How refreshing!"

Donny wasn't sure how to respond. "Yes, sir" was all he could come up with, followed by "Thank you, sir."

Chimera chuckled and released Donny's hand. He leaned over and put his hands on his knees to get a closer look at Donny's face. "And what a pleasant, polite young mortal you are. Consider me fascinated! Might we all have dinner some evening? I'm sure you have all sorts of stories to share about your life in the mortal realm."

"Sure, let's make that happen," Angela said. She put an arm around Donny's shoulders. "We have to move along, but apparently I'll see you around."

"No doubt you will!" Chimera said. He kissed Angela on the cheek and then shook Donny's hand again. "Oh— Donny, let me show you a trick."

Uh-oh, Donny thought. He'd seen unpleasant tricks from the denizens of Sulfur before.

Chimera stepped back, took a deep breath, and plugged the human side of his nose with his human thumb. Then he shot air out the other nostril, producing a long plume of bright yellow fire.

Angela rolled her eyes, but Donny let out a whoop of laughter. "Ha! That's amazing!"

"I have lots more where that came from," Chimera said, winking his human eye. He hopped onto his chariot. Chimera waved as the chariot rumbled away, and Donny waved back.

"I kind of like him," Donny said.

"What do you mean *like* him?" Angela snapped. "Did you not hear the part about the pit?"

"Yeah, I know you don't agree about that. Neither do I. I know how terrible that fire feels. And I don't want my dad ending up in there for even a minute. But Chimera was a lot nicer to me than Ungo Cataracta was. Also, he seems pretty reasonable. You might even be able to change *his* mind."

She sniffed at that notion. "This is politics, Donny. Nobody changes their mind about anything."

CHAPTER 14

Donny was at the Pillar Obscura, deep into a game of Trouble with Tizzy and Nanny. Donny popped a five, and the obvious move was to land on Nanny's peg and send her back to the start. But as he reached for his game piece, Nanny bared her sharp, crooked teeth and growled.

"It's just a game, Nanny," he told her. "And remember, Angela said you're not allowed to bite me." Tizzy held her stomach and giggled.

Before Donny could finish the move, a strange booming sound echoed through the windows carved in the pillar. It was like a foghorn, with a note almost too deep to hear.

"What was that?" Donny asked, lifting his head. He wished Angela were there, but she was a mile away at the latest meeting of the Infernal Council.

"I don't know," Tizzy said. The sound came again, even

louder. Donny felt the noise humming in his bones. Tizzy grimaced and stuck her fingers in her ears.

"I want to go see," Donny said. He ran for the front door, pulled it open, and stepped outside. From that elevated point he saw over the lower buildings that surrounded the pillar. The main avenue was below. Donny spotted Zig-Zag striding quickly along the road.

"Zig-Zag!" he shouted. Both faces looked up. "What's going on?"

"The Ferryman King is coming," Zag called back.

"Is that bad?" asked Donny.

"*Momentous* is a better word," said Zig.

"His appearances are rare," said Zag. "He hasn't been seen for years."

"Are you going to see him?" asked Donny.

"Yes. We think he has come to speak to the council," Zig said. "But we are curious about the reason."

"Can I come with you? Please?"

Zig and Zag glanced at each other and exchanged a few quiet words. Then both heads nodded. "Of course. But quickly!"

CHAPTER 15

Hurry, to the river!" said Zag.

Donny followed as they walked briskly toward the River of Souls. "I didn't know the ferrymen had a king," he said. He had watched those gaunt, ominous beings who manned the barges full of dead souls. He'd even had his own close encounter with one, when he used a barge as a shortcut across the river in an emergency, and he had been fortunate to escape that maneuver alive.

"They do have a king," Zig said. "And it's been the same king for as long as there have been ferrymen."

"He may be the oldest being in the underworld, apart from Lucifer," said Zag.

"If Lucifer is even still alive," said Zig.

"Don't be a half-wit," said Zag. "He is only in hiding or slumbering or wandering the mortal realm."

"You take too much on faith," said Zig. "Besides, if I am

a half-wit, does that make you the other half?"

"The greater half!"

Donny knew that Lucifer had vanished around a hundred years before and that nobody knew where he was. It was a source of much debate in Sulfur. He also knew that if he didn't change the subject in a hurry, Zig and Zag would argue for hours.

That thundering horn blasted again, echoing off the walls and ceiling of Sulfur. Every flying creature was pinwheeling through the air and screeching above, driven into a frenzy. Zig-Zag abandoned their debate and broke into a run, something Donny had never seen before. Zig and Zag had a hard time coordinating their movements at this speed. On Zig's side, the knee rose comically high in the air with each step. On Zag's side, the arm pumped out of rhythm. Donny jogged beside them, prepared to steady them if they stumbled.

It felt good to run again. The smoke damage that had compromised his lungs when he'd first met Angela, because of the fire in Brooklyn, had finally healed.

They made it to the river before Zig-Zag stumbled or passed out, and mounted one of the high arching bridges to catch a glimpse of the Ferryman King's barge. Donny saw it, not far from where they stood. It looked similar to the usual barges, with a huge skull mounted at the prow and a broad flat deck, but there was a tall structure in the center of the craft that the others did not have.

Zig and Zag each held a hand above an eye and squinted at the barge.

"It's stopping!" cried Zag. "Near the ruins of the Council Dome!"

"He's going to speak to the council!" cried Zig. "Hurry—let us go!"

Along the length of the River of Souls, ports were carved into the stony shores. At each port, a short, wide flight of stairs led from the river to the cavern floor. The Ferryman King's ship rested in one port now, gently bobbing in the current.

Now that they were getting close, Donny saw the difference between this craft and the rest of the fleet. There were no dead souls on board—only a crew of the tall, gaunt ferrymen. All the ferrymen looked terribly old, but these seemed even more ancient. Their dark robes were in tatters, shredded at the sleeves, exposing arms that looked like nothing but bone and sinew wrapped in mummified, leathery skin. Donny knew from experience that, while the ferrymen might look frail, they were amazingly strong. During his encounter, he'd been tossed from a barge onto the shore with little more than a flick of a forearm.

The crew was armed with scythes right out of the classic depiction of the Grim Reaper: crooked wooden staffs with curving blades that looked as big as the crescent moon. Heavy chains were looped around their waists, and from those chains hung spheres of dark glass in metal cages, plugged with glass stoppers. The spheres glowed with some kind of twinkling inner light.

In the center of the ship, instead a wide-open space where a crowd of souls could stand, there was a set of tiers leading to a taller deck, like a wedding cake made of blackened wood. On top was a throne that seemed to be constructed of gigantic yellowed bones. Upon it sat the tallest, ghastliest, most ancient ferryman of all. Unlike any of his brethren, his hood was pushed back to reveal his mummified head. The head was so big, Donny could hardly believe the neck didn't snap under its weight. It was more skull than face, with only a few scraps of skin still clinging to it. He had gaping holes for eyes, and a crater of jagged bone for a nose. The lower jaw was enormous and pointed like a beard. There were only wisps of gray hair on his bony head. The ears had withered and shredded like the petals of a dead flower. On his head was a bony crown, studded with dark gemstones. He was so lanky that his knees, poking up under his long robe, rose nearly to the level of his chest.

Imps were running from every direction and collecting in crowds on both sides of the river. Usually these strange creatures were loud and rowdy, but now they stood quietly, peering at the barge and keeping their distance, out of respect and fear. Donny and Zig-Zag found a gap in the crowd and stood among them.

"Why is the Ferryman King just sitting there?" Donny asked.

"The council will come to him," said Zag.

"Huh," Donny replied. He was surprised. That said a lot about the pecking order of Sulfur. He looked over his shoulder, toward the Council Dome.

The dome itself wasn't there anymore. Once, it had stood atop a small hill. But then it had been crushed under a falling stalactite as big as an ocean liner. That was the work of the traitorous council member Havoc, who was currently imprisoned by the survivors of the sabotage.

The Infernal Council still met in the same spot, but for the time being they sat on the fractured blocks of stone. Construction had already begun nearby on the new dome, which would certainly not be located beneath another of those massive stalactites. The imps and demons who had been working on it had rushed to see the Ferryman King as well.

The crimson-robed council members were on their way, heading from that hill of rubble toward the port where the king waited. Donny saw Angela among them, walking beside Formido, the head of the council. Angela was still in her demon form. Her long auburn curls were gone. Now she was covered in sleek, shimmering purple-red scales, with the ears of an elf and pointed fins that curved back across the top of her head.

Donny counted the robed figures. He saw eleven.

There were thirteen before three were lost when the dome was crushed, and when Havoc was imprisoned, that brought the number down to nine. If there were eleven now, that must mean that Ungo Cataracta was here, as well as Chimera. Sure enough, he saw Ungo and his smoking cratered head walking behind Angela, Chimera farther behind.

"Zig-Zag," Donny said. "When was the last time the king showed up here?"

"Seven years, at least," said Zag.

"Every so often he just passes through, looking things over. But it's been much longer since he has spoken to the council," said Zig.

"He will speak to the council if something of great consequence has happened," explained Zag. "Like when Lucifer vanished. And when the war broke out—he was furious about that, especially when a barge was caught in the cross fire."

Zig said, "And when the Pit of Fire was thankfully extinguished—"

"*Erroneously* extinguished," Zag said, and huffed.

"—the Ferryman King came then, too," Zig said. "In fact, that was the last time he spoke."

"Yes," continued Zag. "The Ferryman King turned up quickly after that. Same as now, the council came running—or at least, what was left of the council after the conflict."

"He wanted to know what was going on and where his ferrymen should bring the dead," said Zig. "Angela was as fearless as always. She explained it to him herself, that the dead should be brought to the Caverns of Woe, where the sorrowmongers would force them to contemplate their misdeeds, without all the burning and dismembering."

Zag sighed during that last part. "The Ferryman King seemed annoyed by the development. . . ."

"He most certainly did not," snapped Zig. "Are you pretending that you can tell what's going on inside that skull?"

"But in the end," Zag said, ignoring his other half, "he said nothing despite his misgivings, and returned to his ship."

"On that day and ever since, the dead have been ferried to the port nearest the Caverns of Woe."

Donny nodded. He knew those caverns well—his own father was currently serving his afterlife sentence there.

There was movement on the ship. The Ferryman King beckoned with a long bony finger to one of his crew. The crewman went up the steps and gave him one of the caged glass globes that hung from his waist. The king raised the globe, pried out the stopper, and brought the vessel to his mouth. A blob of twinkly lights flowed out from inside the glass. The Ferryman King opened his mouth, expanded his chest, and sucked the lights down his throat.

Donny felt a chill in his blood. He had seen a cluster of

lights like that before, when Zig-Zag had taken him to the source of the river. When he glanced up at Zig-Zag, both heads were watching Donny, an eyebrow raised on each side, as if waiting for this horrified reaction. "Was that what I think it was?" Donny asked.

"We thought you knew," said Zig.

Donny put a hand across his mouth. It was true: the Ferryman King had just devoured a human soul. "But—what happens to the soul?" he croaked.

"It is gone," said Zig. "The ferrymen exact a price for bringing the souls to Sulfur. On every journey, a ferryman devours a soul. This is the toll on the River of Souls. And this is what sustains the ferrymen. They could not survive without it."

"And the Ferryman King eats what he likes, whenever he likes," said Zig. "Because he can."

Donny's thoughts tumbled as he considered the terrible math. There were two ferrymen on every boat that transported the dead. That meant two souls lost forever on every trip. How many altogether, across the centuries? Tens of thousands? Millions? Sure, these were the wicked dead, people who had done terrible things in life. But still, to be *devoured*. To be gone forever, with no chance at redemption.

"Do they pick the worst souls? Or do they just . . . grab one?" he asked quietly.

"That we cannot tell you," said Zig.

The council members had finally arrived, and they assembled across the top of the steps. Formido was in the middle, easy to spot with his mountain gorilla build and the nautilus whorl atop his head. Angela was on his left.

The Ferryman King rose from his chair, unfolding his limbs. The way he moved was odd. It reminded Donny of a marionette, tugged from above by invisible strings. His tattered robe hung loose over his slender frame. From the way the cloth billowed and sunk in places, it seemed like there was nothing more than a stick figure inside. He seemed to rise forever, and his bones clattered and creaked as he moved. He stepped off the top of the deck, and Donny saw that what he'd thought were tiers on the deck were simply very tall steps, suited to those giraffelike legs.

Two of the crew stepped off the ship before the king, and two more followed behind, guarding their leader with their dangerous crescent blades. They climbed two steps toward the bank of the river and then stopped, facing the Infernal Council.

The imps in the vicinity scuttled backward, hooting like frightened monkeys. Many of them took whatever cover they could find, even crowding behind Donny and Zig-Zag, only their heads poking curiously out.

Donny saw something unfamiliar in the body language of the council members. Apart from Angela, he remembered them for their bold, arrogant demeanor. But now they fidgeted in place and took only quick, furtive glances at the Ferryman King, as if afraid to catch his eye.

There was a long pause where nothing happened at all. Then the Ferryman King lifted his head, looked around, and spoke in a voice that was shockingly loud, like thunder. "Something is amiss."

The archdemons of the council exchanged glances. Finally Formido spoke. Donny couldn't hear what he said, but the Ferryman King solved that problem as well.

"Speak up," the king roared, pointing at his ragged ear. "I cannot hear you."

Formido cleared his throat and repeated himself. "We don't know what you mean. What is amiss? Are you asking what happened to the Council Dome? It was destroyed when—"

"I know what happened to the dome," the king rumbled. "I am not talking about the treachery of Havoc. Something is amiss in the *mortal* realm."

There was another long pause, and another exchange of quizzical looks among the council and the crowd.

Angela spoke up next, loud and clear. "Could you be more *specific*, Your Highness?"

That mummified head turned to look at Angela. He raised a bony finger and pointed. "Obscura. I remember you." Angela stood, put an arm across her waist, and bowed.

"In the mortal realm," the king said, "souls are missing."

There was a long, strained silence. The Ferryman King swayed and creaked. Again, Donny had the impression of a monstrous, loose-jointed puppet. Whispers arose among the crowd. Formido cleared his throat, which sounded to Donny more like somebody starting a chainsaw, and everyone fell silent again.

"What souls, Your Highness?" Formido asked.

The Ferryman King's head turned to one side, his bones grating, and the gesture was somehow terrifying. "Souls that we should have ferried to Sulfur, of course. The others are no concern of ours."

Formido took a half step forward. "May I ask, how do you know they are missing?"

Air whistled through the king's horrid nose, and his head swung from side to side.

"You don't want to aggravate him," Zag said quietly.

Zig nodded. "On that we agree."

"We are the reapers of the dead," the king said. "We watch the crop grow. We sense when it is ripe. And we are aware when the harvest falls short. That is all you need to know, demon."

Formido folded his arms. "But what shall we—"

"I will *tell* you what you shall do," said the king. He stood even taller, as if the invisible strings tugged him high. "You will put a stop to this, and quickly. You will find the vermin that steal our crop. Snuff them out. Or better yet, bring them to me." He pulled a scroll from inside his robe and held it out before him. The crewman beside him took it from his hand and carried it up the last step. With a ghastly hiss, he held out the scroll. Formido extended a clawed hand, and the crewman dropped the scroll into it. All eyes were on the scroll as Formido unrolled it, but the next thing that the Ferryman King said caused every head in the crowd to snap up and turn his way.

"I *warn* you," he bellowed, his voice suddenly sounding like he spoke through a trumpet. "See to this before any more thieves appear to take what is ours. See to this, or there will be consequences."

Formido glared back. His nervous anger was easy to see: The air around him shimmered as heat radiated off his shoulders, like a desert mirage. "What consequences, Your Highness?"

There were hardly any lips still clinging to the Ferryman King's boney face, but the flesh that remained peeled back into a frightening grin. "We took no sides when you battled the Merciless. We did not intervene when you extinguished the Pit of Fire. We brought the souls to the Caverns of Woe as you desired. Perhaps your reformation has led to this new problem. Perhaps we will take sides now and then destroy this council, and let the Merciless punish the reformers."

The only sound was a low, guttural growl that came from somewhere deep inside Formido's chest. As far as Donny knew, Formido wouldn't mind firing up the pit again, but he also didn't like being threatened. Angela defused the tension by stepping in front of him and taking the scroll from his hand.

"And what have you brought us?" she asked brightly. She sounded like she was hosting a cocktail party. She unrolled the scroll, holding it wide with both hands. "Oh look, Formido. It's a map! Just what we need to solve this little kerfuffle." She looked up and smiled broadly at the Ferryman King. "Thank you, Your Highness! Is there anything else we can do for you? Would you like to tour the site of our new Council Dome?"

A horrified gasp went up among the imps and demons who were building the new dome. But the Ferryman King simply stared at Angela for a long moment. He might have been standing three steps lower, but they were still eye-to-eye.

Then he turned and looked toward his royal ship. He gestured with two fingers toward one of the crew who was still on board. That crewman stepped up to the great horn at the prow and blew into it. The booming note sounded out of the mouth of the giant skull. Every rib in Donny's chest hummed as the blast of sound washed over everything. It seemed loud enough to bring another stalactite down. Every imp cowered, low to the ground.

The king and his guard stalked away, back onto the ship, and the Ferryman King returned to his throne high above the deck. The crew cast off the lines that held the ship to the dock, and the barge floated sideways until the current of the river tugged it away. The Ferryman King never looked back.

Nobody spoke until the barge rounded a bend and vanished from sight. Then chatter exploded throughout the crowd. The imps in hiding burst out. Donny put a hand behind his ear, trying to catch what Angela and Formido were saying.

"I'll take care of this," Angela told him.

"What if he was right?" Formido grumbled. "What if this is connected to your reformation, Obscura?"

Ungo stepped forward, leaking smoke like a chimney. "If you ask me, the Merciless are behind this. Intercepting souls before they go to the river." Behind him, Chimera nodded in agreement.

"Maybe they are," Angela said. "Or it might be something else." She rolled the scroll back up and waved it. "But at least I know where to look. Trust me—I'll go up and get to the bottom of it."

CHAPTER 16

The council members returned to their meeting, and Donny and Zig-Zag walked back to the Pillar Obscura.

"I have a couple of questions," Donny said.

"We are here to answer them," Zag replied.

"Okay, thanks. How exactly do souls get from Earth to the barges?"

Zig and Zag looked at each other. "I have never seen it with my own eye," said Zig. "But as I understand it, the soul leaves the human body upon death. It will drift until it is caught up in the nearest current."

Zag nodded. "There are invisible currents called soulstreams. They cover the globe, following the course of human civilization, and sweep up the souls. Think of them as brooks that lead to rivers. Eventually the biggest soulstreams rise into the air and swirl into what looks like a great whirlpool. From there, the souls vanish from the mortal realm. What happens next is a mystery. But the next thing we know, the souls arrive in Sulfur on the barges. You have seen those final stages for yourself."

Donny had witnessed that arrival when Zig-Zag had led him to the source of the River of Souls. The barge slipped through an arch in the stone at the very beginning of Sulfur, its deck filled with globs of twinkling lights. The mist of the river gave the lights shape and form, and turned them into cold copies of the human beings they once had been.

"But how can someone grab souls on Earth before they end up here?" Donny asked.

"That is the mystery," Zig said.

"But it's possible to trap a soul," Donny said.

"It must be," Zag said.

Donny thought about that for a while. "The ferrymen trap souls. They keep them in glass."

"Indeed they do," said Zig.

"So maybe whoever is doing this is trapping the souls in glass."

"Hmm," said Zag. "Whatever the answer is, I'm certain Angela will find it."

"It seems you'll be in for another adventure," said Zig.

"Yeah," Donny said. He supposed it was another chance to get killed, too, like at the Pillar Cataracta, or just about anywhere else Angela took him. He shivered just thinking about how close he'd come to a grisly end—again. "Hey," he said, trying to cheer himself up, "are you guys hungry?"

CHAPTER 17

When the door to Angela's home opened, Donny waved good-bye to Zig-Zag and stepped inside.

"Nanny no bite," Nanny told him.

"I know," Donny replied. "You don't have to keep saying that, but I appreciate it."

"No bite," Nanny insisted.

"Donny!" Tizzy ran over and nearly knocked Donny over with a hug that was more like a tackle.

"Hi, Tiz," Donny said. He ruffled her hair. "Is Angela back?"

"She was, but she went up to the lookout to think," Tizzy said. "She had a big rolled-up piece of paper."

"I know," Donny said. He had so many questions for her, about the missing souls and the Ferryman King. "I'm going to go talk to her, okay?"

"Okay," Tizzy said. "We're playing checkers!"

"Nanny losing," Nanny said.

"I'll be back soon, and then I'll play the winner," Donny told Tizzy. He left, and heard Nanny growl and lock the door behind him.

A ramp circled the great Pillar Obscura, hundreds of feet up until it reached a sculpted ledge with a spectacular view of the world of Sulfur. Angela retreated to that lookout often when she had something important on her mind, so Donny wasn't surprised that she'd gone there. He jogged until he tired and then slowed to a walk. When he was almost at the lookout, he was surprised to hear two voices.

Angela was not alone. A man was with her.

The conversation wasn't quite loud enough to overhear, but the second voice didn't sound familiar. Donny crept forward, around the gentle curve of the massive pillar, until he couldn't go farther without being seen. From there, he heard them clearly.

"I hope you don't mind me surprising you," the man said. His voice was silky and warm.

"Of course I don't," Angela said. "I'm always happy to see you." Donny stopped and listened. He wanted to hear a hint of sarcasm or disdain in her voice, but there was none. She sounded like she meant exactly what she'd said. It wasn't like her.

"It's nice to talk like this, with nobody else around," the man said.

"It really is," Angela replied.

Donny clenched his teeth, hating himself for eaves-dropping. He wondered if he should simply walk around the bend and act like he didn't know anyone was there at all. He also thought about turning back the way he came. But instead he put his back against the pillar and edged forward. He just wanted to get a glimpse of whoever Angela was talking to.

He leaned out just enough to peer around the bend, and saw him. The man was tall and lean, with broad shoulders that tapered to a narrow waist. If he were human, he might have been twenty-five or thirty. He wore dark jeans and a short-sleeved checkered shirt. His blond hair was swept back and hung below his collar. There was something impressive and charming about him at the same time.

Donny disliked him immediately. It was partly because of the way he smiled at Angela as he leaned casually on the balcony, his muscular arms crossed. But it was mostly because of the way she returned the smile. Donny edged away until he was out of sight again, walking softly so he didn't make the slightest noise. He really meant to turn around and tiptoe away. But at the same time, he wanted to hear just a little more. Who was this man? What did he want with Angela?

"Your home is magnificent," the man said. "I always thought this was the greatest of the pillars. It's good that it survived the war with so little damage."

"It was fortunate, wasn't it?" Angela said.

This is wrong, Donny scolded himself. *I can't spy on Angela.* He turned again to leave for real when the man said something that stopped him in his tracks.

"I'm sure your parents were happy here. Perhaps one day you'll find a mate to share your home with as well."

Donny frowned. The tone of the man's voice was unmistakable, and Donny pictured the sly and charming grin on that handsome face as he'd said it. The man, whoever he was, was obviously nominating himself for mate.

Angela obviously sensed it too, because she laughed. It wasn't one of her mischievous laughs this time. This was a shy giggle that Donny had never heard. "Oh, you," she said. "I'm too young for that. I won't take a spouse for another hundred years."

The man laughed too. "Oh, it will be sooner than that. I guarantee it."

This guy, thought Donny. He wanted to run around the corner and punch him right in his perfect complexion. He resolved to leave again, and got two steps away before the next exchange froze him once more.

"I have my friends to keep me company," Angela said.

"I've been meaning to ask you about that," the man said. "These humans of yours. You seem very fond of them." Donny held his breath, afraid to miss a word.

"Fond?" Angela said. "I wouldn't go that far."

Donny clapped a hand over his mouth.

"They're interesting, mostly," Angela said. "The girl isn't very useful. She's more like a toy."

"And the boy?" said the man.

"Useful enough," Angela said. "Having him around helps me learn the human ways. I need to talk like them and act like them so I can pass in the modern world. And some of my missions to the mortal realm require the help of humans."

Donny's knees weakened. He put a hand on the wall to steady himself.

"But you already have human servants in the mortal realm," said the stranger. "It's unusual to bring one to Sulfur to live."

"I need to learn what I can from the boy while he still lives. It's very likely that one of our adventures will get him killed. Then . . ." Donny could almost see her shrugging. "I'll find another. It's easy enough to replace him. Just set a fire or something, put them in danger of their lives, and they'll beg to come with me."

Donny found it hard to breathe. *Just set a fire or something.* He remembered that terrifying moment in the burning building and how Angela had appeared like a miracle when he needed saving. *Was it really her? Did she set the fire that almost killed me?* How could he not have guessed? His heart felt ready to explode. He leaned against the wall and fought to keep his legs from folding underneath him.

"Angela," the man teased. "You can't fool me. I've heard how you act around the boy. You adore him."

"Of course I *act* that way," Angela said. "I want Donny to think he's important to me. How else will I get him to do what I want?"

The man chuckled. "And there we have it. That is the power of Angela Obscura," he said. "You could make anyone believe anything." She laughed with him.

Donny pushed himself away from the wall. His brain was spinning. Part of him wanted to race around the corner and scream at Angela. But he staggered away instead, more afraid of being seen if they should decide to walk his way. He nearly blundered over the edge, dizzy with rage and tears.

If he could choose to undo all of it, to return to that burning building before he'd met her, and choose that fate instead of living to hear the truth, he would have let the fire take him.

CHAPTER 18

When Donny got back down, he told Tizzy he wasn't in the mood for games, and went to his room. He kicked off his sneakers, flopped onto the bed, and stared at the canopy above.

An hour passed, maybe two, and then Angela was at the door. She pushed it ajar and knocked at the same time. "Adventure awaits," she said with a smile. She was back in her human form, this time with an unruly mass of straw-colored hair.

"Okay," Donny mumbled.

"Okay," she mumbled back, deepening her voice to mock his. "What's with you, Mister Grumpy-Pants? Gadzooks, you're not still moping about what happened at Cataracta?"

"Not moping about that," he told her. "And nobody says 'gadzooks' anymore. I'm not sure they ever did."

"Well, fiddledeedee," she retorted. "Get your stuff

together. We're gonna investigate this missing-souls business. Pack for three days. And think tropical."

They stood once again before the cascade of flames. Angela gave Porta their destination, and the diminutive demon gestured at the fire.

Once the globe appeared, Porta waved her hands to spin it until Donny spotted what was obviously the Caribbean Sea, with Florida to the north. He had always loved maps and geography, and knew the islands pretty well. Florida pointed like a finger to Cuba, the largest of a string of islands that reached east like stepping-stones. Haiti and the Dominican Republic came next, and then, before a sprinkling of smaller islands bent toward South America, he saw the place that Angela had named. Porta beckoned the flames, and the island of Puerto Rico grew large in the field of fire.

"There," Angela said. "Old San Juan." Donny saw what she meant: A starlike point shining white against the dark red flames, near the northeastern corner of the roughly rectangular island. A few gestures later, Porta had opened a doorway between Sulfur and Puerto Rico. Donny hefted his backpack and followed Angela into a small, dank, dimly lit room lined with blocks of timeworn sandstone. Just like that, they had stepped between worlds.

The room looked like a centuries-old basement. There was a small bed in one corner, and a little sofa. A desk was nearby, and on it a laptop computer glowed softly. A small desk lamp was the only source of light besides the fire. A dehumidifier hummed in another corner. But nobody else was in the room. There was only one exit, aside from the fire-portal. That was an old wooden door, currently shut tight.

Donny turned to look at the fire they'd stepped through. Like most of the fires that humans maintained for the use of Angela and other travelers from Sulfur, this one came from a pipe connected to a gas tank. He watched as the portal vanished from sight, the supernatural opening filled by flames.

"Someone ought to be here," Angela muttered. As if that was a cue, Donny heard a key scratch inside a lock, and the door creaked open. A dark-haired, middle-aged woman clapped her hand over her mouth when she saw Angela and Donny.

"*Disculpe!*" the woman said. "*Tuve que usar—*"

Angela interrupted with a raised hand. "Do you speak English? *Hablas tú inglés?*"

"*Sí, sí,*" the woman answered in a quaking voice. "I mean, yes. I am sorry. I had to use the *baño*, and I stepped away for only a *momento.*"

"Thank you for that glimpse into your glamorous life-style," Angela replied.

"I am so sorry, *señorita.* I did not think I would miss anything. This . . . this entrance, it is not used so much

.

lately, you understand? We hardly see Señor Fiasco anymore. But we so appreciate the—"

"You're not in any trouble," Angela told her. "But let's keep someone here around the clock for the next few days, all right? I'm not sure when I'll need this fire. *No hay problema?*"

"*Absolutamente,*" the woman said. She took a deep breath. "*No hay problema.*"

The woman led them out of the room. She locked the wooden door behind them, and led them down a stone-walled corridor lit by bare bulbs strung along the ceiling. They passed a plastic porta-potty (the *baño,* Donny said to himself) and came to the bottom of a long set of stone stairs. At the top was an iron gate. When they reached it, the woman unlocked the heavy padlock that secured the gate and pushed it open.

"*Muchas gracias,*" Angela said as they stepped out into a narrow alleyway between a pair of old buildings. The alley was shadowed, but Donny saw bright sunshine beating on a stone-paved street at the far end, and he heard music from afar. Even in the shade, the air felt warm.

"Thank you," Donny told her. He gave her a wave and a smile.

"*Señorita,*" the woman called when they'd walked a few steps away.

Angela stopped and looked over her shoulder, one eyebrow lifted.

The woman looked behind her to make sure nobody else was near, and kept her voice low. "My mother, she has been ill. And my daughters. I have two; they are both very smart."

Angela cocked her head to one side, asking without saying it aloud: *So?*

The woman fanned her face with her hand. "Sorry. I am too nervous. But my mother, she will be well again. And my daughters—I can send them to good schools." She pointed at the locked gate. "Because of the money you give us, to guard that room. So I say, thank you so much." She lowered her eyes. "Or perhaps I should have said nothing."

Angela looked at Donny and shrugged. *"De nada,"* she told the woman. "See you around." She turned and walked briskly down the alley.

Donny lagged behind long enough to say, "I'm glad your mom will be okay." The woman was red-faced, biting her lip. She looked like she wished she'd kept her mouth shut.

Donny jogged up beside Angela. "She was really grateful. You should have been a little nicer."

"Don't be so sappy, Donny. We pay people because somebody has to maintain the fires. If we do something decent, it's by accident."

"But you *are* doing something decent. And that's kind of ironic, right? Considering where you're from?"

"Absolutamente," Angela said.

CHAPTER 19

Old San Juan was broiling and beautiful, a mix of old-world Spain and Caribbean splendor. They walked down narrow, sloping streets paved with blue cobblestones, past rows of three-story pastel buildings.

There were cats everywhere, lounging in the shadows. They were perfectly relaxed until Angela approached. Then they slunk away, their bellies scraping the ground, and occasionally hissed over their shoulders. Angela let out a hiss of her own through her nostrils, a sound of pure exasperation.

Donny thought about something the woman had said that he hadn't understood. "Angela, who is Señor Fiasco?"

"Ah, Fiasco," Angela said with a crooked grin. "An old friend. Fiasco is one of us. He came to Old San Juan a long time ago and refuses to return to Sulfur. We'll go and meet him—I want to ask him something. Also, he might have a clue about the missing souls. His intuition is very strong."

They passed a tall, majestic cathedral and came to a plaza with a tree so wide, its branches nearly brushed the buildings on either side. A handsome hotel, yellow with white pillars, stood before them, and Angela led Donny inside. "This used to be a convent, as long as we're doing irony," she said.

Donny let out a laugh of surprise when he saw two familiar people sitting in a pair of leather chairs in the lobby, sipping icy drinks. One was Howard, the courtly, secretive gentleman who seemed to be responsible for anything Angela needed in the mortal realm. Howard had enormous wealth and resources at his disposal. He arranged for Angela's earthly living quarters, although, thanks to some bad judgment on Donny's part, a luxurious apartment in Manhattan had to be abandoned. Donny shuddered at the memory. He had almost exposed Angela to the police.

The second man was Carlos. Donny had met Carlos in Brooklyn when he helped Angela capture a nasty whispering demon that had stirred up trouble. That was the first time Angela had lured Donny into a near-fatal situation. How many times was he up to now? At least four, he figured. Those awful words he had overheard resounded in his head: *It's very likely that one of our adventures will get him killed. Then . . . I'll find another. It's easy enough to replace him.*

Donny felt his teeth mash together, and he tried to suppress the angry, saddened expression that he knew was twisting his face. He didn't want Howard or Carlos to see it. Donny liked both of these men, although Howard was aloof and intimidating. He forced a smile and gave them a wave as he and Angela walked across the gleaming checkerboard floor. Howard returned a subtle two-fingered salute, and Carlos flashed a grin underneath his sunglasses.

"I didn't know you guys would be here," Donny said.

"Summoned by Miss Obscura," Howard replied as he got to his feet. "We just arrived." He was tall and trim, and dressed in a light cotton shirt and slacks. Carlos wore a flowered shirt, shorts, and sandals.

"I've never flown on a private jet before," Carlos said. He took off his sunglasses, and his dark eyes crinkled as he smiled. "Very luxurious. Have you been on Howard's jet, Angela?"

"Sit in a metal tube thousands of feet in the air with a bunch of nervous, gassy mortals? No, thanks. I like my way better." Angela presented her cheek for a kiss by both men. "Glad you made it, my darlings." She leaned closer to Carlos and talked softly. "I know I haven't told you much yet, but how's your radar? You sense anything here?"

"Not yet," Carlos said. He lifted his chin and shut his eyes. He turned his hands so his palms faced up. Donny got the impression that he was turning himself into an antenna.

A few seconds later Carlos opened his eyes. "Maybe? I am not so sure. I hope I have not come all this way for nothing."

"That's not the spirit," Angela said.

"Let me wander a bit," Carlos said. "I will rent a car and drive around. It helps . . ." His face reddened, and his eye contact with Angela faltered. "It helps if you are not so close by."

Angela smiled as if he'd paid her a compliment. "Jamming the frequencies, am I? Well, have a nice drive. Howard, Donny and I will check in and put our bags away. Then we'll meet you back here in an hour."

"Miss Obscura," Howard said before Angela turned for the reception desk. "I hope you'll keep a low profile while you're on this island?" He shot a sideways look at Donny, who pulled his head between his shoulders like a turtle.

Angela snickered and headed for the front desk.

CHAPTER 20

We have time to kill," Angela said when they were all back in the lobby. "I'm going to find a salon and try to get this hair improved. It looks like, I don't know, a haystack in a tornado or something."

"Do you need any funds?" Howard asked.

"Oh, Donny and I managed to retrieve a bundle recently," Angela replied.

"I wish you'd let my organization handle that," Howard said. He rubbed his temple with his fingers, as if he'd suddenly developed a headache. "May I ask where this happened?"

"Milwaukee, home of beer and bratwurst," Angela replied.

"And were you seen doing anything . . . out of the ordinary?" Howard asked.

Angela glanced at the ceiling. "Not that I can *recall*."

Howard looked at Donny, and Donny shrugged. Then

Howard pulled a leather notepad from his pocket and scribbled something in it. Donny had a feeling that Howard's people would soon be checking out any strange news reports in Milwaukee.

"As always," Howard said, "my advice is to behave as normally as possible. And don't do anything that might draw attention to yourself."

"You're being a fussbudget again," Angela chided. "Donny, you want to watch me get a haircut?"

"Why don't you take a walk with me, Mr. Taylor?" Howard said. "We'll go to the old fort. It's very impressive." Donny was surprised. Howard hadn't shown much interest in him before. If anything, he seemed to regard Donny as a disaster looking for a place to happen, especially since he was still technically a missing child.

"Oh. Sure," Donny said. A few minutes later he and Howard were on the street. As they headed downhill toward the sea, Donny caught a whiff of salty air.

"Mr. Taylor. *Donny*," Howard said when they were a block away from the hotel. "Is everything well with you?"

Donny gulped quietly. Howard must have seen the expression on his face when he walked into the hotel. "Um. Yeah. I'm fine," he lied.

"Hmm," Howard said back. He was silent for a while. The street led to the coastline, and ahead of them, beyond a vast green lawn, stood an ancient, thick-walled fortress. Howard bought bottles of cold water from a street vendor and handed one to Donny. "Hydrate. Do you know what this excursion of Angela's is about?"

"Not exactly," said Donny. "I know there are some souls that should have turned up in Sulfur but didn't. Angela wants to find out what happened to them. She has some kind of map. I guess some of the souls vanished from here."

Howard wore a white Panama hat. He took it from his head and fanned himself with it. "I don't get too involved with infernal matters, but I know a little about these things. That would be a map of the invisible currents that capture human souls."

"Soulstreams," said Donny, remembering what Zig-Zag had called them.

"Really," mused Howard. His eyes twinkled at Donny. "You've learned a lot down there. So you know that those currents are like tributaries, which eventually lead to the River of Souls, which runs through Sulfur." He pointed with the hat toward the fortress. "See that? It's called El Morro. It was built by the Spanish almost five hundred years ago. Back then, San Juan was the most strategic location in the Caribbean, and therefore the most heavily defended. This was the Spanish empire's stepping-stone to the New World." He put the hat back on his head and took a swig of water. "So it's not surprising that one of the soulstreams, as you call them, passes through here. They have always flowed through historically important areas. Come on. Let's go inside the fort. It's remarkable."

They ambled down the paved path that divided the immense lawn. People were everywhere, picnicking, napping in the sun, and kicking soccer balls. Dozens of kites soared in the sea breeze. A spectacular old graveyard, dense with statues and monuments, was visible to the right.

"I want to ask you this again," Howard said as they walked. "And I hope you feel that you can trust me, and you can be honest with me. You don't seem quite the same as the last time I saw you. Not as lively, or happy. Is everything all right for you in Sulfur? Are you healthy? Has Angela treated you well?"

Donny opened his mouth, intending to lie again, but a weird choking sound came out instead. Howard patted Donny's shoulder. "Take your time," he said. "But I want to hear it."

Donny nodded. They walked some more and entered the fortress. After they climbed long ramps and stairs to the highest level, they found a quiet place on the battlements, far from other tourists. The sea sparkled in the sunlight hundreds of feet below. After he stared at it for a while, Donny was able to talk.

"I don't think Angela really cares if I live or die," he said in a rough whisper.

"What makes you think that?"

Donny hadn't meant to say much at all, but as soon as he started to talk, it all spilled out like candy from a piñata. He told Howard everything. He started with the conversation he'd overheard between Angela and the handsome stranger. When he told the part about how Angela might even have set the fire in Brooklyn that had almost claimed his life, Howard made a rare show of emotion. It was a quiet reaction, just a quick intake of breath. Howard rolled his eyes toward the sky and opened his mouth to speak, but then swallowed the thought, whatever it was.

"Do you know who it might have been that Angela was talking to?" Donny asked.

Howard shook his head. "Sorry. I'm not too familiar with the infernal population. But—how many times have you been in serious danger?"

Donny rattled off all his close calls. The whispering demon in Brooklyn. The gunman in Milwaukee. The water imp at the Pillar Cataracta. Howard's eyes widened when he heard about the incident in Havoc's lair, when Donny was subjected to the Flames of Torment.

"This is worse than I imagined," Howard said. "That's not touch football you're playing down there, is it?"

"No, sir," Donny said. "It's tackle all the way."

It was quiet again for a while, except for the distant sound of a park ranger speaking to a group on a guided tour. "Thank you for trusting me," Howard finally said. "I need to trust you, too. Can you keep this conversation between us?"

"Yes, sir," Donny said.

"Good. I'm not sure how Miss Obscura would feel

about it. But let me tell you my opinion on this subject. I don't approve of young mortals growing up in Sulfur. A few years ago it was very troubling to me when Angela found that baby and brought her down."

"You mean Tizzy? Tizzy was abandoned," Donny said.

"I know that. And I've heard that Tizzy is so accustomed to Sulfur that she's afraid to come back to the world where she belongs. There are places on Earth for abandoned children like that. And there are places for you, as well. Living in the underworld—it just isn't right. Especially considering how dangerous it's been."

Donny nodded. His stomach felt sour. "There really isn't a place for me up here, though."

"Let me ask you this," Howard said. He turned and put his shoulder to the wall to look directly at Donny. "Your mother vanished when you were very young. Am I right about that?"

Donny rested his chin on his arms. "You really did learn a lot about me."

"I realize this is very personal. But yes: I had my people look into your history when Angela first brought you down to Sulfur. We dug in a little deeper after that trouble in the apartment. Part of my responsibility is to keep things quiet, as far as Sulfur's intrusions into the real world go. I don't care for surprises, and I like to be informed. So I am aware that you had a mother, and she left you to be raised by your father."

"My mother left because she was afraid of my father," Donny said.

"But she doesn't have to be afraid any longer, does she?"

Donny sighed. That was true. His father couldn't hurt anyone anymore. At Donny's request, Angela had tried to scare Benny Taylor straight. It had actually worked, since his father had made a last-minute attempt to reform himself—but it was too little, too late. When one of his former criminal associates murdered him, Donny's father went straight to Sulfur, where his soul would remain for many years to come.

"No," Donny said. "She doesn't have to worry about that."

Howard leaned closer. "In that case, would you object to us doing a little investigation into your mother's current whereabouts?"

Goose bumps sprouted on Donny's arms despite the heat. "Um," Donny said. "Well. I mean. If you found her, you wouldn't . . ."

"We would never tell her anything until I spoke to you first," Howard said.

Donny looked at the blue sky, and at the great blocks of stone under his feet, and finally at Howard again. "Wow. I guess I'd like to know. Sure, that would be great." He felt a tiny spark of hope kindling deep inside his chest.

"I'm glad, because we already started looking," Howard said as he took another sip from his bottle.

Donny's eyes widened. "You did? Have you . . . ?"

Howard swallowed and shook his head. "We haven't found her yet, but we're close. She covered her tracks pretty well, but we believe she's in Colorado somewhere. My people are very good. I think they'll find her soon—in a matter of days, in fact. But I promise, she won't even know we're looking."

Donny nodded. "So you're saying, maybe I could just stay with my mother? If you find her?"

"Obviously your mother would have something to say about that," Howard said. "And then there's the question of how Miss Obscura would respond. Do you have some sort of agreement with her?"

"When she saved me from the fire, she said I'd have to help her," Donny replied.

"What exactly did she say, and what did you promise? Do you remember?"

Donny thought back to that moment when he'd woken up in the abandoned brewery to discover it was burning. That reminded him of what Angela had told the handsome stranger about setting fires. His anger boiled up again, but he tamped it down and tried to focus on Angela's words that night in Brooklyn.

"She said she would save me if I promised to work for her and do what she asks. For as long as she likes."

"Did you sign anything?"

"We sort of shook hands," Donny said.

"Interesting. I'm sure she considers it binding. And that's her mark on your palm, right?"

Donny raised his hand and looked at the whitish mark that Angela had made with her ring. It looked even less distinct than the last time he'd checked. Soon it might be gone for good. "Does this mean I'm her property or something?"

"I suppose we'll find out. You can't just disappear on her, you know. You will have to ask. If you simply took off, she'd look for you. And she'd ask me to help find you."

Donny stared up at Howard's impassive face. "Would you really do that?"

"Oh yes. Donny, I want to do right by you. But don't forget, I'm loyal to Miss Obscura first. Nobody in my organization wants to find out what it would be like to feel her wrath." Howard smiled grimly. "There is something I always try to keep in mind, and I think you should do the same." He waited until Donny looked him in the eye. "I know what Angela appears to be. But we must remember what she really is. An archdemon. A creature of the underworld. Unpredictable and powerful, and not to be taken lightly. Agreed?"

"Yeah," said Donny. "Agreed."

CHAPTER 21

Donny was in the plaza outside the hotel, scratching the cheek of a purring black-and-white street cat, when the cat suddenly arched its back, puffed its tail, and bolted. He looked down the street, certain that Angela was approaching, and there she was. She had a shopping bag in one hand and wore a new pair of enormous sunglasses. Her unruly haystack of hair had been tamed and cut short, a major change from her usual long, flowing locks.

"*Buenos días,*" she said. She flipped her fingers through the hair on her temples. "Whaddya think? Do I look like a pixie now?"

"Looks nice," Donny said flatly.

"Are you still grumpy? Land's sakes, get over it already. Look, I bought you a present. A swimsuit, in case you want to go in the ocean." She reached into the shopping bag and took out a tiny men's bathing suit. It looked about two inches from top to bottom.

"Oh. Wow. Thanks," Donny said. He wouldn't have worn it in public in a million years. She tossed it to him, and the whole thing was easily stuffed into a pocket of his cargo shorts.

"Let me drop off this bag, and then we'll go find Fiasco," she said.

She skipped into the lobby, and Donny tried to pull himself together while he waited. He wasn't exactly grumpy. He was confused and distressed, trying to figure out what the future would hold. But still, he was curious about this Fiasco character. When Angela emerged from the hotel again, he forced a smile onto his face and followed her along the Calle del Cristo.

They turned a few times, down more lumpy brick streets, and strolled by more colorful buildings with black iron balconies on their second and third stories. The usual thing happened when Angela was out in public: people smiled and tried to catch her eye and then turned to watch her pass.

"I think you'll like Fiasco," she said.

"He's like you? An archdemon?"

"Yes. But he's been in his human form for a long time now. You can tell by his beard. Now, be nice and make a good impression, because I have a big favor to ask of him."

Angela stopped abruptly, outside what looked like an

artist's gallery. The entrance opened wide to the street, with a gate pushed to one side that could be locked at night. The inside was dazzling, with walls ten feet high covered in paintings and crafts. The long, narrow space reached deep into the building, and it was divided into stalls for the artists. Each stall displayed a different style. Most common were scenes of the picturesque streets of Old San Juan, paintings of the abundant street cats, and landscapes of the tropical shores. But there were also colorful masks, painted shells, sculptures of sea creatures, portraits, abstract paintings, and much more.

"I think he's all the way in the back," Angela said. "And that's for the best, honestly."

"He's an artist?" Donny asked.

Angela chuckled. "I guess."

They walked through the long space. Donny saw many of the artists at work or talking to the tourists who'd come in to shop or browse. In one of the stalls, a slender, dark-haired man was painting one of those fantastic masks. It was a grinning lizard face, with long horns that curled from its nose and forehead, and more that radiated from the sides like starfish arms. It was bright with color: white teeth, red lips, and horns of yellow, orange, and green that were covered with spots. The face was something that Donny might have seen among the denizens of Sulfur. He was sure that this artist was Fiasco.

But he was wrong. "Is Fiasco in?" Angela asked the man.

"He should be back soon," the artist replied without much feeling. But then he glanced up and saw Angela. His eyes widened, his posture straightened, and his manner became far more animated. "I think he went for coffee," the man said. "I am Miguel. Can I help you in any way?"

"Nope," Angela said. They walked on until they'd reached the back of the long room. Donny stared at what lay ahead. He didn't quite believe what he was seeing.

"What do you think?" Angela said.

Covering the walls—*defacing the walls is more like it*, Donny thought—was the worst art he had ever laid eyes on. *Amateurish* didn't begin to describe it. Every brush-stroke, every composition, every choice of color, were all woefully misguided.

"Your friend did this? Señor Fiasco?"

"Yup. Aren't they *terrible*? It's, like, a crime against eyeballs," Angela said quietly into his ear.

"It's just awful, isn't it?" A tall, well-dressed woman had walked up behind them. She carried a painting that she'd purchased from another artist. "I never understood why they even allow this fellow's work in here," she said. She shook her head and pursed her lips, and then leaned closer to them, an unpleasant, puckered smile on her heavily made-up face. "The rumor is that he pays the rent for all these other artists, and so they put up with him."

"That sounds really generous," Donny said.

"It's the only way he'd be allowed to stay, I suppose."

The woman looked over her shoulder before whispering to them again with a smirk. "He never sells anything, you know. For obvious reasons."

"You can buzz off now," Angela said.

The woman's head rocked back. "I beg your pardon?"

Angela waved her off like a bad smell. "You're like a fly. Unpleasant, uninvited, unwanted. Buzz off. Be somewhere else."

The woman's mouth dropped open, and she scowled, but something about Angela's manner seemed to tell her that talking back was not the best strategy. She stomped away in a huff and glared back before leaving the building.

"Nobody but me gets to say Fiasco's art is terrible," Angela said. "But it really is, right? Tell me: Which do you think is the worst?"

Donny didn't know what to say. It looked like Fiasco had taken a crack at the styles of all the other artists in this little colony, and failed spectacularly each time. But before Donny could single out any one disaster as the worst, a voice boomed out from behind them.

"*Frituras* for everyone! Enjoy, my fellow artists and patrons, enjoy!" Donny turned to see a tall, wide beast of a man enter the room like a hurricane blowing in. Angela chuckled, folded her arms, and waited to be noticed.

So that's Fiasco, Donny thought. He had to smile just looking at the man (*or archdemon in human form,* he reminded himself). Fiasco held a long skewer in each hand, each lined with a dozen deep-fried golden snacks shaped like fat fingers.

"You're a doll, Fiasco," said a woman in one of the stalls as she plucked a *fritura* off the skewer. Fiasco had maybe the biggest smile Donny had ever seen, with both rows of dazzling white teeth fully exposed. He was easily six and half feet tall, with a burly chest and a big but firm belly. He wore a white linen shirt smeared with a hundred colors of paint, and tan linen pants cuffed almost to his knees. His face was wreathed by a storm of gray hair and a shaggy, pirate-quality beard. A seashell necklace jangled across his chest, and braided leather bracelets encircled his wrists. He had beach sandals on his feet, but with colorful striped socks under the sandals. Donny noticed that one foot was much larger than the other. Around the ankle of that foot was an ancient gold bracelet like the one that Angela wore around her gloved wrist.

The jovial man made his way down the space, offering *frituras* to artists and tourists alike, with a grin and a laugh for all. He finally glanced at the far end, where Donny and Angela stood, and froze. Then he dropped the skewers on the floor, tossed his head back, and let out the biggest, most explosive laugh yet, before throwing his arms wide. "Angela Obscura! How long it's been!" He ran toward them, and Donny felt the footsteps rattle the floorboards.

Fiasco wrapped his arms around Angela, lifted her, and spun her in a circle twice. "As bewitching as ever," he bellowed. She laughed and flung her arms high like a ballerina, and then Fiasco set her down and kissed her loudly on both cheeks.

"Fiasco," she said, "may I introduce my friend Donny Taylor?"

Fiasco smiled at Donny. Then he darted a questioning glance at Angela and raised a shaggy eyebrow.

"He knows *eeeeverything*," Angela whispered past the palm of her hand.

"Aaaaah," Fiasco exhaled. In an instant Donny was swept up in a crushing embrace by the alarmingly strong man.

"Ooof" was all Donny could say.

"To be Angela's friend is to be Fiasco's friend!" the huge man proclaimed. He lowered Donny to the floor and tousled his hair so hard, it nearly broke Donny's neck.

There was a commotion not far behind them. A silver-haired tourist in a parrot-patterned shirt leaned against a post, looking unwell. His wife gripped his arm. "What is it?" the wife asked.

"I d-d-don't know," the man said. His eyes bugged and his limbs shook. "I feel so . . . afraid suddenly." He looked like he was having a panic attack. "I need to get some air!" He and his wife rushed out of the space.

Angela bit her lip and watched him go. "Rats. I think that's us."

Fiasco nodded. "No doubt it is."

"Is there a place we can talk?"

"Of course." Fiasco spoke with a vague accent that wasn't exactly Spanish. To Donny's ear, it sounded like someone putting on an accent in an attempt to sound exotic. But in Fiasco's case, the effect was wonderfully disarming. He had Angela's magnetism, but it was a warmer variety.

They went to the back of Fiasco's stall and through a door that led to a room where artist's supplies filled the shelves on three walls. It smelled of linseed oil and turpentine. In the middle was a round wooden table and brightly painted chairs. "I have to hide in here occasionally," Fiasco confided as he settled his vast bulk into a creaking seat, "when a sensitive mortal wanders in and is frightened by my infernal presence. I should have remembered: the two of us together might be too much for some to handle."

Angela shook her head. "Oh, those canaries." Donny had heard her use that term before, to describe people who sensed her true nature. They could become anything from uneasy to terror-stricken, depending on how sensitive they were, and what sort of mood Angela was in.

"And what about you, young mortal?" Fiasco asked Donny. "Do you feel anything?"

"No, sir," Donny replied. "Not a thing. Does that happen to you a lot?"

Fiasco gave him a chuckle and a wink. "There are some who swear this building is haunted. It is only because of me, of course. But I tell them: 'Oh yes, I have often felt the ghost stand right behind me—he was an artist in life, and has come to admire my work!'" He put his hands on his belly and chuckled. Donny smiled back. He wondered how many other stories of hauntings had started with the presence of a demon in human form.

"Never mind that now. I am so pleased to see you!" Fiasco said. He rocked back in the chair, his hands clasped behind his head. "Did you see my work? I have made great progress as an artist since your last visit."

"Yes," Angela said. "You have certainly . . . done . . . *more* of them."

"Portraits are my latest passion." Fiasco stroked his beard and pursed his lips. "But remarkably, I have sold very few."

"That's hard to believe," Angela said. She shot a wide-eyed glance at Donny.

Donny looked at Fiasco's expression closely, trying to figure out if he was putting them on. But the big fellow seemed completely genuine. *Oh boy,* Donny thought. *He has no idea that his art stinks.*

"True genius can be difficult to recognize," Fiasco mused. Then he thankfully changed the subject. "So, what is it you want to tell me? I hope it is good news, on such a glorious day!"

"News of all kinds," Angela said. "Let's start with the latest happenings in Sulfur."

Fiasco chuckled and raised a hand, palm out. "My dear.

You know I left that world behind forever. I have embraced the mortal world and all of its fragile, fleeting glories. The tropics! Music! Poetry! Fiestas! The sun dazzling in the palms! The moon glittering on the sea! Fiasco the terrible archdemon is no more. Now there is only Fiasco the artist who lives for the moment."

"Bear with me, Fiasco the artist," Angela said. "There are a couple of things you ought to know." She told Fiasco about the recent catastrophe in Sulfur, how Havoc nearly managed to wipe out the entire council, and the idea that it might signal the return of the Merciless. "If everything goes back to the way it was, you know what *that* might mean for the archdemons who've chosen to live on Earth," she told him.

Fiasco angled his head and tugged on his beard. "I do not know. What might it mean?"

Angela rapped the table with her knuckles as she spoke. "They don't like what you're doing. You chum around with humans. You live the mortal life full-time. That risks exposure. They would order you to return, Fiasco. And considering that you fought for the reforms, they might even look for a reason to sentence you to annihilation."

Fiasco slumped in his chair and folded his arms. "You have control of the council, though. You have the majority."

"For now," Angela said. "It's dicey, though. Ungo Cataracta has joined, and he's an ally. But Chimera has

126

joined too, and he wants the pit back. If you joined us . . ."

"No." Fiasco shook his head. "Find another way. Don't ask me that."

"If you joined us, the majority would be safe. You're from an ancient family. They'd have to put you on the council if you asked. You are needed, Fiasco. We need your voice. We need your strength."

Fiasco chuckled sadly and gazed at the ceiling. "Impossible. The butterfly cannot be molded back into the caterpillar. I am transformed."

"You're still an archdemon, Fiasco. Listen—you can have it both ways. You could come down for the meetings, and stay here otherwise. I'm up and down all the time; it's fabulous."

"I never want to see Sulfur again. Or that horrible pit, even though it is extinguished. It reminds me of all the years I spent amid the flames, tormenting those wretched souls. How could I ever have been such a monster? I never want to take on my demon form again—it repulses me."

"Fiasco, you know this can't last forever." Angela reached across the table and took Fiasco's enormous hands in hers. "You've been here so many years already. Your human friends must have noticed that you've barely aged."

Donny looked more closely at Fiasco. It hadn't even occurred to him how old he must be. Archdemons lived ten times longer than mortals, more or less. Angela looked like a teenager but was around one hundred and fifty years old. Fiasco must have been close to five hundred.

Fiasco lowered his gaze. "There have been comments made."

"See? Maybe it's time to come home."

Fiasco shook his head. "No. I'm sorry, Angela. When the time comes, I will leave this island and find another beautiful place. I will make new friends there. Maybe next time I will become a brilliant poet instead of a great artist." Angela stifled a snort. "And when my new friends grow old," Fiasco said, "I will move again. But I will not go back to Sulfur. It is up to you to keep that house in order. Don't ask that of me."

Angela puffed air out of the corner of her mouth. "Well, then. Fiddlesticks."

Fiasco put his hand on his heart and bowed his head. "I am sorry, Angela."

She jutted her chin at him. "You can make it up to me by giving me a hand with something."

Fiasco stroked his beard and eyed her doubtfully. "So there is another card you have not played! A hand with what, may I ask?"

"Not sure yet. Something is amiss on this island. In this vicinity, probably. A lot of souls have been intercepted."

The big man stood and turned away from Angela and Donny. His shoulders rose and fell as he took a deep breath.

"You know something about it?" Angela asked.

Fiasco spoke without turning. "I sensed that things

were amiss. But I tried to ignore it. I feel a presence at times. But never have I seen anything."

Angela looked sideways at Donny. "A presence?"

Fiasco turned back to face them. "An infernal presence. It is wicked and monstrous. That's all I can tell you, and I'm not even sure about that."

Great, Donny thought. He was thoroughly creeped out. It felt like ants were crawling up and down his spine.

"If you seek this thing out, you must be careful," Fiasco said. He looked at Angela and then Donny. Donny nodded vigorously back.

"That's why we could use you," Angela said.

Fiasco clutched the hair on top of his head and gazed at the ceiling. "Angela Obscura," he said. "Why must you shake me from this dream I am living?"

"Come on—it'll be fun," Angela said.

Fiasco looked at Donny and jabbed his thumb toward Angela. "This one has a strange idea of fun."

"That's for sure," Donny replied.

"So you'll do it?" Angela said. She broke out her most beguiling grin, and even batted her eyelashes. "It's the least you can do after you turned me down about the council."

Fiasco pinched the bridge of his nose. "You would charm the rattles off a snake, Angela Obscura. Yes, I will do this." Angela grinned again and tapped her hands together in silent applause. "But," Fiasco said, pointing a finger at her, "I will not transform. You understand me?"

"Come on," she said. "You're such a lovely monster when you want to be."

"I don't want to be," Fiasco said. He folded his arms across his burly chest. "Never again."

"Fine. It'll still be nice to have you," Angela said. She stood up, and Donny followed suit. "We're tracking this thing down now. I'll let you know when we need help."

"I would tell you that I look forward to it," Fiasco said, "but I do not."

He led them out of the storage room, and they said their good-byes. As Angela and Donny walked away, Fiasco suddenly bellowed after them. "Wait! How could I forget? I have something for you! I have saved it for many months!"

"Uh-oh," Angela muttered quietly. Fiasco went to a stack of canvases in the corner, and searched through the pile. "Aha!" he cried. He pulled out a small painting and hid it behind his back as he approached. Then he sprang it on them, holding it up with both hands.

"Oh my," Angela said.

"I painted it from memory, which makes the likeness all the more remarkable!" Fiasco crowed.

Donny bit the insides of his cheeks to keep from laughing. The painting was a portrait of Angela, and it was absolutely ghastly. He couldn't be certain, but it looked like she was standing on a giant open clamshell, rising out of the sea. The paint looked like it had been slapped on with a toothbrush.

"I literally don't know what to say," Angela told him. Her hand was over her mouth, in the manner of someone who was about to be sick.

"Because words are not sufficient," Fiasco said with a hearty laugh. "It is a wonderful surprise, eh?"

Angela nodded. Fiasco thrust the painting into her hands, and she took it. "I can't thank you," she said. "Enough, I mean. I can't thank you enough."

"It is an honor, and a pleasure, to share my art," Fiasco said, patting his broad stomach.

CHAPTER 22

What a catastrophe," Angela said as they walked down the street. She glanced at the painting again, grimaced, and turned it around so the painted side was hidden against her waist. "Worst-case scenario."

"It was really nice of him to do that for you," Donny said.

"I suppose," Angela grumbled, with a scowl that still managed to be appealing. They walked among tourists, past row houses painted yellow, orange, lime, and teal. At that moment Donny could almost forget the rift that had opened between them. Fiasco was right: Angela was bewitching. He had to remind himself about what he'd overheard, and how little he meant to her, no matter how she acted now.

Donny noticed again how Angela drew attention in a crowd. Men and women alike would turn to look. A quick glance often led to a second, longer stare. One lanky young man, maybe eighteen, was using an expensive camera with an enormous lens to snap pictures of an Old San Juan cat, which slunk away as Angela approached. His mouth fell open when he saw her. She bedeviled him with a sly sideways glance and the slightest elevation of her chin.

After they walked by, Donny heard the man call from behind. "I beg your pardon!" His accent was Scottish, or Irish, Donny wasn't sure which. Either way, between those good looks and that appealing accent, Donny found himself grinding his teeth. *If this guy only knew what he was really talking to,* he thought.

Angela stopped and turned to look back. "Yes?"

"I, uh . . ." the man stammered, and lifted his camera. "I wonder if I could take your picture?"

Angela responded with a dramatic sigh of relief. "Would you really?" She thrust Fiasco's painting at the man. "It's all yours. I don't care what you do with it, honestly."

The man blinked rapidly, looked at the painting, and then laughed. "No, miss, I meant I want to take your photograph."

Angela's brow furrowed for a moment, but then she grinned. "Sure, why not? Donny, hold these?"

She handed Donny the painting and her handbag. For a solid minute she ran through a series of poses while the young man snapped pictures. She turned sideways, a hand on her hip, then smiled and looked at the sky, propped her chin on the back of her hands, folded her arms and gave a smoky stare, struck a ballerina pose . . . Donny didn't think it would ever end. Some of it was ridiculous, but all of it was enchanting. The photographer was in a delirium. He flipped the camera horizontally and vertically, leaned forward and back, and circled around her, a bedazzled grin on his face. Donny wished with all his might that a meteor would fall from the sky and obliterate the man and his camera.

"You remind me of something from a poem," the photographer said. "Do you like poetry?"

"All the best people do," Angela said. She pursed her lips and looked over her shoulder at the lens.

"Which poem is your favorite?" asked the photographer, snapping madly.

"Oh, anything by Dr. Seuss, I suppose."

The poses went on until Donny was ready to scream. Even when that finally ended, there was another painful century where the guy showed Angela the shots he'd taken on the screen on the back of his stupid camera. She gazed intently at the pictures and passed judgment on each with a laugh, a scowl, or a happy nod. He stood at Angela's shoulder, looking at her instead of the photos.

After that era had finally passed, he asked, "Would you like me to send you the best ones?"

Smooth, Donny thought, boiling on the inside. To his relief, Angela said, "No, thanks. I know what I look like."

The photographer plowed on. "Are you in San Juan for long?"

"Let's not make this personal."

"It's just . . . it's just . . ." the guy stammered. "Who are you?"

"Wouldn't you like to know?" Angela linked her arm with Donny's, and they walked off together.

Just tell her what you heard, Donny told himself. His anger had mellowed as he walked beside her. He wondered if he should just tell her how he was feeling, and why. But how could he even begin? *So, I was around the corner on your pillar in Sulfur, eavesdropping on you and some guy. . . .*

Before he came close to starting, her phone rang from inside her handbag. She pulled it out and answered it. "Hello, Carlos! Any progress?"

Donny listened to her side of the conversation, and caught just a few of Carlos's excited words on the other end. "What? Already? I thought that might take all week. You're amazing. . . . You're welcome. Where? . . . How far away? . . . Oh. That's so close! But you're not sure what it is? . . . No, I understand. Definitely something infernal, though, right? . . . Okay. We'll check it out tonight. We won't take any action yet, but I'll bring reinforcements, just in case. . . ." She looked sideways at Donny and grinned when their eyes met. "Uh-huh. We'll see you at the hotel. Sound good? . . . Okeydokey. Bye." She ended the call and pumped a fist in the air. "Makin' progress."

"Carlos found what you're looking for?"

"He found something, anyway. We'll check it out tonight."

Donny felt a surge of energy, like an electric current under his skin. It wasn't a terrible feeling. The thrills were a factor in the equation he was trying to figure out. There was no doubt that part of this life he'd fallen into was exciting and amazing, even if it could be horribly dangerous at the same time. If he left Angela's company, he would give all that up too: the weird grandeur of the infernal land, the hidden wonders of the mortal world, and the brushes with extraordinary beings and people with abilities he never knew existed.

"But how does Carlos do it?" he asked. "He just . . . *feels* things?"

"Pretty much. You've seen how some people are sensitive to my presence, right? Like that nasty old woman in Florence?" Donny nodded. He remembered the woman in the crowd who had pointed at Angela and called her a monster. "Well, Carlos is like that, but in a much more sophisticated way. He can sense supernatural things the way a shark smells blood in the water. And he can home in on it, which makes him super-useful."

There was that word again. *Useful.* She'd used it to describe Donny back in Sulfur, when he'd overheard that conversation. Is that all mortals were to Angela? Useful things?

She went on, unaware of the dark thoughts crossing

Donny's mind. "Remember how we found the murmuros in Brooklyn? Carlos tracked him down. There can't be ten people in the world with better radar than him. That's what I call it: radar."

Donny nodded. "Okay. But about tonight—will this be dangerous?"

She smiled with her mouth closed and shook her head. "Oh, Donny. It'll be fine. Not every infernal thing is trying to kill you."

No, Donny thought. *It just feels that way sometimes.*

"How did you find Carlos?" he asked.

"He found *me* five years ago. Chased me all over New York, asking 'What are you? What are you, really?' I told Howard to check him out. He seemed like somebody we could work with."

Donny thought about that for a while. Carlos was still alive after all those years of helping Angela. Still, Carlos had never been to Sulfur, where some of the biggest dangers lay. He wondered if Angela knew what was obvious to him. "You know, I think Carlos . . ." He had trouble getting the words out.

She looked at him with half-lidded eyes. "You think Carlos what?"

"I think he thinks about you a lot," Donny said.

"Oh, you mean he has a thing for me? Ha! Line forms on the right." She gave Donny a sideways grin.

Donny rolled his eyes. It would have sounded

obnoxious coming from just about anyone else. From Angela, paired with that particular expression, it was endearing.

And true, utterly true.

CHAPTER 23

Shortly after midnight they stood outside the hotel. It was still warm, but that didn't bother Donny. It was a lot like the weather in Sulfur.

Carlos leaned against his white rental car, his arms crossed. He wore a dark shirt and pants, and black running shoes. Angela had on a black T-shirt and black capri pants, and the black satchel slung over her shoulder. *You guys don't look too suspicious or anything,* Donny thought. He looked at his striped polo shirt and cargo shorts, and wondered if he should have worn black too.

"If he's not here in a minute," Angela said, "we'll go get him." Before the words were out of her mouth, a low hum arose. It quickly grew to the buzz of a small motor. Fiasco rolled into view on an Italian scooter that looked comically small under his sprawling bulk. His helmet was bedazzled with shells, beads, and bits of glass, but the work was so unappealing and sloppy that Donny instantly knew who the artist must be.

Fiasco rolled to a stop, dismounted, and flung his arms wide. He wore the same paint-splattered clothes, with sandals over his socks. "My friends!" he cried. "And who is this?" He spotted Carlos and rushed at him. Carlos opened his mouth as if to scream, and looked ready to sprint away when Fiasco gathered him up in a crushing bear hug. "This can only be Carlos! A friend of Angela's is a friend of Fiasco's!" He pumped Carlos up and down as if Carlos were a ketchup bottle and Fiasco were shaking out the final drops.

"Pleased-to-meet-you," Carlos wheezed, with the fraction of air still left in his lungs. He wobbled when Fiasco released him.

"So, where do we go on this lovely moonlit evening?" Fiasco boomed.

"Bayamón, sir," Carlos said, rubbing his chest. "Maybe a half hour from here." He cleared his throat and gestured toward Angela and Fiasco. "I am sorry to say this, but it is a little overwhelming for me to have both of you so close."

"Fear not!" Fiasco slapped Carlos on the back and nearly knocked him down. "I will ride behind you. Lead the way!"

"Can I drive?" Angela asked Carlos as they walked toward his car.

"Under no circumstances," Carlos replied.

Donny slid into the backseat and buckled his seat belt. *One last adventure, maybe,* he told himself. The usual mixture of excitement and dread bubbled up inside him. *How bad can it be?*

CHAPTER 24

They drove through a sultry night, crossing a bridge over moon-speckled waters and onto a highway. Donny looked in the rearview mirror. Behind them, Fiasco chugged along on his scooter, hunched over the handlebars as highway lights gleamed off his goggles.

Here and there beside the road Donny saw familiar signs. It bugged him a little, to be so far from where he grew up and to see the same chain stores and restaurants. Maybe the world was getting too much alike. It was differences, not similarities, that made distant places exciting.

Carlos was right—it wasn't far to their destination. Bayamón was another city like Old San Juan, dense with mostly low buildings. It seemed like the tallest things in Puerto Rico were hotels or cathedrals. Carlos exited the highway and navigated deeper into the city. The farther they drove, the less safe it appeared. It reminded Donny of a tropical version of some of the rougher sections of New York. Buildings were decrepit or abandoned. Graffiti covered walls. They passed a group of young men who scowled as they drove by.

After two more turns, Carlos pulled the car to the side of the road and parked it. Fiasco buzzed up behind them. Donny stepped out of the backseat and looked in both directions. The street was poorly lit. At least they didn't have much to fear from humanity—not with Angela and Fiasco there, anyway.

"So, where's the trouble?" bellowed Fiasco. His voice echoed off the walls.

Carlos and Donny both cringed. If stealth was the object, Fiasco might be a problem. "Around that corner," Carlos whispered, trying to lead by example. "I didn't want to park too close. If I can sense *it*, perhaps *it* can sense *you*. Wait here for a moment, and let me go ahead. I'll wave when you can join me."

"Are we jamming your radar?" Angela asked.

Carlos pinched his thumb and forefinger together. "A little." He walked to the end of the block and stopped just short of the corner. Donny peered into the darkness, trying to see what was happening. Carlos hesitated. He leaned back against the wall and closed his eyes for a moment. Was he afraid? Concentrating? Or was he tuning into some weird frequency, like turning a radio dial in his head? Donny thought that might be the reason.

Carlos inched closer to the edge of the wall and poked his head out to look around the corner. Donny had the feeling that an awful thing was about to happen—that something was there, waiting to snatch Carlos by the neck. For a moment Donny couldn't breathe.

He nearly jumped out of his skin when Fiasco spoke up behind him. "They make the most delicious *chicharrones* in this city," Fiasco said in his version of a whisper, which was still louder than an ordinary person's speaking voice. "But I don't imagine any place is open so late," he added wearily.

To Donny's relief, Carlos pulled his head back to look their way, and then waved for them to follow.

Donny followed Angela, and Fiasco lumbered a little distance behind, humming to himself. When they joined Carlos, and Donny saw the building around the corner, he thought to himself: *Not there. Please not that one.*

"That one," Carlos said. He pointed to the same building.

This wasn't anything like one of the old architectural gems that Donny had seen in Old San Juan. This was an ugly concrete industrial beast in a blighted neighborhood, left for dead long ago. It would have been creepy by day, but the moonlight made it even more ominous. The cement had crumbled in places and exposed a skeleton of rusted iron bars. There was nothing but glass fangs left in its windows, and ragged plastic that flapped in the tropical breeze. Trees grew wild beside its mold-stained foundation. Dark vines swarmed up the walls. Even the corner it stood on was in disrepair. Weeds sprouted from cracked and crumbling pavement.

Donny shivered. He didn't have Carlos's radar for the supernatural, but he still sensed something off about the place. He almost jumped again when Fiasco tapped him on the shoulder. "To make *chicharrones*, they deep fry pork skins. Although it can be made with chicken, as well."

"How are you doing, Carlos?" Angela asked. "Got a fix on what's in there?"

Carlos ran his fingers across the dark stubble on his chin. "It's different now. Not as intense. Not as . . . malevolent."

That sounds good, Donny thought.

"That doesn't sound promising," Angela said.

"The thing that was here may be away," Carlos ventured.

"Maybe. Let's investigate, shall we?"

Carlos nodded, and they walked out into the open. A car turned onto the street a block away, and the headlights fell on them like a spotlight. They waited as the tiny rusted car drove slowly by. A thin-faced, mustached man in a white tank top stared at them from behind the wheel. Brakes squealing, the car screeched to a stop, and the driver backed up until he was beside them again. He lowered the window, leaned his head out, and stared at the group. *"Qué están haciendo aquí?"* he asked.

Carlos stepped forward and had a hushed conversation

in Spanish with the man. Finally the man raised his window, shrugged, and drove down the street again.

"What was that all about?" Angela asked.

"He wondered why we were here, and thought we must be lost," Carlos said. "He said it looked like we were heading for that building, and that maybe we should not go in there."

"Ha," said Fiasco. "Why should we be afraid?"

"It was a hospital once, with a sad history. After the hospital closed, bad people hung around in there, but now even the bad ones are afraid to go inside. It is haunted, he says."

Angela rolled her eyes. "For crying out loud. Whatever is in there should be afraid of *us*."

"But what if . . . ," Donny began, but he was afraid to finish the thought. It was the biggest worst-case scenario he could imagine, and it had just occurred to him.

"What if *what*?" Angela asked.

Donny's shoulders felt twitchy. He moved them up and down to work the nerves out. "What if it's Lucifer who's behind all this? The missing souls?"

"Don't get all nutty on me," Angela said. "I told you, it's highly likely that Lucifer is dead and gone."

"Mortals have a clever saying about Lucifer," Fiasco said with a chuckle. "Have you heard it, Angela? It's about the devil's finest trick."

She sighed. "The one where he asks you to pull his finger?"

"No. They say the devil's finest trick is convincing the world he doesn't exist."

"That's clever, all right," Angela said with a roll of her eyes. "Now let's go already." She set off briskly across the street, and the others followed. Dead palm fronds crunched under their feet, and lizards skittered out of their path.

It was easy enough to get inside. The doorways had once been boarded up, but the planks were torn out and lay in pieces on the ground.

"We should follow you, Carlos," Angela said. "You're the bloodhound here."

Carlos nodded and stepped through the opening. An instant later he gasped aloud, and his hands clawed at the air around him. Donny almost screamed, but then Carlos calmed himself and wiped a hand across his face. "Spider-webs," he said. Angela snickered.

It wasn't as dark inside as Donny had expected. Rectangles of moonlight shone through the empty windows above, gleaming on the floor like cards laid out for solitaire. Still, Carlos took out a headlamp and strapped it across his forehead, and then handed a flashlight to Donny. "Thanks," Donny said.

"Maybe we should split up to search the place," Angela said.

"Maybe we should definitely stay together in one group and never ever split up for any reason," Donny countered.

"Don't be such a pantywaist," Angela told him. On another day, when things were better between them, Donny might have teased her about using another outdated expression. This time he frowned and said nothing.

"Just follow me, please," Carlos said. "And I agree with Donny. Stay together. This place makes me nervous. But, Señor Fiasco, it would help if you stayed a few steps behind."

"The moonlight on the floor is quite lovely. I should have brought my sketch pad," Fiasco mused.

The building was just a shell inside. There were charred sticks and black stains on the floor, the only sign of old fires. The beam of Donny's flashlight found moldy magazines, a battered grocery cart, crumpled fast-food bags, bottles and cans, and cigarette butts.

Wherever an opening led to other wings of the old hospital, Carlos paused for a moment, and then shook his head and moved on. At last he stopped at the top of a flight of concrete stairs that led into blackness. He closed his eyes, concentrating, and then looked at Angela and nodded. "Something is down there," he whispered. "But it is not what I sensed the first time, when I drove by this place."

"What's the difference?" Angela asked him quietly.

The headlamp dipped as Carlos furrowed his brow. "It's hard to describe. Before, it was like a foghorn. One thing: loud and significant." He pointed at the steps.

"Now . . . more like a hive. Many things, not so big." Neither one of those sounded good to Donny.

"Let's go down and get this over with," Fiasco said not nearly as quietly as the others. "I know a place back in Old San Juan where the band is still playing, and the dancers dancing."

"I agree," Angela said, and she started down the stairs. Carlos went next. Donny made sure he squeezed in after Carlos. There was no way he'd let himself fall to the back of the line, where something might sneak up and grab him. It was far better to be safe in the middle, between Fiasco and the others.

There was a metal door at the bottom of the stairs. It had been torn from its hinges long before, but somehow it still stood, blocking the doorway. A thick metal chain was wrapped around its middle. Donny didn't like the look of it at all.

"That's weird, right?" Angela said. There was a gap on both sides of the door. She peered in. "I can't see what's in there."

"Maybe we shouldn't touch it?" Donny suggested hopefully.

Angela gave it a push, but it didn't budge. "This is way heavier than it ought to be." She pressed her back against the door, braced her foot on the bottom step, and shoved, baring her teeth with the effort. The door screeched horribly on the floor and slid just an inch.

Donny cringed at the noise. "So much for sneaking up on them," he said.

"Allow me," Fiasco said, and he squeezed past Donny and Carlos. The space was so cramped, he could barely get by. Donny turned and scanned the stairway to make sure nothing was creeping down, alerted by the noise. They were in a dead end with no way out, and would be trapped.

It wasn't a dead end for long. Fiasco threw his bulk against the door, and it slid backward with a shriek and groan. Angela looked at Carlos and Donny and mimed a whistle of admiration.

Fiasco stepped sideways through the opening he'd created and then into the dark room. His voice echoed from within. "How interesting."

Angela followed Fiasco through the gap. Carlos went next, and Donny a split second later. He resisted the urge to clutch the back of Carlos's shirt.

Donny turned his flashlight on the door that had blocked their way. Someone had set tall slabs of concrete against the back of the door, many layers thick, and wrapped the chains around all of it.

"Why would someone do that?" Carlos wondered aloud.

Donny's mouth had run dry. "Maybe to make it so heavy that only someone crazy-strong could move it."

"I think you're right," Fiasco said. "No mortal could budge this. Whoever did this is powerful indeed, and strong enough to pull it shut from the other side, on his way out." To Donny's alarm, the huge fellow set his back to the concrete slabs and shoved the door back into place. He grunted and his face reddened with the effort. Donny looked at Carlos, who returned his wide-eyed glance.

Angela stepped in front of Donny and Carlos. "What're you up to, Fiasco?"

Fiasco slapped his hands together to brush off the concrete dust. "Eh? What am I up to? Oh! Have I made you nervous? I thought I should put this back. Otherwise someone could sneak down and surprise us."

Donny nodded, and remembered to breathe. That did make sense. The whole situation spooked him, though. And the idea that they were now trapped in this room didn't help. He explored the space some more with his flashlight, and his light swept across the long wall that was opposite the door.

"Criminy, what have we here?" Angela said.

The wall was lined with old shelves. On the shelves were jars made of black glass with large openings on top, sealed with thick glass stoppers and wax around the edges. There were hundreds of them.

"I can sense them. . . . This is what I felt," Carlos said. "There are so many!"

Angela took one of the glass jars from the shelf and held it at eye level. She turned back to Fiasco. "Somebody's been busy," she said. She tucked the jar under one arm like a football and dug the nails of her other hand into the wax, prying out the stopper. Her eyes followed something that Donny couldn't see, something that apparently came out of the jar and rose toward the ceiling. Fiasco watched it too, craning his neck.

Donny looked at Carlos. "Do you see anything?"

Carlos shook his head. "There are many supernatural things I can see, but not that."

"Oh, right," Angela said. "Of course you can't." She set the unstopped jar back onto the shelf and dug into a pocket of her satchel, producing a tiny bottle that was capped with an eyedropper. "You'll need drops in your eyes."

Donny had used them before. They were called demon drops, and they allowed humans to see the auras that every human soul emitted. And, apparently, they allowed you to see whatever was in those jars. Carlos raised his face and held his eyes open while Angela squeezed a drop from the stopper into each eye. Donny did the same. When she was done, Angela pressed the tiny bottle into Donny's hand and told him, "Keep it. You should have your own."

The drops felt strange and warm at first, but the feeling soon passed.

"Would you look at that?" Carlos said.

Donny looked at the jars on the shelves. They glowed from within, the light shining dimly through the dark hazy glass. Angela pried the stopper from another jar, and this time Donny saw what came out. He recognized it at once.

The little cloud of twinkling, swirling lights was a soul.

"The missing souls," Carlos said softly. "So beautiful. I never imagined."

Fiasco slapped Carlos on the back. "They *are* lovely, even the wicked ones! Perhaps a fitting subject for one of my paintings, now that you mention it."

"Was that a wicked one?" Donny asked.

Angela peered down the length of the shelves. An angry look crossed her face like a storm front. "That one was. But not all of these are." She shook her head and looked at Fiasco. "Whoever is doing this catches the bad *and* the good."

For the first time, Donny saw the good humor leave Fiasco's expression. "That can never be allowed." His mouth shrunk into an angry circle, and he shook his head.

Carlos was still fascinated by the soul as it slowly drifted up. "Can . . . can I touch it?" He reached out tentatively.

"It won't do any harm," Angela told him. Carlos smiled. His eyes glittered as he carefully brought his fingertips to the edge of the hovering soul, and then slowly moved his hand into the middle of the lights.

"I can see the souls in Sulfur without the drops," Donny said. "Why can't I see them here?"

"Because you're in the mortal realm, silly," Angela told him.

The freed soul floated to the basement ceiling, where it slipped through a crack in the floorboards. Carlos wore a peaceful smile as he watched it go. "What will happen to it now?"

"It'll drift toward the soulstream and get caught in the current. The way it was supposed to in the first place," Angela said. "The wicked ones will end up in Sulfur. The good ones . . . not my problem."

Fiasco tugged at his beard. "The question remains: Who trapped the souls and keeps them here?"

"Let's ponder that while we open these jars," Angela said. She reached for another.

"So all you have to do to trap a human soul is catch it inside glass?" Donny asked.

She shook her head. "Not any glass. These vessels had to be made in Sulfur. Just like the ones that hold our fire." Her brow furrowed, and she looked at the empty jar in her hand. She put her fingers into the top and tugged at it. A quarter of the jar snapped off. She shoved the piece into her satchel. "Cricket," she said, "why don't you take a look around and see if you find anything interesting?"

Donny looked down the dark length of the room. The far end was lost in shadows. He took a moment to gather his courage, and then walked slowly ahead, sweeping the beam of his flashlight into every nook and crevice.

"There are lots of empty jars here," he said. "I guess to hold more souls?" He reached the end of the room and saw something new. "Angela!" he called out. "You better look at this."

Angela jogged over, and he pointed with the flashlight. "I'll be darned," she said.

There was a wall lined with brick that had been blackened by fire. On the floor nearby were different kinds of glass vessels than the ones that held the souls. These were shaped like enormous jugs. Inside the dark brown glass Donny saw something bright and red that glowed and swirled like molten steel. "What is that?" he asked.

"You know how, when people on Earth want to build a fire-portal, they use propane?"

"Yeah."

"This is what someone from Sulfur would do. They'd bring that," she said, pointing to the brown jars. "Just pour it out, and you have a nice temporary fire." She put her hands on her hips and stared at the blackened wall. "So the question is: When someone opens this portal, what's on the other side?"

"Angela!" called Fiasco. "I think you should come talk to your friend."

Angela arched an eyebrow at Donny, and then they both hurried back to where Carlos stood. Carlos looked at his hands as they trembled. His face was slick with perspiration.

"What's wrong? Is that because you touched the soul?" Donny asked.

Carlos shook his head. "No. Something is coming." His eyes bulged as he looked at Angela. "It's close. I can feel it even though you and Fiasco are here. Very strong. *Muy malo.*"

Angela put her hands on her hips. "One thing, or lots of things?"

Carlos raised a finger. "One. One very bad thing."

"Not a problem," Angela said. She smiled at Fiasco. "We're two bad things."

Donny glanced at the door that blocked the entrance, with the massive slabs of thick concrete chained to it. Angela had struggled to move it, and Fiasco had only done it with great effort. Just how strong was this thing? He looked at Fiasco and saw the big fellow staring upward.

There were cracks in the ceiling where moonlight shone through. *That's not just the ceiling,* Donny thought. *It's the floor of the rooms above.* Fiasco put a finger to his lips, a signal to be quiet. Carlos looked up, and his headlamp lit the ceiling, but Fiasco reached over and blocked the light. Donny covered the beam of his flashlight with one hand, leaving only the reddish glow where it shone through his skin.

Now that it was dark, the moonlit cracks were easier to see. Donny heard the creak of floorboards and the shuffle of feet. Something blocked the moonlight in one of the cracks. And then another, and another. Whatever was up there was moving across the floor.

Donny shuddered when he realized where it was going. It was headed toward the stairs that led to this basement room.

CHAPTER 25

Nowhere to hide," Carlos said in a shaky voice. "There's nowhere to hide!"

"Put a sock in it, Carlos," Angela hissed. Donny looked up and down the long room. It was almost bare except for the shelves on one wall. Carlos was right—there was nowhere to take cover.

"Here's what we're gonna do," Angela said. "We get behind the door and stay there when it opens. I want this thing to come in where we can nab it. We do not want it getting away."

Donny *loved* the idea of this thing getting away, especially if it never came down the stairs in the first place. But all he could do was follow Angela and Fiasco as they stood behind the door and waited to pounce. Carlos was behind him, fiercely gripping Donny's shoulder.

"May I suggest we douse the lights?" Fiasco asked. Donny

slid the button on his flashlight but kept his thumb there, ready to flip the light back on. Carlos covered the bulb of his headlamp with a shaky hand.

Donny wondered what he was supposed to do. Angela hadn't given him anything to fight with. The flashlight wouldn't do much damage. *A hand grenade would be nice,* Donny thought.

Angela had done it again. She'd put his life in jeopardy, and he wondered if he'd escape this one unscathed, or even in one piece.

He heard steps on the stairs on the other side of the door. The thing didn't seem to know they were there, because it wasn't trying to be stealthy, from the sound of it. *Or maybe it doesn't care,* Donny thought. *That would be worse.*

He heard something else: The plink of glass against glass. *More of those jars, filled with souls,* he guessed.

The steps grew louder and then finally stopped. A new sound slipped through the narrow gaps between the door and the frame. A moist, ragged breathing. Then Donny heard rustling cloth and more clinking glass. In the darkness he could imagine what was happening: a bag of those jars had been set on the floor at the foot of the stairs. What he couldn't imagine was what sort of creature had put them down.

His eyes adjusted to the dim traces of moonlight that filtered into the room. He bit off a scream as spidery fingertips emerged through the gaps on both sides of the door and gripped the edges. Both sets of fingers were at the level of Fiasco's head. Whatever this thing was, it was tall. Donny had still held on to some hope that they were dealing with a human, but not any longer.

When Fiasco had moved the door, he'd shoved it hard, like a football player hitting a tackling sled. This creature just pushed it inward as if it were on wheels. The stone scraped across the floor. Donny was glad it was noisy, because Carlos let out a high-pitched whimper that only Donny could hear over the grinding of concrete.

The door swung to one side, even though it wasn't hinged. The four of them angled along with the door as it turned, shifting sideways to stay in line and out of sight. Donny thought the sight would have been comical if the predicament weren't so horrifying. Angela turned around to check on the rest of them. From the grin on her face, Donny would have thought this was a surprise party, not an ambush on a powerful, malevolent creature.

The door stopped moving once the threshold was fully exposed. Clinking sounds came again from the other side—the sack of jars being lifted once more. Donny held his breath. Angela crouched like a tiger ready to spring. Fiasco bent low and flexed his fingers.

The thing stepped into the room but was still mostly out of sight behind the door. Donny caught a glimpse of its shoulder—something boney with ragged edges—and then heard the sack of jars being set down again, this time on the inside of the room. *If it put the sack down,* his mind screamed, *it's going to come around to push the door closed!*

Which is exactly what it did.

CHAPTER 26

Carlos took his hands off the headlamp, and a beam of light struck the creature in the face. It froze and glared down from a height of at least eight feet. Time seemed to stop for a moment, along with Donny's heart.

Donny thought he'd opened his mouth to scream, but a gasp came out instead. There was something *familiar* about this thing.

"Golly gee!" Angela shouted. "It's a ferryman!"

Until that moment, Donny had only seen ferrymen on the barges that brought the dead to Sulfur, and among the Ferryman King's company. This one didn't wear the robes that made ferrymen resemble the classic version of the Grim Reaper. Stripped of the robe, it was clad in ancient, moldering rags that had fused to its mummified skin. This gave the already gaunt ferryman an even more lanky, skeletal, and horrifying appearance.

Donny had only an instant to absorb that information. Then the suspended moment ended, and the fight began.

The ferryman's long arm shot out and struck Angela with the heel of a bony hand. She was launched backward into Fiasco, who slammed into Donny, who slammed into Carlos, and the four of them tumbled like bowling pins.

The light from Carlos's headlamp swung wildly as he rolled. Fiasco had fallen hard on top of Donny. It squeezed the breath from his chest and nearly crushed his bones. The weight was off him just as suddenly, as the big fellow shot nimbly to his feet. Donny rolled onto his stomach and looked up, trying to suck air back into his lungs.

Angela leaped to her feet. She pointed at the ferryman. "You're in a lot of trouble, buster!"

The ferryman hissed. His long arm whipped forward again, and he clutched the front of Angela's shirt. He hurled her with absurd strength into the air, so high that she struck the ceiling above. As she fell, pieces of old wood and dust rained after her. She landed roughly on her side and twisted in pain. Her arm was bent at a strange angle and surely broken. The woozy look on her face was a shock to Donny. He had never seen her injured before, and had thought of her as nearly indestructible.

The ferryman reached for a weapon that was slung at his waspish waist—a short-handled scythe with a crescent blade big enough to slice a man in half. Fiasco charged before the ferryman raised the weapon. The ferryman leaned back, lifted a leg, and unleashed a powerful kick. Fiasco was suddenly a blur as he whooshed over Donny's head and straight into one of the shelves of jars. There was a hailstorm of dark glass, and the entire shelf toppled over and buried Fiasco. A twinkling cloud of freed souls drifted from the wreckage.

Somehow Donny still had the flashlight in his grip, his thumb on the button. As he rose to his knees, he slid the button forward and aimed the beam at the ferryman's face. He didn't know what good it would do—blind the monstrous being for a moment, perhaps. The awful face was spotlit in the dim room. The eyes glared from deep within hollow sockets, the only moist things on an arid face. A skeletal mouth grinned horribly. Up went the arm, wielding the wicked blade. It glittered in the dark, poised to strike.

Carlos stepped in front of Donny and hurled a jar at the awful face. The ferryman's other hand flashed up and caught the vessel neatly before it struck. Carlos pulled Donny to his feet and yanked him aside as the blade swept down in a ter-rible arc. Donny heard the weapon whistle through air, and then an awful sound of tearing fabric. Carlos cried out in pain. He clenched his teeth and staggered, a hand pressed against his side. *"Carlos!"* shouted Donny.

Dark laughter bubbled from deep inside the ferryman's throat. Donny put his arm around Carlos and helped him move. A dark stain spread around the tear in Carlos's shirt, and redness oozed between his fingers. It only took one step of the ferryman's stiltlike legs for him to reach them. The ferryman's free hand palmed the top of Carlos's head and tilted it back to bare the neck. The hand with the blade prepared to strike.

Behind the ferryman, the toppled shelf erupted. Something roared up from the glass and wood and spread its massive arms wide. It was Fiasco—but not in the human form Donny had come to know. This was a raging beast clad in bony plates. Fiasco was huge as a man, but as a demon he was even more enormous and breathtaking to behold, like a cross between a dinosaur and a grizzly bear. His paint-splattered shirt was ripped open around his barrel chest, and the thighs of his pants had split. A single lethal horn jutted from his forehead, and his eyes blazed with an orange inner flame. He bellowed and charged, pulverizing wood and glass under his beach sandals.

Before Fiasco arrived, the ferryman had tried to slash his blade down on Carlos's exposed neck—and probably slice through to take Donny's head as well—but Angela sprang up, recovered from her daze. Her wounded arm hung limp by her side, but she hooked her good arm inside the ferryman's elbow and prevented the strike.

Fiasco's shoulder hit the ferryman with the force of a runaway train. The three of them, Angela, Fiasco, and the gaunt ferryman, flew into a wooden pillar and broke it like a breadstick. Part of the floor above collapsed and rained onto their shoulders. Angela rolled to one side, and Fiasco lifted his hands to shield his head.

The ferryman looked up and spotted the gap that had been opened. He scrambled to his feet and leaped, meaning to jump straight through and escape. But Fiasco seized his ankle and whipped him back down. As the ferryman slammed into the floor, he swung his blade again. It bit into the hard plates on Fiasco's thigh and stuck there.

Fiasco, so filled with humor and cheer in human form, was a rampaging monster in his demon state. He plucked the blade from his thigh and flung it to the other end of the room. Steam whistled from where the blade had bit. The ferryman leaped to his feet again, and Fiasco grabbed him by the shoulders.

"Don't kill him, Fiasco!" Angela cried out. If Fiasco heard those words, he did not show it. He snarled and bull-rushed the ferryman toward the concrete wall nearby, and then lowered his horn into the ferryman's chest. The impact shook dust from the rafters. Donny heard Fiasco's horn strike the concrete, all the way through the other side of the ferryman.

The skeletal creature squealed, a sound so piercing and dreadful that Donny clapped his hands over his ears. Fiasco pried his horn from the ferryman's chest. The ferryman slid down the wall and came to rest, his feet splayed. His spidery hands tried to cover the gaping hole that Fiasco had made. Donny beamed his flashlight there, and saw hot mist flooding out of the wound. The ferryman stared up at Fiasco, his eyes wild and frightened. He shivered, and his long gray teeth clacked together. Dust flew from his throat as he coughed.

Angela limped toward the fallen ferryman, cradling her arm. "Boy, Fiasco, you really put a hurt on him."

Fiasco crunched his enormous hands into fists. His breath hissed furiously through his flared nostrils, and he turned toward Angela and growled. He looked ready to do more damage to anyone in the vicinity.

"Easy, sweet pea." Angela took a step back. "You did great. Come back to me now, okay? Why don't you go find your gold band and put it on?"

Donny glanced at Fiasco's ankle. The gold band that was normally around his sock was missing. Fiasco made a concentrated effort to contain his rage. He closed his eyes and breathed deeply. Then he walked toward the fallen shelf and searched the debris for the band that would restore him to his human form.

Donny worried for a moment that the ferryman might have some fight left in him, but the gaunt figure toppled over until his shoulder was on the floor and his head hung at an awkward angle. Angela kneeled in front of him, just out of reach of the long arms and legs. "Looks like the fire's going out of you, old man," she said. She pointed at the vapor wafting from the wound. "Why don't you tell me what this is all about? Where do you go on the other side of that fire? Are you working alone, or did someone put you up to this? I'll try to help you. All you have to do is talk."

The ferryman twitched, and his limbs jerked as if some mad puppeteer were tugging his strings. The jaw opened and shut with frightening speed, and the teeth slammed together until they finally cracked and tumbled loose. He let out a great wheeze as dust and mist flowed from his mouth and his wound. Then every part of his lanky form broke loose, clattering together and finally collapsing into silence. All that remained was a lifeless pile of bones covered with rags.

"Well, phooey," Angela said. "He didn't tell us anything."

Carlos groaned, and Donny suddenly remembered. "Carlos is hurt!" he cried.

"Huh?" Angela said, turning to look. Carlos was on his knees, his face pale and his teeth clamped tight. He pressed his hand against the slash that started on his side and went halfway across his belly. Blood streamed between his fingers.

"Call 911," Carlos managed to get out, gasping.

"Meaning what, exactly?" Angela asked.

"Meaning he needs a doctor right now!" Donny snapped. The ferocity in his voice made Angela's head spin toward him.

Fiasco swooped in, human once more. The enormous beard was gone, revealing an anvil of a chin below. Fiasco kneeled beside Carlos, cradled him like a baby, and lifted him. Carlos winced and groaned. "To the car," Fiasco said. "I know where the hospital is."

Donny lit the way with his flashlight as they raced upstairs, out of the old building, and back to the rented car. Fiasco laid Carlos gently across the backseat.

"I can drive," Angela said.

Carlos's head popped up. "No!" he said weakly. "She cannot drive! I will be dead for sure." He had pulled the keys from his pocket but now clutched them to his chest, away from Angela's reach.

"I can drive a little," Fiasco said. "I think."

"That has to be better than her," Carlos said, and gasped. He held the keys out for Fiasco.

"Take my scooter back," Fiasco said as he wedged his bulk into the driver's seat, his head brushing the ceiling. He tossed a keychain to Angela.

Donny stood by the open rear door. "You'll be okay," he told Carlos, trying to sound confident. Carlos had shut his eyes, and he barely responded except to nod and lick his lips. Donny gulped and closed the door.

"Which one's the gas?" Fiasco shouted.

"The square one on the left," Angela said.

"No, it isn't," said Donny. Even he knew that. "It's the long skinny one on the right!" He started to wonder if he should be the driver, even though he'd never driven before. Carlos raised one bloody hand to draw a cross in the air over his chest. "Maybe I should go with you!" Donny called out, but Fiasco didn't hear him as the engine blasted to life, getting way too much gas.

The car lurched backward and nearly spilled Carlos off the backseat. Fiasco grimaced and shifted from reverse to forward. The car bolted ahead, Carlos thumping into the backrest. From the way the vehicle turned the corner, the brake lights on and the wheels squealing, Donny was pretty sure that Fiasco had his huge feet on the gas and the brake at the same time.

"Hey, Fiasco's driving pretty well," Angela said.

Donny just stared at her. "Carlos is really hurt."

"Oh, come on. It was just a scratch."

Donny's jaw sagged. "Just a *scratch*? It was deep, Angela. He might bleed to death. Don't you even know that? Carlos could *die*."

"You're so dramatic. They'll just sew him back up, right? Put more blood in him?"

Donny was dumbstruck. He stared at her, amazed and horrified. Angela Obscura might look perfectly human, but she wasn't human at all, and that fact was now completely laid bare. She had no real regard for the frailty and mortality of human beings. She couldn't even relate.

He spoke again, his tone colder than ice. "Carlos got hurt because he saved me. He was so scared of that thing, but when it came after us, he put himself in front of me. And now he might die, and I don't think you really care."

She waved the back of her hand at him. "Pshaw. Betcha he doesn't. Come on. We have to clean up down there. Then I'll take you back to the hotel."

Donny fumed in silence as they returned to the depths of the old building. When they were downstairs, Angela flexed her wounded arm and grimaced. "Hang on a sec," she said. She pulled the gold bracelet off her gloved wrist, triggering the transformation to her demon form.

"Why are you doing that?" Donny asked. He was angry but still curious.

"Transforming will heal an injury if it's not too bad," she said. She arched her neck as the skin there turned to scales. The hair fell away from her scalp and rained onto the floor. When the change was complete, she straightened her arm completely. "Much better. One more change will do, but it's exhausting to do them too close together. Come on. Help me pop the rest of the lids off these jars, will you?"

They released all the souls still trapped in glass, the good and the bad. Then Angela went to the corpse of the ferryman.

"I don't get it," Donny said. "How could something like this come and go without being seen?"

"It's like that whispering demon we captured back in Brooklyn. Remember that? There are some things the human mind doesn't want to sense. As long as this guy kept quiet, avoided daylight, and stuck to the darkest shadows, people wouldn't have noticed him. A few sensitive ones might have felt his presence, the way Carlos did. But they wouldn't have *seen* him. The only reason you and Carlos did is because you used the demon drops."

Donny watched with a grimace as she pried the jawbone off the ferryman's skull and set it aside. It resembled the jawbone of the Ferryman King, and perhaps all the ferrymen, with a distinctive point at the bottom, like a beard made of bone. She shoved all the bones and the scythe into a small pile, and took what looked like a flask from her pack.

"What's that?" Donny asked.

"You sound so glum. Cheer up! This is a special blend of flame. Good for getting rid of evidence." She opened the flask and gently tipped it over. Flames poured from the narrow spout like a living liquid, and devoured the skeleton and the garments. When she was done, there was barely a trace left behind, only a shallow crater in the cement floor. She capped the flask and stuffed it back into her satchel, along with the jawbone. Then she stood and walked to the end of the room where the jugs of fire were kept near the blackened wall. She puckered her scaly lips and tapped them with a finger. Then, to Donny's alarm, she reached down, picked up a jug, and pulled out its stopper.

Donny clasped his hands on top of his head. "What are you doing? Why would you do that?"

She tipped the jug over and poured a bright orange

liquid out in a line in front of the blackened wall. "Curiosity, mostly," she replied. Then she stood back and watched.

"This seems really dangerous," Donny said. His legs were electrified, ready to send him out the door at the first sign of anything that came through the fire.

"I just want to see if anyone opens it from the other side," she said. She waited awhile, and then cupped her hands around her mouth and whispered into the flame.

"What? What are you doing?"

"I'm calling Porta, to see if she answers."

"Why wouldn't she answer? She always does."

Angela looked at him over her shoulder. "Silly. It doesn't happen with just any fire. The site has to be prepared."

"Prepared? Prepared how?"

"When I set up a new portal, I mingle some special flames from our portal back in Sulfur. If I don't do that, there's no connection, and the gatekeepers can't sense the fire."

Donny waved a finger at her. "Wait a minute. The first time we met, you rescued me from a regular fire." It came out like an accusation.

"You were a little overcome by smoke, my friend. You didn't see me open a vial of flame. It only takes a second." She stared at the fire. "Hang on. I'll try some other portals." She spoke softly into the fire again, but once more nothing happened. "Wherever this goes," she said, "it's not to any portal I know. Hmmm."

"But there has to be one of those gatekeepers on the other side, right?" Donny asked. He thought of Porta, and the creature like Porta in the Himalayan temple.

"That's right. There has to be," Angela said. Her reptilian jaw slid from side to side as she pondered. "It's always the same kind of demon. Female. Tiny. Foul temper. There aren't many of them, but we've never done a head count or anything. You've got me thinking, Donny. Without a gatekeeper, a fire-portal is useless. So if we want to cut off the flow of lost souls, we really need to grab that gatekeeper."

She stood for a while, watching and waiting. "Anyhow. Let's move on, I suppose. I'll have Howard get a crew in here and tidy up the rest of this mess."

"You're going to leave that fire burning?" he asked.

"I only used a little. It'll go out soon." She clapped the bracelet back onto her wrist, and before long she was human again, at least in appearance. This time she was remade with straight black hair, her most common incarnation.

Donny followed her back out of the old building. She tapped him on the shoulder. "Now that you've got the drops in your eyes, look at the roof."

"I don't see anything," he said. He stared at where the stained cement walls met the night sky.

"Keep looking. It comes and goes."

"I still don't— Oh." Something flickered into view as he stared. It was easier to see if he didn't look directly at it, and even then it faded in and out. A dark line rippled across the sky like a ribbon caught in a gentle breeze. Low clouds had gathered, reflecting the lights of the city, and the line curved up and vanished into the clouds in both directions. Donny only saw it because its waving course brought it close to the rooftop of the old hospital. Tiny lights, as dim as the faintest stars, drifted along that dark vein in the sky.

"That's the soulstream," he said quietly.

"Yes. You can see why the ferryman chose this spot. It doesn't dip this low in many places. He could stand on the roof and grab the souls that drifted by."

Even as Donny looked, the soulstream dimmed and winked from sight. "It's gone," he said.

"Still there, just hard to see. Like the northern lights. That was a pretty good look you got. You're lucky. Now, ready to go?"

They walked down the street, and Donny saw Fiasco's scooter, still on its kickstand in the shadows. He gave some serious thought to walking back to Old San Juan instead of riding with Angela. But it was way too far, and he wasn't sure of the direction. All he wanted was the comfortable bed in his hotel room. So he really didn't have a choice.

"You'll drive carefully, right?" he asked.

"Heck, yeah," she replied.

A light rain began to fall, hissing in the dark.

CHAPTER 27

They buzzed and weaved down the road like a drunken hornet. Wet pavement flashed under the wheels. The drops of rain felt like needles on Donny's skin. He was behind Angela on the scooter, his arms wrapped around her slender waist. Holding her that close, his chest against her back, might have been a thrill on some other night, but something had snapped inside his heart. A plug had been pulled, a connection broken. He only worried that he might not survive this wild ride, and he shouted at her with real anger. "Turn on the headlight! Red means stop! Watch the curb! That's the wrong side of the road again! Don't let go of the handles!"

Every shout was met with fizzy laughter. They didn't pass many cars, but most of them blew their horns as they went by.

Donny's legs were wobbly tubes of yogurt by the time they arrived at the hotel.

"What shall we do now?" Angela asked, still straddling the scooter as Donny hopped off and staggered toward the lobby door.

"I just want to find out if Carlos is okay," Donny said.

"And how do you intend to do that?"

"I don't know. Call hospitals, starting with the one closest to that town."

"Oh, you speak Spanish now? You'd better let Howard's people handle that," Angela said. "I'll text him."

"Howard will be asleep."

"So? This is why he makes the big bucks."

Donny watched her take her phone from a pocket and tap a message with her thumbs, humming all the while. "Good night," he muttered without turning to be heard better. He pushed the door open and went into the lobby. He looked back once before he got onto the elevator. Through the glass in the door he saw her watching him, a mild look of shock on her pretty face.

Once in his room, Donny pushed the door shut, bolted it, swung the second lock into place, and latched the chain. He yanked the bedcover down and flopped onto the sheets. Physically, he was wiped, but his nerves were an electrical storm that wouldn't let him sleep. He sat up and put his head in his hands. There was a picture of a flamenco dancer on the wall, and he stared at it without really seeing it.

Now how many times had this relationship almost killed

him? He could add the rogue ferryman to the count. Since he'd met Angela, he'd been terrorized, clawed, beaten and tortured, and nearly shot, crushed, stabbed, and devoured.

But somehow none of that was the worst of it. The worst was when he'd overheard that conversation. Angela's words came back to him again, like a song he hated but couldn't get out of his mind.

I need to learn what I can from the boy while he still lives. It's very likely that one of our adventures will get him killed. Then . . . I'll find another.

It's easy enough to replace him. Just set a fire or something, put them in danger of their lives, and they'll beg to come with me.

I want Donny to think he's important to me. How else will I get him to do what I want?

It was a sick memory that infected everything. With his stomach churning, he took the phone from his pocket. He had a message for Howard too. It was just six words long, but he stared at it for an hour before his trembling thumb pressed send.

CHAPTER 28

Howard. It's Donny. I want out.

CHAPTER 29

They met outside the hotel early the next morning. Without a word, Howard led him a few blocks away to another blue-cobblestoned street that Donny hadn't been on yet. They went inside a tiny restaurant that was open for breakfast.

"*Café americano, por favor,*" Howard told the server in awkward Spanish. "Anything for you, Donny?" Donny barely heard the question. He stared into space, his arms folded limply in front of him, and managed a weak shrug. "*Huevos y tocineta.* Oh, and, uh, *jugo de naranja,*" Howard said to the server, gesturing to Donny and himself.

"Coming right up," the server replied in perfect English.

Howard waited for the server to walk away and then leaned toward Donny. "About your message. Are you absolutely sure?"

Donny blinked his eyes back into focus and nodded.

"Yes. I have to. You . . . you said you might find my mother soon." His voice clogged with emotion.

Howard's coffee arrived, and he waited for the server to leave again. Then he leaned in even closer. "We were closer to finding her than I let on the last time we talked. I didn't want to get your hopes up too high. But yes. We found her."

Without realizing what he was doing, Donny had plucked a sugar packet from the bowl and twisted it. It tore open, and crystals scattered across the table. "You . . . you found her?"

"She's in Colorado, as we thought. A town called Estes Park, right by the eastern side of the Rocky Mountains. She changed her name. It's not Maria anymore. It's Jessica now. Jessica Dunlap."

"Dunlap?" Donny asked.

Howard nodded. The orange juice arrived, and Howard waited again until they were alone.

"Dunlap is her married name. She got married five years ago."

"Married?" Donny couldn't do much but repeat words back. It reminded him of Echo, a kindly creature who'd died saving Angela.

Howard nodded. "He seems like a good man. Nothing criminal about him. He's a builder who has done well for himself." He paused until Donny looked at him. "She has a child now, Donny. You have a half brother."

Amid all the fear and dread, a strangely alien feeling of happiness washed over Donny. It caught him by surprise. A half brother! He'd always wondered what it would be like to have a brother.

"We can take you there, but the rest will be up to you," Howard said. "I don't want my organization embroiled in this in any way. I'll trust you to keep all this a secret. Every bit of it. We can't have any rumors about Angela or Sulfur slipping out. And we'll take action if it happens. Is that understood?"

Donny nodded. He wasn't sure how far Howard's organization would go to keep their secrets, but he guessed the answer was *pretty far.* "Yes, sir. Definitely."

Howard didn't reply, because their breakfast had arrived. Donny suddenly had an appetite, and he grabbed a fork and stabbed his bacon.

"There's one more complication," Howard said as he shook pepper over his eggs. Donny looked up. "I believe I mentioned this already. You have to ask Angela's permission to leave her service."

Donny's appetite vanished, and the bacon turned to cardboard on his tongue. "Could you . . . ," he began hopefully.

Howard shook his head. "It has to come from you. There's no other way. I can't predict how she'll react, but if the answer is yes, I'll have you flown to Colorado. From there, someone from my organization will—"

Howard stopped in midsentence, because Donny's head had whipped sideways to look out the front window. A tall, broad form had passed by, eclipsing the morning sunlight, and then returned. It was Fiasco. The big fellow framed his hands around his eyes to peer through the window, and spotted Donny. A wide smile that looked bigger than ever, now that his beard was gone, spread across that jovial face. A moment later the door clattered open.

"Fiasco!" cried the server, bouncing up to greet him. "What happened to your beard?"

"Pablo!" Fiasco boomed back. He lifted the server into a crushing hug, his feet dangling off the ground. "Good to see you, *amigo*! Never mind my missing beard; I will grow another. You have special guests in your restaurant this morning. I hope you are treating them well!"

"Of course," Pablo said airlessly as Fiasco set him down.

The silverware on the table bounced as Fiasco rumbled over. He gave a nod and a grin to Howard, and then clapped Donny on the back with brute force. "Donny, you look well this morning! And here is a fellow I have not seen for many years! The mysterious and talented Howard."

Howard stood to shake Fiasco's hand. "A pleasure to see you again, sir. Would you like to join us?"

"Of course!" Fiasco dragged a chair from another table and sat with them. He plucked a piece of bacon off Donny's plate and popped it into his mouth. "So, Donny, you escaped our misadventure without injury?"

"I'm okay," Donny said. "But it's only because you were there to save us." He bit his bottom lip. "But what about Carlos?" He suddenly felt ashamed, because he'd forgotten to even ask Howard about their wounded friend.

"I am happy to tell you that Carlos will recover. It will take some time, because the wound was deep and needed many stitches, or so the human doctors told me." He gave Howard a sly sideways look. "But an interesting thing happened last night. At first the doctors and then the police demanded to know what had happened. They asked many questions, and they were not content with the story I made up for them about finding Carlos after he had been attacked by a crazed man with a knife. Then suddenly the questions stopped and the police left." He put a meaty hand on Howard's shoulder. "I wonder if our resourceful friend had something to do with that."

Howard took a sip of coffee. "I do what I can to help, Señor Fiasco."

A pat on the back sent Howard's coffee sloshing over the rim. "Just Fiasco will do! Come by my gallery today, Howard, and I will gift you with a beautiful painting of our lovely city, one that you will treasure always."

Donny tried not to laugh. "Fiasco, do you miss your beard?"

Fiasco looked like a wounded puppy. "Oh yes. Terribly so." He dropped his voice to a whisper. "I'd hoped I would not have to transform. But that ferryman was monstrously strong, as they all are, so there was no choice. I always return to human form without the beard." He stroked the missing whiskers. "Alas, it will take many moons before such a lush forest can be regrown. Until then, some may not even recognize the great artist they have come to know." Fiasco's eyes widened as he noticed something on the counter beside the cash register. "Pablo!" he cried. He shot from his chair, sending it sliding backward, and ran to the counter, where he gathered a small vase of flowers and a bowl of fruit in his arms. "Pablo! I have been seized with inspiration! May I steal these and paint them?"

Pablo had been cleaning the counter, but he laughed and nodded. "Of course, Fiasco. Anything you want!" Fiasco had already burst out the door, and Donny saw him run down the cobblestoned street, looking as happy as any being he'd ever seen. It was almost impossible to believe that, just sixty years before, Fiasco would have been another terrible demon hunched over the Pit of Fire, tormenting human souls. The changes that had swept over Sulfur had freed him from that life. Just as they had freed Angela.

Angela, he thought. It was time to talk to her.

CHAPTER 30

Angela slept late, as she often did. The DO NOT DISTURB sign, which also read POR FAVOR, NO MOLESTE, hung from her doorknob, and Donny didn't hear any sounds coming from the room. She could snooze well past noon when the mood struck her. This might be that kind of morning, after the battle with the ferryman.

It wasn't too hot yet, so Donny took a walk. He wandered through the bumpy streets, past plazas, statues, and potted palms. At nearly eleven, he found himself close to the building where Fiasco and the other artists worked. It occurred to him that he hadn't thanked Fiasco enough for saving Carlos, so he poked his head inside and looked down the length of the room.

He smiled. Fiasco was at his easel, painting the flowers and fruit he'd borrowed from the restaurant. As Donny watched, a trio of people who looked like college students, two guys and a girl, approached Fiasco and began to look over his work. Donny's smile deflated into a frown as he saw them nudge one another and point. Fiasco looked up from his work and popped off his stool, a warm grin on his face. He held his arms wide and greeted the trio, picked up samples of his paintings, and talked about each with great enthusiasm.

The three were barely able to keep from laughing while Fiasco talked. The girl covered her mouth with her hand, turned away, and pretended to cough. One of the guys talked to Fiasco, but Donny detected the sarcasm in his false grin and body language, even from a distance. The other one snuck cell phone pictures of Fiasco and the art. They finally waved to Fiasco and walked away, and they hadn't gone ten feet before they put their heads together, whispered, and burst into laughter.

Fiasco had always seemed oblivious to how people really reacted to his art, but this time Donny saw the way his gaze lowered to the floor, and his broad shoulders slumped. Maybe it was because the enormous beard was gone, but it was easy to see the warmth and humor depart from his expression. He suddenly looked old and tired, a mountain of a man slightly eroded. He returned to his stool and slowly picked up his brush and palette, but then set them down again and sat, his hand cradling the bottom of his jaw.

Donny glared at the trio as they walked out of the

building. "You okay there, Sparky?" one of the boys said when he caught Donny's glance.

"Nothing wrong with *me*," Donny replied, still glaring. The boy looked at his friends, then shrugged and snickered.

Donny's blood was on fire. He stepped back out of sight in case Fiasco looked his way, and stood in the shade, smacking the wall with his fist.

Then he got an idea.

He patted the pocket of his shorts. There was a lot of money in there still, several hundred at least. He looked up and down the street and searched for a stranger who might help. There were tourists here and there, wandering the old city, shopping and sight-seeing. "But who can I trust?" he muttered to himself.

There was something else in his other pocket, he remembered. Soon he wouldn't need them anymore, or even be allowed to have them. But they could be helpful here. He dug out the tiny bottle of demon drops, pulled the dropper from the top, and squeezed a drop into each eye. He blinked rapidly and felt the liquid encompass his eyeballs and warm them to a nearly uncomfortable degree. The heat faded, and the world took on an amber hue as if he wore tinted glasses. Now when he looked at people, he saw the auras that surrounded them—a halo of light that glowed different colors and revealed to him who was good and decent, and who was downright nasty. It always felt like a violation to see people like this, but right now he just needed a specific kind of person.

As usual, most people were somewhere in between. A sour-looking man went past with an aura so dark and purple that Donny pressed himself against the wall to stay out of his way. A few more went by, including a promising old gentleman, but Donny held out for something better.

Then he saw them. A pair of plump middle-aged women in sundresses, sunglasses, and sandals, each with a shopping bag, ambled down the street. One had short hair, and one had longer hair, but their features were so similar that Donny was sure they were sisters. Better yet, they spoke English. Best of all, their auras were like golden sunshine, some of the brightest Donny had ever seen.

He wondered what to say to them, but they spoke to him first. "Good morning, young fella," one said with a sweet smile and a hint of a Southern accent.

"Um, hi," Donny responded. He scrambled to think of how to ask for what he wanted before they walked by. "Excuse m-me, ma'ams," he sputtered. It was enough to get them to stop and look curiously back. He put on his most angelic smile and pressed his palms together. "I wonder if I could ask a really big favor?"

They looked at each other, their eyebrows raised over the tops of their sunglasses. "Well," said the long-haired one, "I guess it depends what the favor is."

"It's nothing bad, I promise," Donny said. He pointed with his thumb at the doorway of the artist's building. "There's a guy in there, selling his art. But nobody buys any of it, ever, because it's terrible. So I was wondering if maybe you could go in there, make a big fuss about how great his paintings are, and buy some of them." The women opened their mouths, maybe to object, but Donny went on before they could say anything. "You don't have to use your own money. I'll give you the money." He reached into his pocket and pulled out a handful of bills. "Use this! What is this . . . ? It's, like, four hundred dollars. Buy as much as you can with this. Meet me at that plaza right over there, and if you do that, I'll give you a lot more money, just for doing this. Okay?"

They both pushed their sunglasses to the tops of their heads and stared at the bills. Then they looked at each other, amused and a little stunned. "You really have that kind of money to throw around?" asked the long-haired sister.

Donny nodded. "Uh-huh. And I really need your help. It's super-important."

"This feels like one of those hidden-camera shows," the other one said.

"No, this is for real," Donny said. "That guy in there—he really deserves this. I can't do it, because we know each other. Would you please, *please* do this for me?"

The long-haired one chuckled and wagged her head. "This is just the weirdest thing anybody's ever asked."

"I guess it won't do any harm," the other one ventured.

"Great!" Donny said. Before they reconsidered, he shoved the money into the long-haired woman's hand. "He's at the end of that long room, the very last artist. A huge guy. His name is Fiasco."

"Did you say Fiasco?"

"Yes, ma'am. He's nice; you'll like him. And believe me, you'll know him and his art when you see them. Remember, you have to pretend it's really good."

"It can't be *that* bad," the short-haired one said.

"No, it definitely is. Thank you, ladies. I knew you'd help as soon as I saw you."

The long-haired one laughed and repositioned her sunglasses. "All right, here we go. I shouldn't be surprised— crazy things happen to us all the time!"

Tell me about it, Donny thought to himself. He watched them approach the entrance and pause to get a few giggles out of their system. They nodded back at him, smoothed the wrinkles from their dresses, and walked inside.

CHAPTER 31

From the plaza, Donny could see the doorway. He waited, and then relaxed when the sisters had been inside for a while. His biggest fear was that they might come back out and leave without buying anything—either because they wanted to keep the money, or because one of them turned out to be one of those rare people who was sensitive to the presence of infernal beings.

He sat on the wall of a fountain and drummed his kneecaps with his fingers until he started to get nervous. *It shouldn't take this long, should it?* It seemed like almost an hour had gone by. He was about to sneak over and peek inside to see what was happening when the women emerged, each with three or four paintings of various sizes wrapped in brown paper and twine. They headed straight for the plaza, talking to each other in excited whispers. Donny waved them over and backed away until they were all out of sight of Fiasco's building.

"Hold these," the short-haired sister said. She shoved the paintings into his hands, reached into her purse for a tissue, and wiped tears from her eyes. The other sister laughed and shook her head.

"Uh, how did it go?" Donny asked.

"I think that was the happiest gentleman I have ever seen," the long-haired sister said.

"It was wonderful," the other one said with a sniff. She was crying the right kind of tears, where good feelings filled you up and spilled right out of your eyes. Donny reached into his pocket for more of the cash.

The long-haired sister wagged a finger. "You leave that money right where it is. We won't take another dime."

"We just got all the reward we could ask for," said the other sister. They had the type of shared brain where they completed each other's thoughts. Sort of like if Zig-Zag ever agreed on anything.

"What happened in there?" Donny asked.

"Well, that man was in a sorry state."

"He looked like somebody had just run over all his kittens."

"So we wandered over, and I said, 'Look, Loraine, isn't this one nice?'"

"And I said, 'I like that one even better, Brenda.' Then that Fiasco picked up his head, and he looked over and rubbed his eyes like he didn't quite believe what he was seeing."

"Then I said, 'Why, sir, do you happen to know who did all these beautiful paintings,' and he popped out of his chair like he'd been shot from a cannon!"

"I never thought a man that large could move so fast."

"He just went on and on about each painting, and made sure we saw every one."

"*Every* one," said Loraine, with a momentary grimace.

"So we bought all we could with the money you gave us."

"But he insisted on giving us a couple more, because he knew how much we loved them," Loraine said with a chuckle.

"Then he wrapped up the paintings for us, thank the good Lord, because they truly are dreadful."

"He asked for my address so he could send us a thank-you note!"

"Then we both got the biggest hugs we ever got, and I'm half surprised he didn't break all our bones."

"You've never seen such a happy man, laughing and practically dancing."

"He even cried a little, and it was the oddest thing, because I could swear I saw steam coming out of his eyes when he cried."

"You know, I thought I saw that too!" Brenda said.

Change the subject, Donny thought. "I can take the rest of those for you," he told them, pointing at the paintings.

"You know what?" Loraine said. "You just take those

big ones. I'll hold on to the little ones. They can fit just fine on the plane. I know they're awful, but I might want to take them out for a look once in a while so I can remember this day. And you, young fellow."

"Same goes for me," Brenda said. She leaned the bigger paintings against the fountain wall and kept two that weren't much bigger than a cookie sheet.

"Are you sure I can't give you some more money?"

"Don't you even think about it! Why, you're just a little saint, aren't you? Your parents must be so proud."

Donny thanked them again and said good-bye. They walked happily across the plaza and vanished around a corner, giving him a final wave back. Donny was thinking about what to do with the paintings that were left, when his phone buzzed in his pocket. He took it out to see a text from Angela.

Where u at little buddy? Let's have late breakfast or early lunch or whatever. I'm starvin, Marvin.

All his warm feelings vanished in an instant, like a candle snuffed. He stared at the message for a while. "This is it," he mumbled. His thoughts went foggy. He wrote something simple back, but it took minutes to compose because his shaking thumbs kept hitting the wrong buttons.

Be right there. See u in the lobby.

Right before he sent it, he noticed again the ornate letter *O* that was imprinted on his palm. Angela's mark was just a ghost of what it used to be.

He walked slowly back to the hotel, in no hurry for this fateful conversation. Second thoughts bubbled up, but every time he remembered the awful conversation he'd overheard, those bubbles burst.

Down one alley, he spotted a Dumpster that was half full of construction debris. He looked around to make sure nobody would see, and then tossed the rest of Fiasco's paintings into the Dumpster. It made him feel awful. In a weird way, he wanted to keep them, for the same reasons the sisters did. But he didn't know what else to do. He never wanted Fiasco to know why they'd really been bought, and he didn't think he'd be able to bring them wherever he was going. It was safer to just get rid of them.

He turned the corner and saw their hotel. "Oh boy." He stopped, shut his eyes for a moment, and took a deep breath.

When he went inside, Angela was in a flowery blue dress, waiting in the lobby.

CHAPTER 32

Near the hotel was a street that was for pedestrians only. There were restaurants on both sides, and tables and chairs had been set up on the cobblestones.

"This is all very charming," Angela said.

Donny nodded. The best thing about the scene was all the tourists at the tables around them and in the street. He didn't think he was brave enough to tell her what he had to say in private. There was no telling how she might react. Being in public might keep him safe, or save his life, for all he knew.

The server came over and they ordered lunch.

"I heard Carlos will be okay," Donny said after the server left.

"Yes, that's dandy, isn't it? Though he's out of commission for a while, and I wish we had him for the next part of our investigation. We'll sally forth without him, I guess."

Donny nodded, but his head wobbled awkwardly. He looked down at the table. It was suddenly so hard to look at her.

"Obviously we have to go to the other spot on the map. But this time I think we wait and watch, so we can figure out where the . . ." Her voice trailed off. "Cricket, is everything all right?" She leaned forward, elbows on the table, and stared him down, one mischievous eyebrow arched high. "You've been a funny bunny for a couple of days now."

Donny's palms had turned sweaty. He wiped them on the thighs of his shorts, and clutched his shins, rocking back and forth in his seat. "Uh. Yeah. I know. It's just . . . I gotta tell you something."

She put her knuckles under her chin. "Do you?"

He nodded. "I, uh . . ." Time turned to molasses while he paused. "I don't know if I can do this anymore."

Now both eyebrows were up. "Do what? Eat lunch?"

He shook his head. There was a lump in his throat the size of a coconut. "Uh. No. I mean . . . I mean the whole thing. Being with you . . . you know, living in Sulfur. Helping you. Uh . . . all that."

It felt like his heart was stopping, and every muscle in his body was about to snap. He managed to raise his eyes to see her face. She stared back, her mouth pressed in a grim horizontal line. The hand that had propped her chin lowered to the table, and she leaned back in her chair.

Donny dropped his gaze again. His head turtled between his shoulders. The silence was terrible. He searched for something to say, and wished he'd thought this through better.

"It's not you," he said. *How can you say that?* he shouted inwardly. It was *completely* her, the false friendship, and the constant endangerment, but he was so afraid of her temper and what she might do that he was desperate to soften the impact. "It's . . . I found out where my mother is. I wanted to see if . . . you know. If she'd . . ." It seemed impossible to put together a coherent sentence. The table shook, because his trembling knee was touching the table leg.

"Your mother ran away and *left you behind*, remember?" Angela said. Her voice was arctic. Donny glanced at her again and saw a face frozen in rage. He couldn't look at her for more than a fraction of a second. "How could you possibly say that to me?" she snapped. "How *dare* you ask to leave? I saved you, don't you remember? You'd be a crispy corpse if I didn't find you in that fire."

"I know . . . I . . ."

"*What do you know?*" she snapped again. She leaned toward him, almost crawling over the tabletop. He crunched his eyelids shut and slid low in his seat. "We had a bargain, Donald Taylor. An *infernal* bargain. You think you can just walk away from that?"

His resolve shattered. "I'm sorry. I take it back. I take it—"

People must have been staring, wondering what the commotion was about, but Donny couldn't bear to open his eyes. When she spoke again, it was almost a hiss. "I took care of you! I let you into my home! I thought we were . . ." Suddenly her voice twisted with emotion, and her words were strangled. That was somehow worse than her anger.

He had screwed this up in epic fashion. He'd wanted to make her understand how hurt he was, how scared he'd been. "Angela, listen . . . ," he began, but then he felt it. A wave of fear and anxiety hit him like a subsonic noise that he sensed in his nerves and bones but not his ears. "Oh no—please don't do that to me," he squeaked out, but then the panic was on. It was like he'd been dropped out of a plane without a parachute. His heart thumped wildly, his limbs jolted, and his brain went berserk. He heard people get up from tables nearby, gasping and moaning, their chairs screeching on the stones.

The wave ended suddenly. Donny clutched the front of his shirt and gulped for air. He gripped the table with his other hand so he wouldn't topple over. And then he heard steps, and her voice was at his ear and her lips brushed his hair. "Maybe I should put an end to you," she whispered. "Not here. When I catch you somewhere, alone."

"I'm sorry," he whispered. It barely made a sound.

She stood tall and glowered down. "It's not even worth the effort. Get out of my sight. Don't cross my path. Don't go anywhere we've ever been. If I see you again, I'll crush you and feed your soul to the flames. Starting in thirty seconds."

He sat there, eyes shut, heart pounding.

"I renounce you! Go!" she shouted.

He scrambled out of the chair and stumbled down the street, blind with tears.

CHAPTER 33

Time had ceased to have any meaning, but Donny thought that he'd turned the nearest corner before thirty seconds had passed. Still, he looked behind him, and even at the rooftops, to see if she'd changed her mind and had come to stalk him.

He tried to orient himself and remember which way was back to the hotel. Was it safe to go there? *Not really,* he figured. His extra clothes and money were in a bag in his room, but it wasn't worth the risk to retrieve them.

He stepped out of sight behind a van that was parked on the narrow road and dug his phone out of his pocket. There were only two contacts in there. He called the one that wasn't Angela. It rang for so long that Donny was afraid he'd have to leave a message. What if Howard never responded? What if he didn't pick up because Angela was already on the phone, ordering him to cut Donny off from all contact, all assistance? Did she even know that Howard was planning to help him? Would she figure out that Howard's organization had tracked down his mother?

"Mr. Taylor," Howard answered. Donny was so dizzy with relief that he put a shoulder against the van to steady himself.

"Hi." He wanted badly to call Howard "Mister something," but all he knew was Howard, and Howard probably wanted it that way. "Uh, Howard . . . I talked to Angela. About leaving."

After a pause, Howard replied. "I'm impressed. That took a lot of courage. How did it turn out?"

Hard to say, Donny thought. "Well. I think she's going to let me go. But if she sees me again, I'm pretty sure she'll kill me. And then do something even worse."

"There's that fiery temper. You'd better take it seriously. Stay out of her way."

No kidding, Donny thought. He craned his neck around the side of the van. "Yes, sir."

"Are you still in Old San Juan?"

"Uh-huh. Yes."

"Do you remember El Morro, the fortress we went to?"

"Yes."

"Can you find your way there?"

His nerves settled a little. It felt good, being told exactly what to do. "I'm pretty sure. I mean yes. I can do that."

"Good. If you recall, a long footpath goes across the

lawn to the fortress itself. I'll meet you there, where the road ends and the footpath begins, within an hour. Stay calm, and obviously keep out of sight. Come out when you see me. I will be in a black car."

"Right. El Morro. The footpath. Black car. Thank you. Thank you so much, Howard. Sir."

"Miss Obscura is trying to reach me."

Donny's eyes popped.

"I need to take that. See you soon, I hope," Howard said, and he ended the call.

It took a while for Donny to collect his wits. His imagination sped to awful destinations. He wondered what Angela and Howard might talk about. Did Angela change her mind? Would Howard tell her where Donny could be found?

"Don't get paranoid," Donny whispered aloud. Then he looked both ways around the van and squatted low to see if she lurked underneath.

There really wasn't a choice. He had to meet Howard as planned. Otherwise he was trapped in Old San Juan with just the stuff in his pockets, and no way to get to his mother. Even the fake passport that Angela had given him was in the hotel room.

Finding El Morro was easy enough. At the end of the street, Donny glimpsed the ocean. He headed toward it, and it was obvious that he had to turn to the right and follow the centuries-old wall that once guarded the old town from invaders. Soon he saw the fortress with its dark, time-stained walls looming over the sea.

There was a yellow building with a pretty red dome nearby. He went into the building's courtyard and stood in the shade of a broad green tree, where he had a clear view of the beginning of the path.

The road ended in a wide circle. He watched every vehicle that drove through and turned around, dropping people off and picking them up. Tour buses arrived and passengers got out, and he looked at all the tourists just in case Howard was among them. All the while, he kept an eye out for Angela, too.

His hand went into his pocket and touched his phone. He took it out and looked at the last text he'd gotten from Angela. There was an ache inside his chest. He started to compose a message of his own. While he typed, he looked around after every few words to watch for Howard.

I am so sorry. I really liked you, but I know you didn't feel the same about me. I will never forget you, but don't worry, I'll never talk about you either. Good-bye.

A long black sedan pulled to the edge of the circle and idled there. Donny tried to see who was inside. The back door opened and Howard stepped out, held a hand up to the driver, and told him to wait. Donny sent the message and shoved the phone back into his pocket. He jogged out from his hiding place in the shade, looking again for Angela in every direction. Howard spotted him. He waved Donny over, ushered him into the backseat, and slid in beside him.

"Isla Grande airport," Howard said to the driver.

Donny sagged low in the seat, from relief and the need to hide. There was something soft at his feet. He looked down to see his travel bag. "You got my stuff!"

"I thought you might need it," Howard said. "Your passport is in there, I presume?"

"Yes, sir," Donny said. "But how'd you get in my room without a key?"

"Money will open almost any door."

Donny pulled a baseball cap from the bag and tugged it low over his eyes. "Thank you, Howard. I really mean it."

Howard nodded and held out his hand. "I should take your phone."

"Oh." That caught Donny by surprise. It was his final connection to Angela, the only way left to reach her.

"Right now, please," Howard said without inflection, keeping his hand there to receive it.

"Sorry. Sure. Of course." Donny took the phone out and gave it to Howard, who dropped it into the bag by his side. Donny wasn't certain, but he thought he heard the phone vibrate a moment later.

The car zipped through town. Soon they crossed the bridge that separated Old San Juan from the main island. The driver immediately turned onto a street that led to a small airport.

"You'll take my private jet to Colorado," Howard said.

"One of my associates will meet you there and bring you to the town where your mother lives."

"Wow," Donny said quietly. "Does . . . does she know I'm coming?"

Howard shook his head. "It will be up to you to reintroduce yourself. Are you comfortable with that?"

Of course not, Donny thought. "I guess so," he said. They pulled into the airport. Flying usually meant going through a crowded, noisy terminal, but they just stopped at a security checkpoint and were waved through after a few words from Howard.

Donny looked out the window toward Old San Juan. "It just occurred to me: I won't ever see Angela again."

"Or me, for that matter," Howard said. He held out his hand once more, this time for a handshake.

Donny stared at the hand, stunned. Of course he wouldn't see Howard again, he realized. He reached out and shook it. "Right. Thank you, sir. Thank you so much."

"This was the right thing to do, Mr. Taylor," Howard said. "You seem like a fine young man. I hope you can put all this behind you and enjoy a normal existence. It won't be easy, of course. Life will seem dull compared to your recent adventures."

"Dull" felt very appealing at the moment. "I think I'll be okay."

"Excellent. Now, I'll say this one more time: you must

not speak of what you've seen and what you know."

"I won't. People would just think I was crazy anyhow," Donny said.

"We would make sure they did."

Donny almost laughed, but he noticed that Howard wasn't smiling when he said it.

CHAPTER 34

It was weird, getting to fly in a private jet. There were no tickets to show, and no waiting for the plane. They drove right onto the tarmac where the plane waited for Donny.

There were two pilots, a man and a woman. Howard spoke quietly to the woman while the man took Donny's bag and stowed it in a rear compartment.

"Come on in," the woman said to Donny. Howard raised his hand in a farewell gesture. Donny waved back, and then he walked up the short flight of aluminum steps and entered the plane.

It was all wood and leather inside, not plastic like a typical commercial jet. It smelled new and clean. He was the only passenger, and that made it even weirder.

The pilots barely said a word when Donny climbed on board. The man told him to sit in any of the six white leather chairs, and asked him to buckle his seat belt. He pointed out the bathroom and a basket filled with snacks if Donny wanted anything after they took off. Then he joined the woman in the cockpit, closing the door behind him and leaving Donny alone in the cabin.

The takeoff was nothing like Donny was used to from commercial flights. The ascent was much steeper, and he gripped the armrests tight. The runway ended at the sea. He saw giant cruise ships in the harbor below, and Old San Juan from above. Then a wispy curtain of clouds flowed by the oval window, as if closing on an act of Donny's life.

Everything hit him at once: all the things he'd given up and hadn't really thought about until now. He wouldn't see Tizzy anymore. Or Zig-Zag. Or Arglbrgl. Or any of the other denizens of the underworld. He would never again stand amid fiery clouds and feel their gentle warmth, or watch the mist of the river restore human shape to arriving souls. He wouldn't behold the magnificent pillars that propped up the underworld, with ancient cities that circled their roots like wreaths. He wouldn't see all the wondrous ways that flames could be engineered. He wouldn't explore any more unknown quarters of that cavernous universe. All that strange grandeur was forbidden to him now. It would be dangerous even to speak of it.

Maybe one day he'd think it was all a dream.

But there was a new life ahead, or at least he hoped. A new life that might erase the old one. His mother was out there. And a half brother who he'd never seen. And the man his mother had married. Did they live in a cozy little house? Was there a room for him there? He'd share one with his brother. He wouldn't mind at all. Maybe you could see the Rocky Mountains right out the window. *That's a different life,* Donny thought. He could learn to snowboard. Or climb mountains with his new father and his little brother, or catch fish in a crystal alpine river. Maybe he'd grow up to be a park ranger.

Florida appeared on the horizon, and they left the blue seas behind. Donny fell asleep and dreamed of snowcapped mountains.

CHAPTER 35

A tap on Donny's shoulder woke him up. "We'll start our descent pretty soon," the male pilot said. "Sorry to wake you up, but I thought you might be hungry."

Donny rubbed his eyes and looked down. A tray had appeared in front of his seat, unfolding right out of the wall, and on it was a silver platter with a turkey sandwich, salad, cheese, grapes, a brownie, a green bottle of fancy mineral water, and a can of juice. "Thank you," he said.

His appetite didn't kick in until he'd taken a few bites, and suddenly he was starving. He ate everything on the plate and guzzled the juice. The man came out and took the platter away, folding the tray back, and soon after that there was a change in the sound of the engines. They were descending. Donny peered out the window. The sky was clear again. The land below was flat, but when he looked out the windows on the other side, he saw a great mountain range in the distance.

The plane touched gently down and rolled to a stop. Donny waited for one of the pilots to come out of the cockpit before he unbuckled his seat belt.

The woman came out first. "We're in Denver. You ready, Mr. Taylor?"

"Yes, ma'am," Donny replied.

The man opened the door. "Right this way," he said. They stepped through the open door and walked down the metal steps to the tarmac. There was a ceaseless roar of planes overhead.

The man got Donny's bag from the storage compartment, but he didn't hand it to him. A big black car approached their plane, driving slowly across the pavement and pulling up right next to them. The door opened, and another man stepped out. He had a kind of military look about him, with short-cropped hair and a solid build. He wore a jacket and slacks.

"Donald Taylor?" he asked.

"That's him," the pilot replied before Donny could respond. The pilot held Donny's bag out, and the driver took it.

"I'll take it from here," the man said. "Right this way, Mr. Taylor."

Donny got the slightest of nods from the pilot, who returned to the plane without another word. The driver opened the door to the backseat, and Donny got in. "How far is it, sir?" he asked when the driver got behind the wheel.

The driver tapped out a text message on his phone before he replied. "Seventy-five miles to Estes Park," he said flatly.

That was it for small talk. Donny had already gotten the signal. This was all business, and neither the pilots nor the driver were there to make friends. Donny never even got a name from any of them. Even Howard had acted that way at the very end—not unfriendly but not friendly, either. They were cutting ties. As they drove, Donny just stared through the windshield and watched the mountains get closer.

An hour and a half later the car pulled off the highway and into a town with snowy peaks looming high in the west, and pine trees and rocky outcroppings on the rolling hills nearby. Donny had pictured a sleepy little town, but the place was bustling with visitors and busy with restaurants and shops. They turned off the main drag and headed into a neighborhood, and that was when Donny's hands started to shake. *Get a grip,* he told himself.

The driver pulled a sudden U-turn in the middle of the street and accelerated in the other direction. "What happened?" Donny asked.

"Your mother just drove by," the driver said.

Donny's eyes bugged. There was a blue SUV just ahead. "You're following her?"

"You're supposed to meet her, isn't that correct?"

"Uh . . ." Donny tried to get his breathing to slow to

normal. "Yeah. Yes . . . I am." The moment was close and he wasn't ready.

"There's an envelope in your bag with some extra money from Mr. H."

"Mr. H. Is that Howard?"

"She's parking," the driver said. "I'll pull over here."

Donny opened the door, stepped out onto the sidewalk, and put the strap of his bag across his shoulder. The driver lowered the power window and leaned over to speak through it. "You all set?"

Donny's mind swirled as if someone had pulled a plug and his brain was circling the drain. A hundred yards away he saw a woman get out of the blue SUV and take a stroller out of the back. "I'm . . . I'm good," he said, barely thinking while he spoke.

"You sure?"

The woman—*my mother,* he said to himself—opened a rear passenger door and leaned in. She emerged again, a toddler in her arms. She gently settled the boy into the stroller and buckled him in.

"What?" Donny said to the driver. It was hard to listen and panic at the same time. "Oh. I'm good. All set." He moved along the sidewalk toward his mother, so numb that the simple act of walking felt strange. Behind him, he barely heard the sedan's wheels grind on pavement and then accelerate away.

CHAPTER 36

Donny kept his distance for a while, keeping pace as his mother pushed the stroller down the sidewalk. She wore blue jeans, pink-and-gray sneakers, and a white fleece jacket. He stared at the back of her head like he'd never stared at the back of anyone's head before. She was taller than he expected. He watched the way she leaned to one side to say something to the boy in the carriage, and he caught a glimpse of her profile. *That's my mother,* he told himself again. He walked a little faster, drew a little closer.

He stuck his hand in his pocket absentmindedly, and his fingers closed around the tiny bottle of demon drops. He'd forgotten about them completely, and was sure that he wasn't supposed to still have them. Howard wouldn't even let him keep the phone. So there was no way he'd want Donny to hold on to actual evidence of the infernal world.

His gait slowed for a moment as an idea came to him. He took the bottle from his pocket and stared at it, cradled in his palm. There was plenty left inside. If he used the drops right now, he could find out for sure. What kind of woman was his mother? Was it really such a good idea, to reunite with her after all these years? It would be so easy to find out. A drop in each eye, and the secret would be revealed.

He pulled the stopper out of the bottle and poured the liquid onto the pavement. As he passed a garbage can, he tossed the bottle inside. All that infernal magic was behind him now. It was time to join the mortal realm. And that meant fumbling in the dark to understand another person, until hopefully the years brought you closer.

His mother turned on a side street that led downhill. She looked both ways as she crossed the road. Donny's heart got a jolt when she glanced his way, but she just went on pushing the stroller, and jogged across the intersection.

As Donny walked, it occurred to him that he might have made a mistake when he told the driver he could go. What was he supposed to do if this didn't work out? "But it *will* work out," he whispered to himself.

The street led to a park beside a river. The river tumbled by with dangerous force, as it frothed and hissed away from the mountains. A paved walking path ran beside it, and a railing kept people safe from the current. Donny followed his mother, now just a hundred feet behind her, as she walked along the path toward a children's playground. She sat on a bench and turned the stroller to her. The little boy inside had fallen asleep.

Donny ambled closer. He pretended to look up at the mountains and down at the river when he wasn't staring at his mother's face. Seeing her was like finding the missing pieces of a puzzle. He always knew which features he'd inherited from his father: the shape of the face and the ears, the color of the hair. But there, for the first time, he saw the rest of himself. The nose. The set of the mouth. The eyes.

He had eyes like his mother.

She turned and looked directly at him, gave him a little smile, and then took a paperback book from a bag under the stroller. That little smile stopped Donny cold in his tracks. He recovered a couple of seconds later and sat at a bench that was just a few feet away from hers.

It was time to say something, he knew. But his throat was so dry, he had to clear it first. He gulped and coughed, and felt sweat sprouting on his head and palms.

He looked at her again, and this time he was sure that she had been looking at him. She turned back to her book.

Donny cleared his throat again. "Your son is really cute," he said with a shaky rasp.

She smiled a little wider this time. It was like the smile Donny saw in the mirror.

"Hey, thank you," she said.

"You're welcome."

She went back to reading again, but then her gaze rose slowly and she looked right at him. Maybe because he seemed somehow familiar. Or maybe because of the way he looked at her.

Her eyes crinkled at the corners. The smile was uncertain. "Do I know you?" she asked.

"Uh . . . not really," he replied. "But sort of." His fingers were twitching. She leaned toward him and studied his face. Then her eyes opened wide, and the color drained from her cheeks.

"Um, hello," Donny said. He felt like he might get sick all over the sidewalk.

"Are you . . . ?" she said. "You're not . . . ?"

"You're Jessica," Donny said. He had to choke out the next words. "But your name used to be Maria."

The book slipped from her fingers, and she sucked in a tiny gulp of air.

"I'm Donny."

She opened her mouth and closed it again, then took a bigger breath and held it.

"I'm your Donny."

For a second Donny thought she would tip over. She put a hand on the stroller to brace herself.

Donny walked to her bench and sat beside her. He left as much room between them as he could. They sat side by side for a moment, neither of them making a sound except for her quiet sniffs. "Oh, Donny," she finally said. She reached for his arm and squeezed it. He slid closer and leaned toward her, and she put her arms around him. Her hair fell across his face. "My Donny. How are you? How have you been?"

Donny hesitated, trying to figure out what to say next. Did she even know that his father was dead? He didn't think so. What exactly could he tell her about everything? "Oh, I've been all right."

She let him go, reached for a pocket in the stroller, and pulled out a pack of tissues. She yanked three for herself and offered one to Donny. He took it—his eyes needed dabbing. Hers were full of tears, and she blotted them and blew her nose. "I figured this would happen eventually," she said with a weak smile. The smile faded, and her forehead wrinkled. "Does this mean your father knows where I am?"

She doesn't know anything, he thought. Again, he chose his words carefully. "No. You don't have to worry about him."

She gave him another long stare.

"I'm not with Dad anymore," he said.

"You're not?"

He shook his head. This was getting tricky. If she was going to take care of him, he wanted it to happen because she wanted to, not because she felt obligated. And not because he had nowhere else to go.

"So that's my brother," he said. He smiled into the

stroller and saw a round face with eyes shut, and one limp arm across a stuffed dinosaur.

"Half brother," she said.

"Right," Donny answered.

"I'm sorry. This is . . . such a shock," she said. Her gaze darted back to the street and across the river, as if she expected Donny's father to show up at any second.

"You don't have to be afraid," Donny told her. "I . . . I just wanted to meet you."

Her voice quaked. "If you found me, he can find me."

"No. He's not going to find anyone," Donny said. "He's not around anymore." He wanted to say *Mom* at the end, but it didn't feel right. Not yet.

She fixed a long, blank look at him, and then she leaned back against the bench. "What? Oh my. Oh . . . I've been worried for so long."

"You don't have to worry now," he said.

She let her head roll back, and blinked at the sky, and then the oddest laugh sputtered out. Her expression flattened again, and she looked at Donny. "But what about you? Will you be okay?"

Donny repeated the question inwardly. *Will I be okay?* The way she phrased that, and the things she didn't say, implied so much. He wanted to let the words flood out of him. *Will I be okay? Isn't that up to you now? I don't have a father. I had a place to stay, but I can't go back. How could you think I'd be okay?*

But he didn't say any of it. Instead it was like a ventriloquist taking hold of his body. He heard himself say, "I'll be all right."

Her chin trembled and her eyes jittered as she stared at him. "Donny . . . I don't know what you need from me. Or if you even need anything. Or . . . I don't know what to say. My head is spinning right now." She folded her hands in her lap and stared at them. "You . . . you have to understand. I left because your father scared me so much. And he would never have let me take you, and he would have found me somehow if I did; I just knew it. So I hid from him, far away, and I started all over." She shivered and then looked at the little boy in the stroller. "I have this whole life now, Donny. I have a new son, and a husband who loves me. He doesn't know anything about my past. I made up a story and didn't say anything about another husband, or another son. It was a huge lie, but I had to do it that way. And now . . . if you came out of the blue . . . I . . . I don't know what I would tell him. What would my husband think?"

Donny took another look at his sleeping brother and then looked away. "Yeah. No, that makes sense. I get it."

She sniffed again and blotted tears. "Do you need help? Is there anything I can do for you?"

Donny stood up. Another thing he wasn't brave or cruel enough to say popped into his head. *Anything you can do for me? Besides saying, "Come with me and be my son," you mean? No. That was the only thing I wanted.* "I'm fine. Bye, Mom," he said. The word *Mom* was like a bomb busting a dam, and she broke down into sobs. He walked away.

Still a chance, he mouthed, his back to her. If she called to him now, and they talked some more, maybe it would work out somehow. He could be part of a new family and have a normal life. He'd be a good son, and the best brother ever, and never cause any trouble, and study hard and do the dishes and walk the dog and go to college and make them proud.

But all he heard was her quiet weeping.

CHAPTER 37

Donny walked awkwardly, suddenly unsure of how to move his limbs like a normal person. His brain had gone offline. Sullen clouds blew in from the other side of the Rockies and blotted out the sunshine. Wind stirred the trees, and the air felt damp with rain.

With no idea of where to go next, he followed the path by the river, pausing now and then to look at the turbulent water.

Now what?

He had enough money to get a room at some motel. Did motels rent rooms to kids without asking questions? Even then, what was he supposed to do next? Call the police in New York and tell them, *Hi, I'm that missing person?* Maybe it was time to find out what this world did with kids who had no place else to go.

There was another bench up ahead by the side of the

river. He could barely summon the energy to walk that far. He dropped his bag and slumped onto the seat as his body deflated.

A father and son walked his way along the path. The dog whimpered and changed directions, straining on the leash. They let the dog lead them away.

Birds burst out of a nearby tree, wings thumping. Donny felt the hairs on the back of his neck go electric. He sat up straight.

A shout came from across the river. "Hey! Hey, you little jerk!"

The sound couldn't have hit Donny harder if it had been a thunderclap. It was simultaneously the most welcome and unnerving thing he'd ever heard. He stood up and turned to see Angela on the opposite bank. She wore an electric-blue tracksuit with yellow stripes down the sides, and bright orange sneakers. Her long black hair was in a ponytail.

She glared at him, her fists on her hips. A spidery feeling crawled from the hairs on his neck to the bottom of his spine. She wasn't even directing her fear-beam at him. This was just her anger, leaking out like radiation. He was glad there was a moat of raging water between them.

His throat cinched up and his mouth quaked, but he managed to choke out a syllable. "Hi."

"Don't you 'Hi' me. Don't you *dare*. I'm *furious* with you. I came all this way and ran all over this stupid town looking for you, just to tell you how much you *stink*." She punctuated her words with a stabbing finger.

He tried to say something, but his jaw flapped feebly. She cut him off with a wave of her hand. "Don't even *talk*! Just shut your candy hole!"

She folded her arms and glared at him. Donny felt compelled to say something, anything, to break the tension. "You ran around to find me? Is that why you're wearing that?"

"I couldn't find a taxi, and I wasn't going to run all over in heels and a dress," she snapped. She looked at her outfit. "It's pretty comfy though; I kind of like it." When she looked at Donny again, her gaze was fiery once more. "Don't try to distract me, you filthy pip-squeak. You know why I'm here?"

"Um," said Donny. He looked left and right to see if anyone was nearby, but they were alone. The dog walkers were long gone, and the cloud of fear she was producing probably warded anyone else away. "You wanted to see how I was doing?"

Her eyes narrowed. "I wanted to exterminate you, is more like it. The more I thought about it, the madder I got. We had a deal, remember? When I saved your butt from that fire in Brooklyn? You agreed to come with me and be my helper. That was supposed to be a binding agreement. You don't just walk away from something like that!"

"But . . . I asked, and you told me to get out of your sight. You renounced me."

She lowered her head like a bull. "With good reason." Another wave of furious energy washed over Donny. He took an awkward step back.

"We can't have mortals wandering around who know too much about Sulfur. I should end your sorry life," she said.

"Please don't." He took another hopeful look around to see if anyone was within shouting distance. Then he looked back toward Angela and gasped, because she hopped onto the railing and leaped high into the air and across the river. Before he could move, she landed in front of him and used both of her hands to clutch the front of his jacket. Donny squeaked.

"How could you just *leave* me like that?" she snapped. "And that stupid text you sent—it didn't even make any sense! What did you mean, I didn't feel the same? I was your *friend*."

Donny shut his eyes and waited for the end. "That's what I thought," he whimpered. "Until I heard the truth."

She lifted him high and spun around. He was suddenly over the side of the railing, his legs dangling. Donny cracked his eyes open and looked at the water that raged under his feet.

Her lips were pulled back, baring perfect teeth. "*Heard the truth?* The truth is, you left me after everything I did for you. How many times did I save your stupid life?"

Donny clenched his teeth. "I don't even care," he said. "I have no life anymore. I have no home. My dad is gone. My mother didn't want me. You don't really like me. You don't even care if I live or die."

She shook him back and forth. "I don't *what*? What are you *talking* about?"

"I heard you talking about me to someone, in Sulfur. You said you didn't have any feelings for me. That you faked being my friend. You said if I died it wouldn't matter. I heard you, Angela. You didn't know I was there, up there near the lookout, but I heard all of it. You said—"

He didn't get the rest of the sentence out because she'd lifted him up again, but only to turn and drop him roughly on the grass. He landed on his rump and scrambled back to give himself some distance. When he looked up, she was leaning forward in an odd crouch, her hands on her knees. For a moment Donny thought she was going to puke. She seemed to convulse, and made a choking sound, and then a snorting sound, and then finally the first laugh shot out of her mouth like a cannonball: *"Haw!"*

She staggered sideways, dropped to her knees, and laughed like a lunatic until she could squeeze out some breathless words. "Ha! Ha-ha! You heard *that*? Oh my stars. Now I get it! *Haw!*" The laughter tumbled out, and it was a solid minute before she was able to talk again. She walked on her knees to where Donny sat. Then she plopped down beside him and shoved him on the shoulder with one hand.

Donny toppled over. "What?" he finally said, when he thought she could hear him over her own guffaws. "What do you get?"

Her words were punctuated by giggles. She put her hands over her mouth and talked through them. "You ding-dong! Do you even know who I was talking to?"

Donny was dizzy, unsure where this was going. "No. Some guy. Tall. Sort of handsome."

"That was Ungo Cataracta, you dope! In his human form!"

"What? No, I know Ungo's voice. It wasn't him."

"Yes, it was! He sounds completely different when he changes. Donny, I didn't mean any of that! I was trying to get Ungo on the council, and I know how he dislikes mortals! You're such a goose. I don't want anyone on the council to think I care about you. What if my enemies knew? They might try to hurt me by hurting you. Jiminy Crickets, you heard *that* conversation? *That's* why you were such a jerk?" She fell onto her back again, holding her stomach, and turned red with laughter.

Donny felt like helium had been pumped into his head. He had to double-check the facts and make sure it was real. "Seriously? That was really Ungo? That guy with the smoke coming out of the holes in his head? I didn't even know he had a human form."

She nodded, laughing too hard to answer.

"So when you talked about starting a fire . . . that wasn't true either? You didn't start the fire in Brooklyn?"

She snorted and stomped the grass with her heels. "That's right, I forgot I said that, too! You thought I was some kind of arsonist? *Haw!*"

Donny stuck his hands in his hair, and a wide smile spread across his face as a wave of relief surged up from somewhere deep inside. He fell back onto the grass beside her and waited for her to stop laughing.

She propped herself on her elbows, tears streaming from her eyes. The tears turned to steam as they trickled down her face, and the wind swept it away. "Wait," she said as the laughter finally ebbed. With a titanic effort, she flattened her smile into a sympathetic frown and made a halfhearted attempt to sound serious. "Did you say your mother didn't want you?"

Donny sat up and shrugged, and plucked the grass by his feet. "Yeah. I mean, she didn't come right out and say it. But she didn't ask me to stay. She didn't even ask for my phone number, for crying out loud. She's got a new life now, and I would have messed all that up."

Angela grinned wickedly and rubbed her hands together. "You want me to do something really awful to her?"

Donny glared at her and pointed a finger. "No. Seriously, do not do that."

"Fine," she said, and sniffed. "But you had it all wrong, Donny. You do have a home. You know what home is? Home is where you're wanted."

Donny put his face between his knees and took a deep breath. "'Home is where you're wanted.' Did you just make that up?"

"Maybe," she said. "Who knows? Hasn't everything already been said or written by now?" She put an arm around his shoulders and tugged him closer.

Donny looked up as a voice called out from the distance. Finally another human being was in sight. A man in jeans and a polo shirt jogged toward them, short of breath. He called out while he was still several strides away. "Excuse me, miss! Can I talk to you for a second?"

"That guy," Angela moaned. "I saw him a couple times when I was looking for you, and he kept shouting at me. I just ignored him, and he couldn't keep up with me."

"Who is he?"

"I don't have the foggiest."

"Wait, how far did you run before you found me?"

"Not sure," she said, "but it feels like I covered every square inch of this burg at least twice."

The man slowed to a walk as he got to where they sat. He was out of breath and bent over, his hands on his knees. "Miss . . . what is your name?"

"Millicent Stroganoff," Angela said. She gestured to Donny. "And this is my brother, Biff."

The man's jaw slid to one side. "Okaaay," he said slowly. "Very funny. I get it. I'm interrupting. But I just wanted to know: Are you in high school or something?"

"Something," she replied.

The man cocked his head at her. "Listen—it's just that I saw you running. Everywhere. Really fast. It was amazing. I think you sprinted a marathon. And . . . well, I don't know if you're in college, or you plan to go to college, but I'm a track and field coach at the University of Colorado. And I'm pretty sure we could offer you an athletic scholarship."

Angela gave him a fake gasp and an openmouthed smile. "Isn't that nice!" She stage-whispered to Donny. "What is an 'athletic scholarship'?"

The coach answered for him. "Don't you know? It's a free ride."

Angela clapped her hands. "Now you're talkin'! Can you drive us to Denver?"

CHAPTER 38

The track coach declined to drive them the seventy-five miles to Denver. Donny explained to Angela that you could call for a cab, and you didn't just have to wait for one to drive by like in New York. When the cab arrived, they got inside just ahead of the rain that spattered the windshield. Angela read an address off her phone to the driver, and they sped out of town and onto the highway, the mountains shrinking behind them.

Donny reached forward and closed the opening in the plastic partition between them and the driver so they couldn't be overheard. "How did you know where I was?" he asked Angela.

"Howard told me. I mean, he didn't want to tell me, but I sort of made him."

Donny rubbed his forehead. "Ugh. Tell me you didn't."

"Oh yes, I did," Angela said. "I was in no mood for

resistance. I might have overdone it a little."

"Oh no," Donny said. Howard was not a young man. At least he had a strong heart, apparently.

"So, are we okay now?" Angela said.

"Yes. Sure."

"You don't sound a hundred percent convinced."

Donny squirmed in his seat. "Well . . . I know you didn't mean what you said about me to Ungo. I get that. But still, sometimes . . ."

She twisted in her seat to look directly at him. "Donny. Cricket. I need you. I told you that I need a human to assist me sometimes, and that's true. But it's more than that. You make me modern. You help me learn how to fit in better. But mostly, you're my friend. So, what do you want from me? Just come out and say it."

Donny froze. There were so many ways to answer that question. Some of the ways, he'd barely started to understand. But there was one thing he could say right now with confidence. "You have to be more careful with my life," he said. "I think you forget how easily humans get hurt. Like Carlos. He was seriously wounded, but you didn't seem to think so."

"But you guys have doctors who stitch you right back up!"

"It's not that simple. We're not like the dead down in Sulfur. We might die before the doctors can help us. Or we can get hurt so bad that doctors can't do anything."

She nodded vigorously and pointed at her temple. "Right. Point taken. I'm storing that tidbit away."

"Great. Also, you need to understand how scary some of this can be for me."

"No doubt about it." She kept on nodding. "But you have to remember something too, okay?"

"Sure. What?"

"I'm a beast from hell, Donny. Sometimes you gotta cut me a little slack."

Donny sighed and nodded.

Angela leaned back in her seat. "I think I need a nap after all this excitement." Her cell phone rang, and she extracted it from the pocket of her tracksuit. "Speak of the devil," she said, waving the phone toward Donny. He saw the name of the person calling: HOWARD. For his profile picture, Angela had selected a picture of an aging billy goat. She answered the call and put the phone to her ear. "Howard, darling," she said. She grinned sideways at Donny. "Are you feeling better? Oh . . . Hmm. Yeah . . . Sorry about that . . . Yes, it probably was uncalled for. Maybe you should spend a couple of extra days at the beach. . . . Yes, I found him, all right. In fact, he's right here next to me. . . . What's that? Of course you can. Here's the little rascal." She handed the phone to Donny. "Howard would like to say hello."

Donny took the phone. "Hello?"

"Donny. This is Howard." He sounded weary.

"Hi, Howard."

"Is everything okay?"

"Actually, yes it is. We had a big misunderstanding. I'm glad Angela found me."

"Is that so? Is she making you say that? If you're in trouble, use the word *wonderful* when you answer so I can tell."

Donny felt a wave of guilt. He had put Howard through all this for nothing, it turned out. "It's all fine. I know that sounds weird, but it really is. Um . . . Sorry about this. I don't know what to say."

"Neither do I, exactly. We'll just move on, I suppose. Can we keep what I'm about to say between us?"

"Oh." Donny glanced at Angela, who had shut her eyes, a contented smile on her face. "Sure. Yes, definitely."

"First, I want you to know that Miss Obscura confronted me and demanded to know where you were."

"Yeah," Donny said. "And I think I know what happened next."

"Oh, did she inform you? Yes, I resisted at first and told her it was for the best, letting you go. She did not like that answer, and forced me to tell her as only she can."

"Yeah. I know how that feels. I'm really sorry about that."

"As am I. That was my first experience with her, shall we say, primary weapon. And I hope it is my last. I believe it shaved a good five years off my life expectancy. The funny thing is that all she got out of me was the name of the town before she dashed off. If she'd been a little more patient, I could have called and had my employee pick you up."

"I feel really bad about this, sir."

"Never mind. I just want you to know that I tried. Apparently she is quite attached to you after all, young man."

Donny glanced at Angela again. She looked like she had nodded off, her head turned his way and her red lips slightly parted, gently breathing. At times like that, she seemed almost harmless. "I guess so," he said.

"Did you get to meet your mother?"

"I did. I don't think it was going to work out though," Donny said. "She . . . she couldn't handle me just turning up after all those years."

"That is unfortunate. But it brings me to the other thing I wanted you to know."

Donny waited for a moment, expecting Howard to continue. Finally he said, "What was that?"

"When you asked to leave Angela's company, I wanted you to believe that reuniting with your mother was your only option. I thought you'd give it your best shot that way, if you didn't hold back. But in fact, my man stayed close to you all the while. We would have retrieved you. There was a backup plan that involved a new identity, an excellent boarding school overseas, and eventually your employment in my organization in a very quiet position, well out of Miss Obscura's path."

A warm, pleasant feeling filled Donny's chest. "I . . . wow. That was really nice of you."

"Yes. Well, that all went out the window once our

mutual friend went berserk. I told my man to keep his distance. But you were never on your own. And that's all I had to say. I didn't want you to think I'd leave you homeless in Colorado. I hear the winters are brisk."

"Thanks. Thanks so much."

"Shall we say good-bye for now? It seems we'll meet again."

"I think so. Bye, sir."

The line went dead. Donny put the phone on the seat. Angela murmured something, then reached over and gave Donny's arm a gentle squeeze. Her hand slipped off, her breathing slowed, and she didn't wake up again until they'd reached the address she'd given the cabdriver.

CHAPTER 39

Angela sprang to life as they pulled up to a mansion that looked like it had seen better days, maybe about a century ago. She stuffed some hundred-dollar bills into the delighted driver's hands. "Is that enough?"

The driver gaped at the cash. "That is so generous! I can buy my wife something nice for her birthday."

She gave him two hundred more. "Make it really nice." The driver pulled away, giving them a huge grin and a friendly farewell honk.

A nervous elderly man opened the door to the mansion as they approached. "You can calm yourself," Angela told him. "I'm in a much better mood now."

Donny tried to imagine the state she was in when she'd arrived to hunt him down. The old man gave Angela a wary look and a wide berth as they stepped into the house. "Hello," Donny said.

"Everything is ready for you," the man said.

"We'll let ourselves out," Angela said. Donny followed her downstairs to the basement, where a gas fire filled a brick cavity in the wall. Angela whispered into the fire, and a dark space appeared amid the flames. They stepped through a thin sheet of ash and into the familiar stone corridor. As usual, Donny was at the receiving end of some menacing body language from the little gatekeeper Porta.

"We have so much to talk about, Cricket," Angela said as she stomped merrily along the passage.

"We do?"

"Oh yeah," she said as she knocked on the ancient door that led to the cavern world. Grunyon, the imposing armor-clad guard, peered through the peephole and unlocked the door.

"Howdy, Grunyon. Sorry, no snacks," she said as they walked by. "Yes, Donny, we have to talk. You know what we need? A recap. Go ahead—lay it on me. What do we know so far?"

"You want *me* to recap?"

She stopped and gripped him by the shoulders. "Yes, Cricket. You're part of this operation. I want to know what you think." She gave him a wink and a vigorous shake, and set off. Sulfur was in full wondrous, cavernous, luminous view ahead as he trotted after her down the stairs. Somehow the place that human beings feared most was a welcome sight.

"Okay, so it turns out that the souls in Puerto Rico were stolen by a ferryman," Donny began. "Which is weird, because it was the Ferryman King who told you to find out what was happening."

"Yuh-huh."

"So maybe the Ferryman King has something to do with this—although why would he ask you to stop it if he did? Or maybe he knows one of his own guys was involved. Or he didn't know anything, and this will be a big surprise."

Angela led Donny down a different, less-worn path than the one she usually took to her pillar home. This way led to where the River of Souls slithered by. She sat on a thick bed of black moss that grew on the bank. "Let's wait here."

Donny settled beside her. "For what?"

"The next ferry. I have something to say to those mummified clowns."

They sat quietly for a while, and then Angela chuckled. "I can't believe you thought I was Ungo's girlfriend or something."

Donny smirked. "That's what it sounded like. He asked about you taking a mate."

"A mate! Sheesh. That's not happening anytime soon, I can tell you that. I'm not getting married till I'm at least two hundred. And no kids until I'm three hundred. If ever."

Donny ran his fingers through the thick moss. "But . . . have you ever been in love, though?"

Angela lifted her chin and half closed her eyes. After a pause, she said, "Sort of. I guess."

"Who was it? Can you tell me about it?"

Angela smiled wistfully. "He was famous. Before your time, though."

"Famous? Really?"

"Yeah, really. You like old movies?"

Donny tilted his head. This was getting interesting. "Some. My dad used to."

Angela tugged her legs into a pretzel and leaned toward him, her hands on her knees. "Ever see *Destry Rides Again? The Philadelphia Story?*"

"Nope."

"*Mr. Smith Goes to Washington? It's a Wonderful Life?*"

"Yes! I saw that one. It's on at Christmastime a lot. About the guy who sees what life would be like if he never existed. Zuzu's petals, right?"

"That's it."

"Wait, you mean *that* guy? The George Bailey guy?"

She frowned. "He had a real name, you know. Jimmy Stewart."

Donny had heard the name before. "Seriously? You knew Jimmy Stewart?"

She turned away and stuck out her bottom lip. "I *tried* to get to know him. Here's what happened. I went to the movies one day, and there he was up on the screen. This . . . perfect angel. The sweetest, dreamiest, cleverest, most darling human I'd ever laid eyes on."

"How long ago was that?"

"I dunno, 1930-something? Maybe 1940? It was *Destry Rides Again*. He was a cowboy in that one. Total infatuation! I wanted to be in the movies with him. I went to every showing for a solid week."

"What did you do?"

"Nothing for a while. I just dreamed about meeting him. Saw everything he was in. Then I couldn't take it anymore. I had to see him in person. Say hello, whatever."

Donny felt his heartbeat quicken. "Really? And you did?" He did some quick math in his head. It was seventy years in the past, maybe more. "Wait, you must have looked like you were ten years old, though."

She gave him a narrow-eyed glance. "It doesn't work exactly like that, you know. I didn't look two years old when I was twenty, for crying out loud. But yeah, I looked young. More like thirteen. But adorable, of course. Listen, I knew I wasn't going to be his girlfriend. I just wanted to meet him. Okay, maybe in the back of my head I thought he'd want to adopt me, and I would have rolled with it, I tell you. Anyway, I started reading the Hollywood trade papers and magazines, and I found out he was shooting a movie. I had a simple plan. I was gonna put on a cute dress, stick a bow in my hair, bring some flowers and a framed picture for him to autograph, and go find Jimmy Stewart."

Donny gaped. "This is my favorite story ever."

"I jumped a fence and got onto the lot easy enough. A guard saw me and tried to stop me, but I induced a panic attack on him—"

Donny groaned.

"He was *fine*," Angela snapped. "Probably. Stop interrupting. So I went to where they were all eating lunch. I looked around, and a couple of people looked back at me, and they smiled because I was just the cutest thing. I saw some other famous faces, but I didn't care about any of them; I wanted *him*. And there he was. He had his back to me, but I still knew him. So lanky, so trim, so perfect. I had the flowers, and the picture pressed to my chest, and I walked toward him. Everything felt weird, like it was slow motion. The woman sitting across from him was some other movie star, I forget who, but she saw me coming. She figured out what I was there for, and gave me this big smile, and she reached over and tapped Jimmy's hand, and I watched her mouth and I could tell what she was saying: 'Jimmy, I think you have a fan.'

"And then Jimmy Stewart turned around and looked at me. He *looked at me*. I was two, maybe three steps away from him, just standing there. I remember how the flowers were shaking." Angela paused and shut her eyes.

"What did he do?"

She opened her eyes again. "He sat there. He saw a darling little girl holding his picture, a goofy grin on her face. He smiled very kindly, like I knew he would, a really warm and genuine smile. He pushed the chair out and stood up, because he was about to be wonderful to me. But by the time he was standing, I saw the terror in his eyes."

"Oh no."

"Oh yeah. His chest started heaving, he clutched his shirt, his eyes bugged out. He stumbled backward, into the table, knocked stuff over, trying to get away from me. Jimmy Stewart was a big-time canary."

Donny's heart twisted. He knew that, in every crowd, there might be one person who was sensitive to her presence and might even panic if she got too close. How cruel it was that the one person she wanted to meet the most would turn out to be that one in a crowd.

"So I ran. I got away from him. It was the best thing I could do for him. And I never tried to see him again, not even from a distance. I saw every movie he ever made though, and every time he was on TV, even when he was just a sweet old white-haired man reading silly poems to Johnny Carson."

Donny didn't know who Johnny Carson was, but that didn't matter.

"It's funny watching humans get old. It happens so fast. One day he was this wonderful star, and then one day he was gone. I cried for weeks when he died. So much steam coming out of my eyes."

Donny's throat felt tight, and he watched as Angela

stared into the distance, looking at nothing at all, just see-ing whatever was inside her head. "Well, that was morose," she finally said. She forced a smile onto her face.

The mood was broken by the familiar, bone-rattling sound of a great horn. It came from upriver.

CHAPTER 40

A nd here comes one at last," Angela said. She stood and
wiped bits of black moss off her tracksuit. A barge
glided down the river, manned by the gaunt, creepy
ferrymen and filled with hundreds of souls freshly formed
into icy, waxy echoes of their former living selves.

Angela dug the jawbone of the Old San Juan ferryman
out of her satchel. As they waited for the barge to draw near,
she flipped it in the air and neatly caught it again. At last the
barge rounded the nearest curve. The great skull and horn
at its prow drifted into view first. There were two ferrymen
on each barge, one fore and one aft. The dead were crammed
shoulder to shoulder between them. Under the thrall of the
ferrymen, they were unable to move except to turn their
heads and gape with fear at their new surroundings.

The barge reached the spot where Donny and Angela
stood. "Hey, you!" Angela shouted. The hooded ferryman

at the front of the barge swiveled his head in her direction. Angela tossed the jawbone, and it clattered at the ferryman's feet. The remaining teeth broke loose and skittered across the deck. Angela crossed her arms and scowled. "Show that to your boss, and let him know it was one of *you* that was stealing the souls in Old San Juan. And tell him Angela Obscura wants to know what exactly is going on here!"

The ferryman said nothing. He looked at the jawbone and then locked his gaze on Angela as the current took the barge past them. She stared back, unflinching, until another curve swept the barge out of sight. Then she turned toward Donny, wearing a satisfied smirk.

"What do we do now?" Donny asked.

"First, we go home, grab Tizzy, and see what's cooking at the diner. And then I think we head to the Hall of Elements and get some supplies. When we meet the next soul thief, we'll be ready."

CHAPTER 41

Donny gazed over the side of the rolling chariot. The road followed the rim of the old Pit of Fire, where millions of souls once bathed in flame. He had never been this way before, and it was his first look at this section of the massive hole in the floor of Sulfur. He saw wisps of smoke still rising, a few tiny pools of fire still burning, and more tall spires of rock topped with thrones where the archdemons once oversaw the suffering.

The shape of the pit was irregular, and he was surprised to see a place ahead where it narrowed to a width of only a few hundred yards. That space was spanned by a stone bridge, which was supported by great arches below. The runner imps turned onto the bridge and raced across the span. Donny leaned over to look at the floor of the pit. Far below, he saw a dark, oozing shape. It was a massive herd of wriggling, giant worms. He'd encountered a herd like that before, on his first day in Sulfur. He didn't know whether to laugh or groan at the memory. Once, those worms helped torment the dead. Now they wandered aimlessly across this subterranean land. He wondered if they missed the fire and wanted it back.

As soon as they crossed the bridge and crested a gentle rise on the other side, Donny saw a lone building ahead. Sulfur was full of strange wonders, and here was yet another. The building looked like a giant stone beehive, maybe fifty feet tall. Dozens of chimneys bristled up from its roof and out through the upper reaches of the walls. As Donny watched, a black burst of smoke belched from one chimney, and a shower of sparks spat out of another.

But the feature that set this building apart from anything Donny had seen was the solid curtain of flame that surrounded its blackened walls, lapping halfway up. At the bottom, the fire was a purple as dark as grape jelly. At the tips it was neon pink.

Donny raised his voice to be heard over the clatter of the wheels. "Is that where the chemist lives?"

"You got it," Angela replied. "Behold the Hall of Elements."

"How are we supposed to get in?"

"She has to let us in. On account of the moat of deadly fire."

"Does *she* have a name?"

"It's Ellie. Ellie Mental."

Donny gave her a suspicious glare. "That's a joke, right?"

"It started as a joke a hundred years ago. Then we all forgot her real name. But she's fine with Ellie."

The chariot came to a stop in front of the hall. Angela and Donny hopped onto the ground. "We won't be too long," she told the runner imps. She pointed to the right. "Help yourselves to the field of mushrooms over there." The runners unfastened their own harnesses and trotted off, licking their scaly lips.

Donny stared at the deep-purple flame. "What kind of fire is that?"

"Special blend," Angela said. "It'll melt anyone who tries to get through, whether they're infernal, mortal, or already dead."

"I guess the chemist doesn't like visitors."

"Just being prudent," Angela said. "Her works are valuable and potentially destructive. During the war with the Merciless, the bad guys raided this place and used Ellie's stuff to fight the reformers. That's when she created the moat. Now nobody gets in unless she lets them in."

"How do you let her know you're here?"

"We ring the doorbell, silly," she said. "Come on." Donny followed her forward, a wary eye on the flames.

A chain emerged from the burning wall at eye level. A pole was embedded in the ground, and the chain passed through a loop at the top of the pole and hung down, a fat metal ring at its bottom. Angela grabbed the ring and tugged. Somewhere beyond the flames, Donny heard the clang of a bell.

Angela stepped back and peered at the wall, a hand across her brow. A dim light glowed in one of the narrow windows above, in the center of the hall. A few seconds later Donny saw a silhouette step in front of the light.

"Hello up there!" Angela called out. "It's me. I have some favors to ask." She patted her satchel. "And I brought Ellie something!" The silhouette moved. A minute later Donny heard a sound beyond the fire, like doors creaking open. He squinted into the flames but couldn't see.

"Seriously," he said. "How do we get in there? Is this going to be dangerous? Because I can wait out here."

"It's not going to be dangerous," Angela replied in a weary, singsong voice. "In fact, I think you'll love it. It's tubular."

Donny was ready to chide her for using weird, outdated surfer slang, but then he saw an enormous glass tube emerge from the fire. A few wisps of neon flame that had been trapped inside slithered out and rippled into the air.

"Let's go," Angela said. She had to duck her head, but the tube was still big enough to allow her to jog through. Donny eyed the passage doubtfully. It looked sturdy enough. The sides were inches thick, obviously strong enough to hold his weight without shattering. But still, he could see those dangerous flames on all sides of the milky glass. What if the tube chose this moment to break? What if a rock came loose from above and fell on it, right when he stepped inside?

Angela peered back from the other side. "Come on, before it gets too hot."

Donny shook his head, exhaled heavily, and entered the tube. It was awkward, walking on a curved surface. He put his hands out to steady himself. The glass was already almost too hot to touch. When he looked down, he saw the moat under his feet, filled with swirling, billowing fire. The hiss and sizzle of the flames pulsed through the glass. He didn't breathe again until he emerged on the other side. "That almost melted my sneakers," he said. "Why does—"

He cut himself off when he saw the creatures on either side of the tube. They were squat but powerful imps, about his height. Their bumpy alligatorlike hides were charred and sooty. As Donny stared, the imps drew the tube back into the room. He stepped quickly aside to avoid being run over. They rolled the tube against the far wall and chocked it with triangular stones, and then trotted back and closed and barred the front door. Every movement was efficient, as if they'd done it a thousand times before.

Donny looked around at the space they'd entered. It was a simple entryway, not much bigger than a parlor, with only a few stone benches for furniture. There were exits from the hall on both sides. One was a ramp, and the other was a stairway. Both curved gently up into the innards of the building.

One of the imps waved for them to follow. When they walked up the stairs, the other imp trailed behind. They emerged on a landing above a tall, round room that encompassed the entire core of the beehive. Donny's lips puckered into a silent whistle when he saw what was in there.

It looked like a primitive laboratory, with a riot of equipment crammed into a space not much bigger than a school gymnasium. There were tables all over the floor, littered with glass vessels, ceramic jars, boxes, racks of test tubes, mortars and pestles, crucibles, and old-fashioned balance scales. A dozen cauldrons of all sizes were suspended over flames. Everywhere Donny looked, he saw solutions that steamed and bubbled inside glass spheres, their vapors rising into the air or passing through an octopus tangle of glass pipes. Freestanding chimneys stood over brick ovens, kilns, and open hearths. They rose up and pierced the domed roof or angled sideways to jut through the walls.

Among all that equipment, a dozen or more imps were working. Some supervised the experiments, and some were busy crushing crystals or stones into fine powders. One imp was making glass objects by blowing into a pipe with molten glass at the end. All around that imp were his creations: tubes, bowls, pipes, beakers, and more.

The reek of brimstone was strong inside, along with a hundred other bitter, pungent, or acrid smells that assaulted Donny's nose.

Blobs of fire drifted overhead. They were smaller but thicker, more liquid versions of Sulfur's luminescent clouds, and each was a different color. A yellow blob drifted past a blue one, and where they touched, both turned green until they separated again. *It's like being inside a giant lava lamp,* Donny thought. As he gazed up, something strange emerged from a blob: a miniature hot-air balloon with an imp in a leather seat suspended below, using something like swim flippers to guide the craft through the air.

Half of the floor below had been paved with flat stone, and the rest was the natural ground of Sulfur. In the center of it all, a beautiful, almost liquid plume of multicolored flame rose from underground. Donny knew that type of flame, because he had seen it before. That was the Crude, the one that could be refined into all the other forms of infernal fire. He had no doubt that the Hall of Elements was built on this site to take advantage of that spout.

The stairs that brought them to this landing continued to the floor of the hall. There, staring up at them, hands on hips, stood the chemist.

Ellie Mental was a tall, slender, imposing archdemon, dressed in baggy overalls, a fire-damaged short-sleeve shirt, and a heavy leather apron. Her shape was more or less human, but she was covered in scales that might have been mostly gold at one time, but were now burnt or stained by years of chemical mishaps.

She pointed at Donny. "Who is *that?*" she asked. It was a rich, imperious voice.

"Oh, him? Just my worthless human servant," Angela replied. "Or pet. Or whatever. He's sort of useful but likely to die before long during one of my missions. Not that I care."

Donny stared at Angela, his mouth twisted. She winked at him with the eye that was turned away from the chemist.

"*Likely* to die?" asked Ellie. "You mean he's not already dead? That's a *living* mortal?"

"That's right."

"Hmmm." The chemist gave Donny an avid, hungry stare. "Can I have him for some experiments?"

Donny looked at Angela. He shook his head in tiny but rapid movements. She bit her cheek to keep from laughing. "Sorry, Ellie, but no. I need him undamaged for the time being," she said. She walked down the stairs. Donny followed, eyeing the chemist with a newly heightened wariness.

"Lamentable," said the chemist. She raised both hands and beckoned with her fingers. "But you brought me something?"

Angela pushed the satchel behind her back. "Only if you can help me out."

Behind the chemist, a screech erupted from one of the cauldrons and rose in pitch. "Better cover your eyes," Ellie said.

"Why——" began Angela, but that was all she got out before, with a mighty whistle, a burst of brilliant white light shot out of the cauldron. It was worse than looking into the sun. Donny closed his eyes and raised his forearm a fraction of a second too late. The light was so strong that it passed right through his eyelids. When he blinked his eyes open, the world looked like it had been bleached. He saw lights pulsing everywhere.

Even Angela rubbed her eyelids with her fingertips. "Sheesh, Ellie, a little more warning would be nice."

"Eh, you'll recover soon enough. Now, what do you need from me?"

Angela squinted and blinked. "I have a question first, actually. Do you happen to have a vessel for catching souls on hand?"

Ellie's head rocked back. "We don't make those. Why would you ask?"

Angela unzipped her satchel and reached into it. Ellie leaned sideways and tried to see what else Angela had in that bag, but Angela angled herself to shield it with her body. She took out the piece of glass that she had retrieved from the basement in Puerto Rico and handed it to Ellie.

"Can you tell me anything about this? Like, where it was made?"

Ellie held it high so the lights of the fiery blobs shone through it. "This is amateurish work. Look at how irregular and murky the glass is. Not my glassblower, for certain." She handed it back to Angela. "As for where it was made, it could be from anywhere in Sulfur. There's nothing special about it, really."

"Hmph." Angela pursed her lips.

"But what have you really come here for?" Ellie asked.

Angela stuffed the fragment back into her satchel. "A few things. First off, we might have a rogue ferryman to deal with."

The chemist angled her head to one side. "Rogue ferryman? Never heard of such a thing."

"Well, I can assure you they exist. We cornered one recently and barely survived the encounter. Do you have anything that can help? If we meet another one, I'd rather avoid a battle. A knockout would be nice. Or temporary paralysis. Or something."

The chemist rubbed her chin hard, like kneading dough. "There's a challenge. A ferryman is a powerful creature. An ordinary knockout solution won't fit the bill. I'll be guessing, but I think I can make something potent enough." She pulled a notepad and a ballpoint pen from her pocket. Donny expected that she'd use parchment and a quill, but it looked like somebody had gone to an office supply store for her at some point. Another, closer look around the room showed Post-it notes stuck everywhere, and three-ring binders, calculators, and markers and whiteboards covered with scribbles.

As the chemist wrote furiously in her notebook, Donny took another look around the Hall of Elements. Behind them, in a hollow area under the stairs, something that looked completely out of place startled him: a plush reclining chair and a pair of couches, arranged in front of a huge television with a DVD player and an old VCR on a shelf below, and tall speakers on both sides. He wondered where they got electricity to run the equipment. Then he saw the electrical cords that ran along the floor and were wired at the other end onto a metal rod that stuck out of a huge ceramic urn. *Some kind of battery,* Donny thought. He shook his head. *A home theater, in a chemical laboratory, in the underworld.* The pure weirdness of Sulfur never ceased to amaze him, when it wasn't putting his life in danger.

The sound of paper being torn from the pad brought his attention back to Ellie Mental. With her notes clutched in her hand, she looked at a table halfway across the room. There, a grizzled old imp sat examining a glass container full of a frothing green liquid. "Quibble!" she shouted. "Put that beaker down and come over here."

"This is a flask, not a beaker," Quibble called back. "Beakers have straight sides."

"Just get off that chair and come here," snapped Ellie.

"Chairs have backrests. This is a stool."

"*Quibble!*" the chemist roared. The grizzled imp sighed, hopped off his stool, and waddled over.

Ellie shoved the paper into the imp's gnarled hand. "Assemble these ingredients. But don't combine them. Off you go." The imp plodded away. Ellie turned back to Angela and eyed the satchel, an eager smile on her face.

"Hold on," Angela said. "I have two more requests."

The chemist crossed her arms. "You've already asked for a lot."

"The next one's easy," Angela said brightly. She unbuckled her sword from her side and handed the whole thing to the chemist, still in its sheath. "The flame has gone dim. It needs a recharge."

Ellie pulled the sword partly out. Where the blade touched the air, it became cloaked in a dull orange flame. "Yes, it does. Not a problem. An overnight bath in vat number seven will refuel it," the chemist said. She shoved the sword back in and set it on the table.

"Hey!" Donny shouted. His fingertips had an odd, tingly feeling. When he looked down, he saw another imp, who had snuck up from behind and held a jar of pink fire under his hand. Donny jerked his hand away.

"Did that hurt?" croaked the imp.

Donny scowled and flexed his hand, then raised it to keep it out of the imp's reach. "No," he said.

"Huh," said the imp. He sniffed at the flames. "It was supposed to hurt."

Angela snorted back some laughter and then assumed a serious expression when Donny whipped his head around to glare at her. "Ellie!" Angela said. "Tell your staff: absolutely no experiments on my human."

Ellie mouthed, *Shoo,* and waved the imp away.

"Now then, one more thing," Angela said. She flashed her most charming smile and tented her hands in a pleading gesture. "I could really use a fire escape. Type two."

A fire escape? thought Donny.

"A fire escape?" said the chemist. "You've gone too far. You know how tricky those are. And the ingredients are priceless!" She flung her hands in the air. "You ask too much!"

"Fire escape, type two," Angela repeated. She swung her satchel around to the front and then unzipped it. Ellie's eyes grew wide. Angela reached in, took out a DVD, and held it in front of the chemist, who froze as if in a trance.

Donny looked at the DVD. It was some movie from the forties or fifties. The cover showed grinning sailors in white uniforms, a dancing woman, and the New York City skyline across the bottom. The title was in big red letters: *ON THE TOWN*. Under that, it said, *They Paint The Town With Joy!*

The scales on Ellie's face bristled. "What's it about?"

Angela looked at the back of the case. "This is a musical

about 'three sailors on shore leave in New York City, searching for fun and romance before the day is up.'"

"Aaaagh!" the chemist said. Her hands trembled. "But . . . what are *sailors?*"

Angela shrugged. "Men in little white hats who sing and dance."

Ellie's voice rose in pitch and volume as she grew more fevered. "Is it as good as *Singin' in the Rain?*"

"Of course not," Angela said. "But it's good."

"It has songs? And dancing?"

"It wouldn't be much of a musical if it didn't."

"Give it here!"

Angela held the DVD farther back from Ellie's grasping hands. "Fire escape?"

"Yes, yes! You'll have it by tomorrow!"

Angela tossed the DVD to Ellie, who snatched it out of the air with cobra-quick hands.

Donny was suddenly aware that the chatter in the room had stopped. Every imp stared, frozen, at the DVD that the chemist held high above her head. "A musical!" Ellie bellowed. The imps shrieked in reply, abandoned their work, and followed her as she dashed for the home theater.

"Remember, you said tomorrow!" Angela called out between cupped hands.

"I'll have it all sent over!" Ellie bellowed. She switched on the television and DVD player as Quibble clawed at the cellophane wrapper on the DVD case, trying desperately to find the seam. The imps piled onto the couches. They left the recliner directly in front of the television for Ellie.

"We'll let ourselves out, then," Angela said, not bothering to shout. She and Donny headed back up the stairs. The two imps at the entrance opened the door and slid the glass tube through the flames.

Soon they were back outside the Hall of Elements, and Donny was finally able to ask the question. "What's a *fire escape?*"

"Exactly what it sounds like," Angela chirped. She was in an excellent mood, practically walking on her tiptoes. "It can open a temporary fire-portal just about anywhere, instantly. Handy to have in an emergency."

"Are we planning to have an emergency?"

"Planning? I don't think that's how emergencies work. It's nice to have in our back pocket, just in case. Come on. Let's go find our runners so they can take us back home."

CHAPTER 42

As the chariot approached the Pillar Obscura, Donny saw Zig-Zag running down the street to intercept them, his arms waving over his heads.

"Hold it, guys," Angela told the runners, and the long-legged imps complied. The chariot rolled to a stop beside Zig-Zag.

"He's here!" Zig said with a huff.

"To talk to you!" Zag said with a puff. "Not the whole council. He showed up and demanded to talk only to you!"

"Who is this 'he' we're talking about here?" Angela asked.

"The Ferryman King—he's at your door!"

"I can't imagine why," Angela said, tossing Donny a smirk. "Hop on." Zig-Zag climbed onto the chariot. They sprinted the short distance to the pillar and took the narrow road that spiraled up to her front door. A full circle around the great stone column brought them to where the

Ferryman King stood, flanked by four of his ghastly guard.

The runner imps stopped a short distance away. The chariot rocked as they shifted nervously from foot to foot. "Calm down, boys," Angela told the runners. "Once we're off, you can go." They hopped off the chariot, and the runners swung it around and hustled away, glad to retreat.

Angela flicked her eyebrows up and down at Donny and Zig-Zag, then walked over to stand before the Ferryman King. "This is an unexpected visit," she said brightly.

The Ferryman King sneered with what was left of his lips. With one hand he raised the jawbone high, and with the other he pointed a bony finger at Angela. "You killed my son."

That's not good, Donny thought.

Angela put her fists on her hips. "How do you know it's your son?"

"They are *all* my sons."

If Angela was intimidated, she didn't let it show. "Well, let me tell you something about *that* particular offspring. He trespassed in the mortal realm, and he captured souls from the soulstream."

The Ferryman King's neck made a bony, crunching sound as his enormous head listed to one side. His breath whistled through his clamped teeth like a graveyard breeze.

"Kids today, right?" Angela said. "It gets worse. He didn't just collect the wicked souls that belong down here. He grabbed anything he could get, the good and the bad.

When we found his hiding place, there were hundreds of souls already trapped."

The king cradled his forehead with his spidery hand. "That cannot be true."

"Oh, it certainly is. I know we don't have too many laws down here, but capturing good souls has to break one of them. When we caught him in the act, your little acorn attacked us. We had to defend ourselves. Either he was going to let the fire out of us, or we were going to let it out of him."

The Ferryman King turned his back to them. His head lowered and practically disappeared beyond his shoulders.

"You know it's true. I think you knew some of your own were involved all along," Angela said. "So what was he doing? Was he feasting?"

The Ferryman King stood clutching his head. He bent a little at the knees and waist. When time went by without a response, the tallest of his guards spoke for him. "You said hundreds. He couldn't devour all those souls. Not that many. They were meant for something else."

"But what?" Angela asked.

The guard shook his bony head. "That is unknown."

The king finally spoke again. He raised a hand, two long fingers extended. "Two were missing," he said. He turned to face them again. "Two sons."

Angela scratched the back of her head. "But why? Since when do your ferrymen go rogue?"

That seemed to anger the king. He rose from his slump to his full height, swaying a little as if tugged by invisible wires. Donny heard a muffled clatter of bones inside those robes. The king loomed over Angela. "Do you think arch-demons are the only ones who fight and disagree? This revolution of yours was a topic of dissent among the ferry-men, as well. Some of my sons believed that the Pit of Fire should still burn and that the souls should be cast inside to suffer forever, as they always had."

Angela's face grew hot and red. Talk of restoring the pit had a way of doing that to her.

"During the war," said the king, "some of my sons even wished to join the Merciless in battle. I told them it was not our place to interfere. I said we would bring the dead to you, and let you decide how to punish them. But the two that are missing now, including the one that you have slain—they were the loudest and angriest of the dissent-ers."

"You might have mentioned all this at the beginning," Angela said.

The king leaned closer and glared down, his enormous head almost directly over hers.

"Find my other son, near the second place I showed you on the map," the Ferryman King said. "Destroy him if you must."

"It might be more complicated than that. There was a fire-portal in his lair in Puerto Rico. I'm guessing I'll

find the same thing at the second location. Your other son may be the one who's down here somewhere, on the other side of that portal. Or it might be somebody else whom we haven't seen—someone in Sulfur who's behind all this, and is helping them."

Bones creaked as the ferrymen swayed and turned to look at each other. The king joined the others as they gathered in a circle. The ferrymen put their heads close together. They whispered in some strange tongue that Donny could not understand, a language of hisses and clacking teeth.

"What are they saying?" Donny whispered to Angela.

"Ya got me," she replied. "I don't speak ferryman."

The conversation among the ferrymen ended. The king stepped over to speak to Angela again, a second ferryman close behind him. "I am troubled by your news. Ferrymen do not take sides. That was my decree. We ferry the dead, and that is all. If this second dissenter is in league with other beings, this must end now."

"Ditto that," Angela said.

The king gestured to the ferryman by his side. "This one will go with you." It was the tall one who had spoken to them before. "He is the strongest of my sons, and he will subdue the dissenter. You deal with the others."

Donny gulped. Angela's eyebrows rocketed up. "Are you serious?" she asked.

The new ferryman took a step forward, frighteningly close. "I am ready for this hunt," he said.

267

"Sorry, but no," Angela said. She put both hands up, palms out. "You see, my whole thing is keeping infernal beings out of the mortal realm. Bringing one with me . . . well, I have a policy against that."

"You will make an exception to your policy," the Ferryman King said. Without another word he strode past them, and the others followed, except for the tall one.

Angela folded her arms and scowled as she watched them go. Then she looked up at the lone ferryman.

"So, what's your name?" Angela asked.

He stared and clacked his teeth before answering. "If you must have a name, call me Agony."

Angela giggled and then covered her mouth with her fingers. "Agony. Isn't that lovely?"

"I am ready for this hunt," Agony said again.

"Yes, you mentioned that already. But we are not. We won't leave until tomorrow. Do you want to come inside?"

"I will wait here," Agony said. He straightened to his full height and stiffened like a statue. It made a faint sound, like ice freezing.

Angela looked at Donny and shrugged. "At least we'll have plenty of muscle."

CHAPTER 43

A ngela was absent until the following afternoon. "Plans and preparations" was all she said before she left.

While she was out, an urgent, insistent knock came at the door. Donny and Tizzy looked down from the window above. The ferryman still stood frozen in the same spot. Beside him, ready to rap on the door again, was an imp with a long wooden case tucked under one arm. His scales were burnt, bleached, and discolored.

"Hi down there!" Tizzy shouted. She smiled and flapped her hand furiously in greeting.

Arglbrgl was with them in the pillar. He squeezed between Donny and Tizzy and growled at the imp below. "GRRBRGR."

The imp squinted up, searching for the voices. "Ah. There you are. Delivery for Angela Obscura. From the Hall of Elements."

"She's not here, but you can leave it for her," said Donny.

The imp cast a wary sideways glance at the frozen ferryman and shook his head. "These are precious and valuable items. I can hand this over to only Angela Obscura. By order of the chemist."

"Okay. You'll have to wait, then," Donny said. "She'll be back eventually."

The imp sighed heavily, set the wooden case down, and sat on it, beside the towering ferryman. Donny rolled his eyes. Now two strange beings waited at the door, one tall and gaunt and silent, the other short and squat and muttering complaints to nobody in particular.

Angela came through the front door an hour later, the case under her arm. "We got the stuff," she said as Arglbrgl ran around her in circles. "Let's take a look."

She set the case on the long table in the main hall, flipped the latches, and swung the lid open. Everything inside was nestled in a thick layer of stringy black moss. She reached into the padding and found her sword in its scabbard. When she pulled the blade partway out, it glowed fiercely. The room was awash in rippling yellow light. She pushed the blade back inside, snuffing the flame. "Much better!"

"GLRGL," said Arglbrgl.

Next she pulled out what looked like a tall, narrow

bottle of dark brown glass. It was sealed with a cork that had a thick ring sticking out of the top. A piece of paper had been taped to the side. Angela read the note and then passed it to Donny.

KNOCKOUT GAS. MAXIMUM POTENCY. PULL THE CORK AND DIRECT IT AT THE ENEMY. DON'T SHOOT INTO YOUR OWN FACE.

"Yeah, let's not," Donny said.

Angela found something else: a pouch with tiny jars of demon drops. "Oh look, something extra. I guess they liked the movie." She handed one jar to Donny and set the pouch aside. Then she dug into the moss again. "Ah, here's the main attraction." This item was larger and tucked into a soft pouch like a baby in a papoose. When she extracted it, Donny saw another glass vessel. This one was dark red and shaped like an oversize bowling pin. It was easy to grip at the narrow neck, which was wrapped with leather lace. Another note was taped to the side, and she scanned it and handed it to Donny. This one he read out loud.

"'Fire escape. Immediate access to portal. No incantation necessary. Shatter against solid surface and stand back.'" He tried to see within the red glass. It looked like liquid boiling in slow motion. "This is nuts, Angela. What does 'no incantation necessary' mean?"

"Don't be dim, Cricket. I already told you how portals work: you have to prime the site with the flames of the portal you want to use. Then you have to whisper the incantation for the gatekeeper to hear. Those are just some hocus-pocus words in the ancient infernal language. This little cocktail has the portal flames, plus the incantation, plus the fuel to keep a fire going. So whammo, instant fire-portal. Got it?"

"Oh yeah, now that you've explained it, it makes total sense," Donny said. *Except that it's still nuts,* he added to himself.

Angela shoved the red vessel back into the pouch, then reached out and put her hand on his wrist. "Donny, I know we've gotten into some scary stuff recently. So it's your choice if you want to come with me or not."

He took a deep breath. "Where exactly are we going, anyway?"

"It's in Cyprus."

"Cyprus? Really?"

"Uh-huh. You know where that is?"

"Um." Donny tried to picture a map. "In the Mediterranean, right?"

"Correct. Off the coast of Syria and Turkey. Another island."

Donny had traveled a lot in his short life, even before he'd started to hop the globe with Angela, but he'd never been to any of those places. He remembered things from school: ancient lands. Some of the earliest civilizations. Amazing antiquities and fabulous ruins.

"Why do you think it was islands both times?" he asked.

"If I had to guess? On an island, the soulstreams would

converge. Kind of like highways that meet in a city. And both of those islands are historically important, so the stream would be powerful. That makes for good fishing, if you know what I mean."

Donny nodded, trying to picture the soulstreams coming together. "But you have to find the exact place where the ferryman is stealing, right? And you don't have Carlos to help you, like in Puerto Rico."

"We have someone else on the case. Some local specialists—a guy and his brother, who is supersensitive and probably can't get anywhere near me. Those two will meet us in Cyprus and put us in the vicinity. This time we'll move more cautiously. This is our last chance to see who's behind the whole scheme, so we can't mess up. We'll stake out the scene for a while and wait for the rogue ferryman to open the portal. If we can make a move, we will. Sound okay?"

Donny thought about it. It sounded like another one of those absurdly dangerous situations. But now, for the first time, he'd been given a choice. And that made all the difference.

"Yes. Sure, I'll come with you."

CHAPTER 44

When they opened the front door to leave, Agony the ferryman was still there, as motionless as ever.

Angela shouted up into his face. "Time to go!"

The cloaked head swiveled toward her, making the unpleasant sound of neck bones grinding. Agony nodded. Angela and Donny headed down the road that spiraled around the pillar, and the ferryman followed without a word. He stayed far enough behind that it was easy for Donny and Angela to talk quietly between themselves.

"This is kind of unusual, right?" Donny asked.

"How so?"

Donny looked back at the tall, gaunt figure that strode behind them. "Well, I thought you tried to keep a low profile when you go to Earth. But we have something that looks like the Grim Reaper with us. And you have your flaming sword. And I'm carrying the fire escape, and you've got a big bottle of knockout stuff. What if someone sees Agony, or any of the magical things?"

She nodded. "I know what you mean. But these are special circumstances. Apparently, we're headed for a ghost town of some kind, so we're not likely to run into any people."

"Ghost town? There's a ghost town in Cyprus?"

"Yes. Our contact says it's a forbidden zone. It's fenced off and illegal to enter."

"So of course we'll go in," Donny said.

"Makes sense though, right? It's an easy place to capture souls without getting caught in the act."

They reached the steps that led to the guarded door. At the top of the steps, Angela paused and waited for the ferryman to join them on the landing. "You don't talk much," she told him when he arrived.

Agony let out a slow, hissing breath. "When we find him, leave the ferryman to me."

"He's all yours," Angela replied. She flexed the arm that the last ferryman had broken.

They went down the short passage to where Grunyon guarded the door. Donny wished Grunyon could join them. He had a feeling that, in a fight, Grunyon might be the best warrior of them all.

"Pop Rocks?" Grunyon asked Angela.

"Sorry, buddy, I don't think we're going to any stores. Next time though, for sure."

Grunyon's helmet drooped a little. He sighed and unlocked the door for them. Angela, Donny, and the ferryman stepped through, and the door closed heavily behind them.

From there it was a short walk to where Porta the gatekeeper sat beside the ruby-red wall of flames. Donny wondered if she ever moved from that spot.

"Mediterranean Sea, island of Cyprus," Angela told her. Porta worked her magic on the flames. When a globe of the world appeared, she spun it until the Mediterranean was in view and then drew the island of Cyprus closeup. Three lights twinkled on the island.

Angela pointed. "That one. The new one, right by the shore."

Porta nodded. With a gesture of her hands, she conjured a dark shape within the flames.

"Here we go," Angela said. Donny followed her through the flimsy barrier of ash.

They stepped into an old parking garage in a terrible state of decay. The paint on the concrete walls had flaked and peeled. Rusted pipes dangled from the ceiling. There were a few dust-covered cars nearby, all their tires flat.

A man leaned against the hood of one of the cars. He stared in amazement at Angela and Donny. "I didn't believe it would really happen until I saw it," he said. He glanced at his watch. "You're very prompt. I thought it might—" His eyes bugged as he looked past them, at the gas fire that burned against the concrete wall. The ferryman had just stepped through, bending low to fit through the space and then clattering upright, nearly eight feet tall. Agony was terrifying enough, but there was something strange about his appearance here in the mortal realm. He looked blurry, transparent, and not entirely *there*.

"Don't mind him," Angela said cheerfully.

The man threw his hand in front of his eyes and turned his head. He had broken into an instant sweat. "What . . . what is that?"

"Nothing to worry about," Angela said. She turned to whisper to Agony. "Can you blend into the shadows and stay out of sight? I need to talk to this guy, and you're freaking him out." Agony grumbled and moved to a shadowy area of the garage, behind a thick pillar. Donny watched, amazed, as the ferryman fused with the darkness. It was like pouring ink into coffee. As long as Agony avoided the light, he was nearly invisible.

"He's gone now," Angela called to the man. "And besides, he won't hurt you."

The fellow peered between his fingers as he slowly turned around. He looked left and right, searching for any trace of the ferryman. Finally he relaxed enough to speak, although his voice quavered. He spoke with a gentle accent. "I should have been prepared for anything, I suppose. Forgive me for being such a coward. You are Angela, I assume?"

"And he's Donny. You're Osman?"

"I am. It is nice to meet you both. And to see you, Angela, after only hearing your voice until now." Osman had a likeable face, with a dense crop of dark hair and a broad mustache. He was dressed for stealth, in dark jeans and a black long-sleeve shirt. A camera bag was slung over his shoulder.

"Welcome to Varosha," Osman said. "This seemed like the safest place to have the fire, without burning the whole town by accident or being seen by the authorities. It's important to stay out of sight. You could get arrested, or even shot, just for being here."

Donny tried not to groan out loud. As if the rogue ferryman wasn't enough of a problem, they had to worry about the local police, too. "But why?" he asked. "Why is this a ghost town?"

"You do not know?" Osman said. He looked surprised, and a little discouraged. "In 1974, Turkish forces came to Cyprus. The armies met here, and all the residents of Varosha fled. Tens of thousands of them. The town has been fenced off since then. It is a buffer zone between the sides. There is hope that the dispute will be settled soon, but for all the buildings here, it is too late. They have fallen into such decay that nothing can be saved. Everything must be demolished if we ever want to use this place again. What a shame, because before that happened, this was a beautiful resort town. The beach is one of the Mediterranean's finest. Long ago many movie stars came here."

Angela gasped. "Jimmy Stewart?"

Osman's brow wrinkled. "I do not recall if Jimmy Stewart was here."

"Never mind," she said, waving her hand. "So, do you have a bead on what we're looking for?"

"My brother does," Osman said. "He is very sensitive, and wanted to keep his distance from you. He waits for us, down the street. Follow me."

Osman led them out of the depths of the garage, past more decades-old cars. They neared the exit, where a payment booth still stood, its glass blurry with age and dust. Donny couldn't see Agony, but he was sure that the ferryman was close behind.

They stepped out of the parking garage. It was late at night, but the moon was bright overhead, and so Donny could see clearly. Directly across from the garage was the ruined side of a tall hotel. The windows were gone and shutters hung askew. The elements had gnawed at the walls and balconies. The city may have been off-limits, but people had clearly snuck in over the years, spraying graffiti wherever they could reach. The pavement of the street had fractured, weeds and trees sprouting in the cracks. Over the top of another building, an old construction crane still loomed high.

"This whole city is fenced off?" asked Donny.

Osman nodded. "Chain-link fencing and barbed wire, all the way around."

"How did you get in?"

"You can swim around the fence in the sea. Or there are holes in the fence, if you know where to find them. We crawled through the holes in the dark."

"What if you got caught?"

"Big trouble," Osman said.

"That's why we pay you the big bucks," Angela said.

"This is true," Osman said. He tapped his camera bag. "If we are seen, I tell them I am just an innocent photographer here to take pictures for fun, and hope for the best." He pointed to a white building, a block away on the other side of the street. It was maybe twelve or fourteen stories tall. "Do you see that building over there? That is where we are going. I don't think we'll be seen, but let's stay out of the open as we move."

"Just a sec," Angela said. She leaned close to Donny and whispered. "Put some drops in, okay? I want you to be able to see."

Donny fished the tiny bottle out of his pocket. He tilted his head back, squeezed a drop into each eye, and blinked slowly while they soaked in. When he looked around, his heart thumped a little faster as he spotted Agony. The ferryman was clearly visible where before there had only been shadows behind them, watching and waiting.

"Look up," Angela told him. He peered at the top of the

buildings across the street. When he squinted, he noticed the slimmest thread of darkness in the sky. It curved down like the track of a roller coaster and veered close to the roof of that tall white building.

"Just like in Puerto Rico," Donny said.

"All set," Angela told Osman. They crept quietly down the sidewalk, staying out of the moonlight.

"There is my brother," Osman said when they were across from the building he'd pointed out. It was another hotel. A circular driveway where cars would have pulled in was on the other side of the street. Just outside the doors of the hotel, a dark figure stood, half hidden behind a cement column. The man raised a hand in greeting.

"Let me go and speak to him," Osman said. He darted across the street, looking furtively around him. The brothers put their heads close for a minute and talked quietly. Then Osman's brother walked back the way they had come, but on the other side.

Osman waved them over. His face looked a little paler when they arrived.

"My brother was confused. He said he felt the presence of something terrible, up there, on top of the building." Osman's hand trembled as he pointed to the rooftop. "But then he felt something similar, which came from where we stood. The feeling was too strong, and he could not stay. His heart was racing, and it was hard to breathe."

"That all makes sense," Angela said. "The first thing

he sensed is what we're after. The second one was the tall, scary guy you saw in the garage. This is good stuff, Osman. Is there anything else you can tell us?"

Osman gulped and nodded. "Yes. We learned this yesterday. When the presence is not up high, on the roof of this building, it is down low. In the basement, maybe."

"Perfect," Angela said. "I think that's all we need from you. Howard will be in touch. Good luck getting out."

"And the same to you," Osman said.

Yeah, Donny thought. *The same to us.*

CHAPTER 45

One large pane of glass in the lobby doors had shattered long ago. The shards crunched under their feet as they stepped inside.

A once-beautiful lobby had turned into a nightmare. Wallpaper was peeling off in sheets. Pieces of the ceiling had rained down. A chandelier lay on the floor, its crystals scattered everywhere. The lobby furniture remained, but the cushions were rotting. The smell of must was overpowering.

"Our quarry is up top, but the lair is below. So how do we get there?" Angela mumbled.

Donny saw elevator doors in the corner of the lobby. Obviously they couldn't take the elevator. But a sign next to the elevator had a little map that showed what he was looking for. "Over there," he said. "The stairs."

"Right," Angela said. "Let's go."

She turned the handle of the stairwell door and pushed it slowly inward. The rusty hinges squealed in protest, and Donny gritted his teeth at the sound. Angela didn't open it any farther than she had to. She just turned sideways and scraped through the opening. Donny and the ferryman went in after.

When they closed the door behind them, it was pitch-black. Angela took out a penlight and shone it around. Donny had brought a powerful flashlight of his own, but for now he decided not to use it. A brighter light might give them away.

Below them, the metal stairs descended under street level. Above, they climbed all the way to the roof. There was a narrow rectangular gap in the middle, an empty shaft around which the steps rose, flight after flight. Donny leaned over and looked up through the stairwell. The upper reaches vanished into darkness.

Behind him, he heard a fierce whisper from Angela. "Hey!"

Donny turned to see Angela, her hand gripping Agony's arm. Agony had one foot on the stairs that led up. Angela glared at the gaunt ferryman. "What do you think you're doing?"

"This is foolish. I know he is there. I will go and take him," came the hissed reply.

"Nuh-uh," she said. "This is my operation, mister. If you go up there, we could lose him on the rooftops. We're going downstairs, where he'll be trapped. And we'll wait for him to open that fire-portal before we do anything. Then you can have him. Understand?"

Agony leaned over and put his head directly over hers. She had to crane her neck to meet his seething stare.

"Don't test me, ferryman," she said. "You wouldn't be here if my people hadn't tracked him down."

Agony tapped Angela on the shoulder with the tip of his blade. "Who are you to tell me what to do?"

Angela put two fingers on the side of the blade and turned it away. "I'm Angela Obscura of the Pillar Obscura. Member of the Infernal Council. Instigator of the Great Reform. And if you go up those stairs, I'll scream so loud, your brother will be sure to get away."

Donny felt rage emanating from the ferryman. Agony's spindly fingers curled tightly around the handle of his weapon. "I could silence you first."

"Then my little friend here will scream for me."

Agony's cloaked head turned to look at Donny. Donny nodded. "Yes. I would definitely scream, super loud," he said. That was a perfectly honest threat, because a lot of loud screaming was exactly what he would do.

"Enough already," Angela said. "We're wasting time." She went down the stairs, trusting that the ferryman would follow. And he did, but Donny made sure to tuck in behind Angela first. There was no way he would let himself be the last one down, or the first, for that matter.

It was hard to walk on the creaking metal stairs in complete silence, but they did their best. "Oh yeah," Angela said. "This is the place." She waved at what was below. A flight of steps had been torn out, creating a gap. "An obstacle to keep the curious out," Angela said.

"Just like in Puerto Rico," Donny added. The whole situation was eerily similar. "Angela, I'm not sure if I can make it across that—" Before he finished the thought, she put an arm around his waist, lifted him, and leaped across the gap. She was nimble and came down softly, but the steps still groaned when they landed. Agony came next. He covered the gap in a single long stride, with much less noise. They paused there and peered up the stairwell, listening for any sounds from above.

The bottom of the staircase was one more short flight below. Donny peered into the darkness, which wasn't as dark as it ought to have been. "There's light down there," he said.

Angela switched off her penlight. "Hmm." They crept down the remaining steps and entered a stark hallway, dirty cement walls on both sides, wires and plumbing above. The ceiling was low, and Agony had to hunch to pass through. They went by a bathroom, and then a storage room with janitorial supplies, where all the shelves had collapsed. On the other side was what looked like an old office. Inside was a desk covered with moldy papers and stacks of manuals. Paint was bubbling off the walls.

Angela stopped, tapped Donny on the chest with the backs of her knuckles, and pointed at the floor. In the dust were long, narrow footprints, twice as long as Donny's feet. "Definitely the place," she said.

The meager light came from just ahead, through an open doorway at the end of the hall. Angela reached the threshold, put her back to the edge, and leaned her head over to peer in. Then she smiled and waved them in.

Donny sighed. Here they were, in another disgusting room that felt like a deathtrap. This one was an eerie maze of mechanical things, surrounded by walls of brick. It smelled like oil and grimy rags. There were silvery ducts and pipes and valves everywhere, a corroded electrical panel mounted in one corner, and a table covered with fat wrenches and other rusted tools. A boiler that was nearly as big as a school bus was at one end of the room, shedding its paint in long curls.

On the far side of the room, Donny saw exactly what they had expected to find: shelves full of dark jars with twinkly souls inside, and a clear space along the brick wall that was covered in scorch marks where a fire-portal had been lit. The light that they had seen came from a couple of clear bottles with flames inside. They weren't earthly flames, Donny was certain. That fire, burning in a closed bottle with no oxygen to feed it, could only come from Sulfur.

"This is abhorrent," Agony said as he surveyed the jars.

"Right. But you know what? I think we're in luck," Angela said.

Donny wasn't feeling very lucky. "How's that?"

She pointed to the shelves. "All those jars are full of souls. If those are meant for the other side of the portal, maybe it's time for a delivery."

They gazed around in silence. Then all three of their heads turned as a faint, echoing, metallic sound rolled down from the far end of the hallway.

"What did that sound like to you?" Angela said.

"Like a door slamming shut, way at the top of those stairs," Donny said.

"I'm picturing our quarry," Angela said. "He finished up on the roof, closed the door behind him, and now he's making his way downstairs."

"Yeah, I'm picturing that too." Donny reached behind him to pat the container with the fire escape, which was nestled inside his backpack. He wanted to be sure it was still there.

Agony unleashed a long, slow, chilling hiss. Dust fell from his hands as he compressed them into fists.

"Time to hide and see what happens," Angela said.

CHAPTER 46

They stood behind the boiler, where they could peer out between thick vertical pipes. Donny's eyes were already accustomed to the gloom, and the meager light that the bottled fire provided. He closed his eyes to focus on his hearing, and thought he detected the faint scuff of footfalls on the metal stairs.

Then came a screech and groan of metal bending. *He just stepped across the gap,* Donny thought. Beads of sweat sprouted along his hairline. The footsteps grew more distinct, and added to them was the muffled clink-tink of glass. *More jars of souls, inside a sack,* Donny thought. His hands shook, his heart thumped, and his lungs screamed for more air. He had to breathe through his mouth to keep the air from whistling out his nose.

The silhouette of the rogue ferryman filled the threshold, and then he entered the room. He let the bulging sack droop to the floor, and then dragged it the rest of the way toward the charred wall and the shelves filled with souls. Donny glanced at Angela, who kept a firm hand on Agony's wrist.

The ferryman paused near the wall. Donny held his breath, certain that the ferryman was about to start the fire. He sensed Agony tensing, ready to rush out from hiding. But then their quarry stepped to the shelves, ran his fingertips across the surfaces of the jars, and selected one. He pried the top off the jar and held it to his chin. A twinkling cluster of lights drifted up. *A human soul,* Donny thought. His stomach curdled as he watched the ferryman open his mouth and draw the soul in with a horrid slurping sound.

Donny had to turn away. *That used to be a person,* he thought. But worse still, the soul that drifted from the jar had been a bright, almost angelic color. It was never meant for Sulfur. It was someone like the sisters in Old San Juan who'd been so kind to Fiasco. Or somebody's kindly grandmother. And now it was extinguished forever. When Donny looked at Angela, her lip was curled, her nostrils were flared, and her body swayed from side to side. She was like a cat ready to spring. Agony's knuckles crackled as he tightened his fists.

The rogue ferryman sighed, long and deep, as if he'd

taken a cold drink on a hot day. He set the empty jar down and then returned to the spot where the portal would be lit.

This is it, Donny thought.

And this time he was right.

CHAPTER 47

Next to the charred section of the wall stood a huge brown glass jug, like the ones they'd seen in Puerto Rico. The rogue ferryman pulled the stopper and tipped the jug. A glowing liquid spilled out and filled a long narrow trough that had been gouged into the floor, next to the wall. Flames sprouted from the liquid and rose high. The fire hissed, like waves washing up on a beach.

Angela leaned over and whispered to Donny. "You, stay behind me. Use the fire escape if I call for it. Remember, all you have to do is smash it against a wall." She leaned the other way to whisper to Agony. "You take care of him. I'll grab the gatekeeper on the other side."

Donny slipped off his backpack and took out the fire escape, still cushioned inside its pouch. He peered out from between the pipes again. A dark shape grew in the center of the flames. The rogue ferryman picked up the bag of souls and stepped through. Ash fell around him like filthy snow. All Donny saw beyond the portal was a narrow tunnel without another being in sight.

"Go," Angela said to Agony. "Hide next to the fire. Grab him when he comes back."

Agony hissed and raced out from behind the boiler.

"Just like we planned! Come on," Angela said to Donny. She bolted and followed in Agony's footsteps. Her hand slipped into her pack and came out holding the knockout bottle.

I can't believe this is happening, Donny thought for maybe the hundredth time since Angela had appeared in his life. He kept up with her as well as he could, careful not to trip or kick some debris and make too much noise, but she was halfway down the room before he'd taken three steps.

Agony reached the fire-portal and pressed his back against the wall beside it. His curved blade hung at his waist. Angela stood beside him. Donny arrived just in time to see the rogue ferryman step back out of the portal, pushing what looked like an enormous, ancient wheelbarrow.

There was a blur of motion as Agony reached out, seized the rogue ferryman by the neck, and dashed him to the ground. Donny wasn't sure if the splintering and crunching sounds came from the ferryman's bones or whatever was scattered on the floor beneath him.

Angela made a quick sideways leap to the portal, and

another directly through it. Donny raced after her. With one step, he was in the basement of a forsaken hotel in a historic island off the coast of Turkey. With the next step, he was somewhere else completely. And the first thing he heard was Angela's shout.

"Duck!"

When Angela leaped through, she had guessed that the gatekeeper sat to the right, where Porta would have been found. But the keeper of this portal sat on the opposite side, and when Donny stepped through, he'd put himself right between them.

This one was like Porta's twin. It was a tiny, fearsome creature with a plump body but long spidery arms. One of those arms held a double-headed ax.

Donny dropped to the ground as the keeper brought the blade over one shoulder, ready to swing it. Angela pulled the plug from the knockout bottle. A jet of sparkling green flame shot over Donny's head. Angela had aimed it in the general direction of the gatekeeper, but the stuff acted like a heat-seeking missile and shot straight into the keeper's mouth and nostrils. The effect was instantaneous. The ax clattered to the ground. The keeper went as limp as a wet tissue and fell with a thud.

Angela plugged the bottle. "That's good stuff," she said. She tucked it into her satchel and turned around, scanning their new surroundings.

"This must be somewhere in Sulfur, right?" Donny

asked. They had stepped into a chamber at the end of a long tunnel. The wall of flame on this side emerged from a crack in the floor, much like the portal they used near Angela's home. The ferryman's sack of souls had been left to one side, next to a long shelfful of empty bottles.

"Definitely," Angela said. "That's a natural fountain of infernal flame. This is a portal that we never knew about. Someone's kept it secret."

"How long will that stay open?"

"I'm not sure. Long enough for the ferryman to cart all those bottles in, anyway, and that would take a while." She stared at the empty bottles. "At least they recycle."

Donny was in no mood for jokes. "We should get out of here, right? Before someone comes?"

"It doesn't seem like anyone noticed our little scuffle," Angela said.

"Which is awesome," Donny observed. "Now we can leave, right? You got the ferryman, and you caught the gatekeeper. So it's over."

Agony stepped through the portal, ducking to fit into the chamber.

"That was quick," Angela said. "Where's the rogue?"

"He is dust and smoke," Agony said.

"My assistant thinks we should leave," Angela said. "I suggest that we look around and find out who's responsible for this nasty enterprise. What do you think?"

"I prefer your idea, Angela Obscura," Agony replied.

Of course, thought Donny. "But hold it," he said. "Something might go wrong. The keeper could wake up. Or the fire in Cyprus could go out faster than you thought. We'd be trapped."

"You have the fire escape, silly," Angela said.

"Yeah, about that," Donny shot back. He still kept his voice low, just in case. "Will it even work? We're in Sulfur now. But you told me we can only travel from Sulfur to Earth and Earth to Sulfur." He lifted the red bottle, still inside its protective case. "We can't use this to get to Porta's gate, can we?"

Angela smiled back. "Remember I asked the chemist for a type two fire escape? That's what type two means. Sulfur to Earth. This will open a door to the temple in the Himalayas. We're all set, Donny. Just keep it handy."

Agony quivered with impatience. His bones rattled musically. "Do we stand and talk, or do we find out what lies down that passage?"

"We find out," Angela replied. "Follow me. Quietly, my friends."

CHAPTER 48

Almost as soon as they'd set off down the low, narrow tunnel, Donny heard a terrible noise start to grow louder.

Shrieks, moans, and screams.

The closest he'd heard to that sound was when he'd stood next to a scary roller coaster in an amusement park. But when screams came from a ride, you knew they came from joy and exhilaration. The cries he heard now were born from terror and pain.

He bit his lip and looked at Angela, wondering what she was thinking. Her features were arranged in a way he hadn't seen before: eyebrows high, a tightly cinched mouth, and a crinkle of pain around the eyes. Then it was all wiped away by a look of rising fury. "I know that sound," she said in a cold and lethal voice.

Donny felt anger emanate from her. Gooseflesh erupted

on his arms. He tightened his grip on the neck of the pin-shaped vessel. "What is it?" he whispered back.

"Someone misses the old days," she said. She started to walk a little faster, to Donny's dismay.

"Angela, what is that sound? How do you know it?" She whipped a hand through the air, telling him to be quiet. But Donny was pretty sure that none of them had to worry about making noise. The screams grew in volume and multiplied. At first he thought they came from a dozen sources, but now he was sure they were the screams of hundreds, or even thousands, as the sound echoed in the narrow passage. A red, pulsing glow leaked in as well from the far end. The air grew warmer.

They bent around a final curve of the passage, and what lay beyond came into view. Donny saw a lone figure at first, standing with his back to them. He wore black pants, a red vest, a black shirt, and the kind of hat you'd see in a movie about old-time gangsters. The brim of the hat hid his head from sight. Rippling red light washed over him. He stared at something they could not yet see.

But when they took a few more steps, they could see it all.

The passage ended in a cavern, not much bigger than a domed stadium. A thousand points of stone hung from the ceiling above. In the floor of the cavern there was a massive pit filled with brilliant orange flames that twisted and writhed like living things. Donny had seen only a tiny sample of that flame before, but he knew it at once. Those were the Flames of Torment, meant to agonize human souls.

The screams of thousands rose from the pit. The sound made Donny want to shove his thumbs into his ears. He tugged at Angela's sleeve. "We should get back, out of sight," he said, close to her ear.

Angela stared at the lone figure. "I know him." She didn't bother to whisper.

"Great," Donny said. "But let's hide." He tugged harder, but she didn't budge. She let her satchel slip off her shoulder and onto the ground, then reached for the hilt of her sword. Beside them, Agony took his curved weapon from his belt, flexed his neck, and rolled his shoulders.

Donny wasn't sure if the figure heard the crunch and grind of Agony's bones, or if he turned around at that moment by chance. But he looked over his shoulder, and his body jolted in surprise. Then he turned and faced them.

Donny realized that he knew who it was too. It was a face that was impossible to forget, with human flesh on one side and demon scales on the other.

"Chimera, looks like you've been busy," Angela said.

"Angela Obscura, the one and only!" he cried. Chimera clapped his hands, one of flesh and one of scales. He took his hat off and held it to his chest, and a wide smile spread across his face. When he spoke, he sounded as pleasant and reasonable as ever. "I can't believe you found us. You must have come from Cyprus. Would you believe, this was the last night of that operation? We knew you were on our trail, but I thought we were safe for at least another day." He squinted at Agony, who was running his blade across the tips of his bony fingers and emitting a low growl. "That's not my ferryman, is it? Oh dear. I can only imagine what happened to him."

Agony gave the same answer as before. "He is smoke and dust."

"Is he really?" Chimera said. He shook his head and clicked his tongue. "Well, now you've gone and killed both of them. And that's a shame, because we had room for many more souls. I guess we'll make do with the thousands we already have." Chimera's gaze landed on Donny, and he smiled again. "And look who else has joined us! The little mortal! It's Donny, isn't it?"

The greeting was so warm that Donny opened his mouth to answer, but Angela spoke before he found any words.

"Where exactly are we, Chimera?" Angela asked. "Are we in the Depths? Is this the hole that the Merciless slunk into after the war?"

Chimera frowned and folded his arms. "There's no need to insult me. You're not in the depths. You're in a cavern under my pillar. This has nothing to do with the Merciless."

"All that talk about getting along, understanding one

another better," Angela said. "And here you are with your personal Pit of Fire. You lied to my face!"

Chimera put his hat back on and took a step toward them. Donny noticed an instrument slung around his neck—it looked ancient, like something carved from the horn of an animal. "I never lied to you, Angela. I told you that if the council was in favor of the Caverns of Woe, I accepted that ruling." Chimera tapped his fingertips together. "But nothing prohibits us from building a pit for our amusement."

Angela stomped a foot. "Chimera, this ends now. You will surrender the dead at once. We had an entire civil war over this, or perhaps you've forgotten."

Chimera chuckled and rolled his eyes. "Oh, Angela. Why can't you understand? I'm not being unreasonable here. *You're* the inflexible one. You won't even talk about compromise! Why can't you have it your way, and let the true believers have it our way? This pit isn't hurting anyone!"

The screams of the dead poured from the flames. Angela sneered. "Not hurting anyone? Did you really just say that?"

"Oh, you know what I mean," Chimera scoffed. He pointed toward the pit. "Do I have to remind you? Those are the wicked dead in there, Angela. They murdered! They robbed! They were cruel and selfish! They preyed on the weak and defenseless! This torment is what they deserve. From the beginning, this is what the underworld was meant to be."

"It wasn't just the wicked souls, Chimera," Angela snapped. "Your ferryman friends captured good souls too."

Chimera frowned and raised his hands in a little gesture of surrender. "That is a perfectly valid point. Believe me, I asked them to stop. Apparently the good souls were more delicious than the bad ones, and my ferrymen insisted on that reward. I'm as disappointed as you about that."

That remark triggered a rasping, furious breath from Agony. "Enough of this," he growled.

"Time's up, Chimera," Angela said. She drew her sword. Flames swarmed along its length, brighter than ever. "Let those souls out of that hole, and I won't slice you like a stick of pepperoni."

Chimera took another step toward them. "Angela," he cooed. It was the voice of calm and reason. He cupped a hand behind his ear. "Listen to those cries! That is the song of infernal justice! I don't think you understand what this means to some of us. Just because you could leave it behind doesn't mean that we could. We *need* it, Angela. We crave that music, and we must have it. Even those two ferrymen left their brothers and joined this cause because they wanted to hear it again."

Angela whipped the blade through the air. "Ask them how that worked out."

Chimera rubbed his human eyebrow, as if he'd developed a headache. "You wound me deeply, my old friend. I don't imagine you'll just walk away and let this be my secret?"

"There's not a snowball's chance of that," she replied.

Chimera sighed. "Well, I suppose I don't have any choice."

"Out of choices. Out of time."

"This is a real shame. I've tried to reason with you. But when reason fails . . . well, there are always other ways. As you might have guessed, I am not alone in this." Chimera lifted the horn to his lips.

CHAPTER 49

When Chimera blew his horn, it was so much louder than Donny had expected. The notes rose high and clear over the cries of the dead.

There was a rumble of chains and squealing metal behind them. Donny spun around to see a gate of bars fall over the mouth of the tunnel. It crashed to the ground and cut off their exit. There was a large, toothy imp in an alcove above the tunnel, who had dropped the gate. The imp raised a spiky club and leaped out, meaning to land on top of Angela. It was a poor decision. Agony snatched the imp out of the air by the leg, whipped him in a half circle, and flung him against the bars of the gate.

By the time Donny turned back around, dozens of demons and archdemons had emerged from the pit, bounding up steps that were hidden by the fire. Each had a sword, a spear, a trident, or some other nasty weapon.

"There is something else in the flames," Agony said. He pointed with his curved blade.

At the far end of the pit, Donny saw a disturbance in the fire. Something huge moved toward them under the surface. Hot waves rippled aside in its wake. The flames bulged upward and broke like water, and an enormous creature leaped out of the pit. Donny felt the ground tremble when the creature landed. Ribbons of flame poured off the towering monster and slithered back into the pit like snakes. This creature was bigger and more horrible than anything Donny had seen so far. And yet he knew what it was.

"Donny," Angela said, "remember when the water imp attacked you, and I said it could have been worse, it could have been a titan imp?"

Donny couldn't talk at the moment, so he nodded.

She pointed with her sword. "In case you still wondered." The titan imp looked just the way she'd described it. *Absolutely massive. Insanely strong. Dark purple with yellow spots. Claws like garden spades.* This was the King Kong of imps.

Chimera sidestepped out of the path of attack. "My friends!" he shouted to the demons and archdemons behind him. "Angela Obscura has forced this upon us. We must kill all these intruders to keep our secret safe—Obscura, the ferryman, and the mortal!" The demons hissed, and the titan imp bellowed.

"Agony," Angela said. "We can't handle that titan imp,

even together. But don't worry: we have a way out." She backed toward the wall of the cavern.

Agony seemed perfectly content to retreat alongside her. "I am glad to hear it," the ferryman said.

Donny finally managed to get his voice working again. "Fire escape?"

Angela nodded. "Absolutely. Just throw it against the wall."

Before he could draw the red vessel from its pouch, he heard a thunderous crack. When he looked up, the titan imp had reached for one of the hanging stalactites and snapped it off. In the same motion, he hurled it at them. It came in a blur, spinning like a propeller.

"Donny!" Angela screamed. She threw herself in front of him. The stone hit the ground and broke into fat chunks that rolled like dice. One struck Angela hard. It knocked her sword from her grip, and she slammed into Donny. They tumbled across the ground.

Donny rolled to a stop and lifted his head, seeing double. The largest chunk of stone had tumbled on top of Agony and pinned him there, his arms and legs twitching on either side. Angela was barely conscious. Her eyes were closed and her teeth were clamped tight. Steam leaked from a gash on her temple. She pulled the bracelet off her wrist, to start the transformation that would help her heal.

The ground trembled. As Donny got to his feet, he looked back to see the titan imp coming at them. The red bottle was still in Donny's hand—he had managed to hold on to it when he'd fallen. He tugged it from its pouch and lifted it over his shoulder like a football, ready to dash it against the wall.

If he did that, a fiery portal would open instantly, and he would be able to escape. Angela was still on the ground, unable to rise, barely aware of what was happening. Could he open the portal and drag her through before the monster was upon them? There was no chance of that. Angela was doomed, and if he tried to save her, he would only die with her.

A shadow fell across him as the titan imp blotted out the light of the pit. The beast was two steps away. Donny looked again at the vessel of glass, and a wild idea came to him. Before it was even half formed in his head, he acted on it. With all the strength he had, he hurled the vessel at the titan imp. The red bottle spun through the air and smashed into the imp's chest. The beast was reaching for Donny, those deadly claws inches away, when a great circle of flame blossomed.

A cloud of smoke exploded from the spot. Donny heard the imp roar, and then the roar ended with a sick, soggy gasp. The sooty cloud shot past Donny. As it passed, he was sure he heard a whispering voice amid the smoke. He'd heard that sound before, when Angela spoke her incantation to open a fire-portal.

Of all the insane sights he'd seen since meeting Angela

Obscura, this was the craziest yet. The titan imp rocked unsteadily on his feet and stared dumbly at a gaping hole in his chest. The hole was round, ragged, and ablaze at the edges. It was covered with a thin membrane of ash that was suddenly clawed open from the other side. When the ash was gone, it revealed a familiar sight. Donny was looking into the lost temple in the Himalayas. As the titan imp staggered, the vision of the temple shifted with him, as if it were on a television lodged inside the beast's body.

The temple was currently occupied by a small army of heavily armed, glossy white and black imps, some large and some small, who stormed forward and leaped out of the hole, two by two. *Ungo's chessmen!* thought Donny. Even the titan imp seemed to be astonished as he witnessed the bizarre sight of armed imps leaping out of his torso. He even reached out and grabbed a black pawn around the waist, but he was too feeble to hold on for long. The monster's strength gave out completely. He fell, his back against the wall of the cave, and his head wobbled and sagged to one side.

Chimera and his gang were stunned by the sight. As more and more of the chessmen emerged, they paused, as if wondering how many opponents they would be facing.

Ungo Cataracta was the last to leap from the portal. Steam blasted from the cracks in his skull. He looked startled for a moment to see what he had stepped out of. Then he noticed Angela on the ground.

"Angela!" he cried.

Angela was fully transformed into her sleek-scaled demon form. She was still weak, but at least more alert. "I'm fine. My human saved me. Do me a favor and put Chimera in chains, will you?"

Ungo turned toward Chimera, his gaze furious. Chimera stood at the center of his small army, armed now with a pair of long daggers. Ungo pumped his long-handled, ax-headed weapon in the air. He screamed and charged, and his chessmen followed.

Donny felt a hand on his ankle. He saw Angela looking up, her eyes just starting to focus again. "Genius move," she said.

"Thanks," said Donny.

Her voice was still thick and groggy. "Not your move. Mine. I had Ungo and his chessmen waiting in the temple. The fire escape was to summon them." She rubbed the side of her head and surveyed the situation. Chimera's demons had backed away and made their stand on a narrow ledge on the far side of the pit. The chessmen charged and slashed, pushing them back. The pawns fired crossbows, and Chimera's demons shrieked with fury when the arrows struck.

Donny saw Ungo and Chimera in a duel, apart from the others. Ungo had lost his weapon, and they grappled for control of Chimera's daggers. Then something else at the near edge of the pit caught Donny's attention. He tapped Angela's shoulder and pointed. "Look!"

Human souls stumbled and crawled up the stone steps, out of the pit. Even when they emerged, the flames reached out like tentacles and wrapped around their ankles. When they finally broke free of the flames, the souls rolled on the ground and swatted at their bodies, as if the pain was still fresh, before looking around in a daze.

"Get them all out of the pit and through the portal, before it goes out," Angela said. She sat up and winced with pain, and then put the bracelet back on, to heal herself further with another transformation. "If we lose this fight, that's our only chance to set them free."

Behind them there was a rough crash. Agony had finally pushed the rock off his body. He got to his feet, bent and limping, and groaned with pain and fury.

Donny ran toward the growing crowd of souls. "This way!" he shouted. "You'll be safe if you come with me!" None of them moved at first. Donny grabbed one man by the arm and screamed into his face. "You want to go back into the fire? You will if you don't follow me!"

The man's face crumpled with fear. "Not the fire!"

"Then run this way!" Donny shouted. Some of them came running, but the rest looked confused and dazed. "Come on!" Donny screamed.

A long, bony hand rested on Donny's shoulder. "Leave this to me," Agony said. He stared at the lost souls and began to whisper and clack his teeth in that strange and ancient language of the ferrymen.

The souls stood up, straight and stiff. Every head turned toward Agony in unison. And then the dead began to walk in almost perfect lockstep. Thousands more marched out of the pit. "Wow," Donny said quietly. He remembered the way the souls stayed rooted in the barges, and how they walked to their fates in the Caverns of Woe, unable to do anything except what the ferrymen wished. That was the power the ferrymen held over the dead.

Donny ran to the front of the line and waved them toward the fallen titan imp. "Right in there!" he shouted.

The man who he'd spoken to was first in line. "This is madness," he said as he approached the burning hole. His body was under the ferryman's spell, but he was able to turn his head and speak.

"It sure is," Donny said, and he pushed the man gently through the portal and into the temple beyond. He reached out and tugged at the next soul, a wide-eyed woman. *"Gracias,"* she said hoarsely. Donny stepped back to let more souls through. He peered through the hole, into the temple on the other side, and saw what happened when they stepped into Tibet, into the mortal realm. The cold, waxy figures vanished within seconds. Only the twinkling lights of their souls were left behind.

CHAPTER 50

The fight was over. The last few hundred of the dead filed into the portal. Along the edge of the fiery pit, Donny saw the slain bodies of Chimera and most of his demons and archdemons, and a few of the chessmen, too. The rest of the chessmen came back toward him and Angela, helping their wounded along.

"Oh no," Angela said. Donny saw one of the largest chessmen with Ungo in his arms. Smoke billowed from wounds in Ungo's chest and arms. Angela ran to meet them, still woozy and unsteady on her feet despite the second transformation. She was back in her human form, this time with pure white hair that brushed her shoulders.

The chessman laid Ungo gently on the stony ground. "My dearest Ungo," Angela said. She knelt by his side and clasped his hand.

Ungo smiled. "So this is all it takes for you to speak with

such affection and to hold my hand? I would have gotten a fatal wound much sooner."

"Don't talk nonsense," Angela said. There was a ring on Ungo's longest finger. She tugged it off, and his metamorphosis began. It started with the hand and crept toward the wrist. The scales vanished inward and left human flesh behind.

"Too late for that," Ungo said, and wheezed. "I can feel the fire going out of me, Angela."

"Shut your mouth," Angela said. "You feel no such thing."

Donny watched the transformation lose momentum as it moved up Ungo's neck. By the time it made it to his chin, it stopped altogether. Donny gulped. *He's not going to make it,* he thought. He looked at Ungo's eyes and was shocked to see Ungo staring back at him.

"Did you say that your human saved you?" Ungo asked Angela.

Angela sniffed and nodded.

Ungo smiled and winced at the same time. "Maybe . . . he's not as worthless as I thought." The steam that flowed from his wound grew weaker. He gripped Angela's hand between both of his. "I slew Chimera for you," he said.

"Thank you," she whispered.

"But it appears he slew me, too." Ungo's voice faltered. "Angela Obscura, I am the last child of the Cataracta line. I bequeath to you my pillar and my chess set. They are brave and loyal, and will serve you well."

Angela shook her head. "Stop this at once. Dying is the worst. I won't allow it."

"I am sorry I will not join you on the council," Ungo said as the last trickle of steam wafted from his wound. "I would have . . ."

The cavern was suddenly almost silent, except for the snap and whistle of the Flames of Torment. Every lost soul had vanished into the portal. The chessmen gathered around them in a circle. They watched, as still as statues, as Angela folded Ungo's hands across his chest and ran her palm across his still-craggy head.

Ungo had treated him poorly, but now Donny felt like his heart was in a vise. Angela stood, cleared her throat, and looked at the chessmen. "Down that tunnel is a gate-keeper, fast asleep. She is a traitor. Bind her up and bring her to me." One of the white pawns nodded and sprinted away.

"Which of you is in charge?" Angela asked the chess-men. The tallest of the white and black pieces, emblems of kings on their chests, stepped forward. "You fought well. Did any of them get away?" she asked.

"A few," said the tall black chessman.

"Some of you, track them down," she told them. "Some of you, take proper care of Ungo's body. The rest of you, seal the entrance to this pit and guard it until we can have it extinguished."

She turned to Donny and brushed her hand across his hair. "Let's get out of here. The fastest way is through the fire escape, before it goes out."

"Okay," he said.

Agony still stood beside the portal. "Our work is done," he said.

"You coming with us?" Angela asked.

Agony shook his head. "I will find my way out of here and to the river. That will take me home."

She stuck her hand out. "I enjoyed our collaboration."

His long, bony fingers could have wrapped twice around her hand. They shook, and Agony strode away, creaking and groaning, limping from his injuries.

The white pawn returned with the gatekeeper, and Angela slung the unconscious imp across her shoulder.

The ring of fire around the fire escape sputtered. "Quick, before it goes out," Angela said. She and Donny hopped through. In a single bound, they traveled from a remote corner of Sulfur to the lost Himalayan temple.

CHAPTER 51

A hot-fudge sundae was normally the finest thing Donny could imagine eating. Cookie had even slathered it with melted marshmallow and a mountain of real whipped cream. But Donny's stomach was too sour, and he just pushed the toppings around with his spoon.

"I'm sad about Ungo," he said. Arglbrgl was beside him on the seat. The imp whined a little, said, "GRBLRGL," and then leaned over and gave Donny a sympathetic nudge.

"Even after he was so mean to you?" Angela asked. She stared off at nothing, dipping her tea bag up and down in a steaming cup of water.

"Yeah, even after that." He shoved the spoon deep into the ice cream so it stood up, and sat back in the booth. Ungo's death wasn't the only thing that bothered him. It was the discovery that Chimera was behind the missing souls all along. Chimera had seemed so reasonable, despite their disagreements. And yet he overlooked the loss of innocent souls and was ready to kill to protect his secret.

"It's a bummer, all right," Angela said. She dropped the tea bag onto the saucer and then sipped her tea. Neither of them said anything for a while, until she set the cup down and spoke again. "And it creates a brand-new problem."

There was a smear of hot fudge on the back of Donny's thumb. He licked the chocolate and then wiped off the rest with a napkin. "Are you talking about the council?"

"Yeah. Ungo was on my side. Now I've lost him, and I'm not sure who I can get to replace him."

"Right, but you don't have to worry about Chimera, either," Donny said. "And he was against you."

"I know. But if I don't fill at least one of those seats with an ally, we'll be worse off than where we started." She put her elbow on the table and rested her cheek on her fist.

Donny was wondering how to reassure her when he heard a booming voice in the street outside the diner. Whoever was out there was attempting, and failing badly, to sing in operatic style.

Cookie was behind the counter, reading a paperback book. She scrunched her face. "Sounds like a moose going under a steamroller," she said. Arglbrgl slid out from the booth and puffed himself up, his spikes jutting. He bared his teeth and growled.

Angela and Donny looked at each other. "Is that who

I think—" Angela started to say as the door to the diner burst open. Fiasco stood there and vomited his last note, his arms flung wide. Arglbrgl yelped, deflated, and hid under the table.

"Fiasco!" Angela cried. She ran to the door and leaped into his arms. Fiasco laughed and whirled her around.

"Angela Obscura! That charming two-headed fellow told me I'd find you here."

Donny walked to the door to greet him. "Hi, Fiasco."

Fiasco lifted Donny by the armpits and kissed him on both cheeks. "Donny Taylor! How good to see you again!"

Donny didn't feel at all like smiling a minute before, but now he couldn't keep the grin off his face. "You too! But I thought you said you'd never come back to Sulfur."

Fiasco put one hand on Donny's shoulder, another on Angela's. "Let me explain. But first . . ." He looked at Cookie, who watched warily from behind the counter. "Madame," Fiasco said. "What masterpiece of the culinary arts can you produce on a few minute's notice?"

Cookie puckered her lips and thought for a moment. "Grilled cheese?"

"*Perfecto!* Let there be grilled cheese!" Fiasco boomed. He looked from Donny to Angela and lowered his voice, as if sharing a secret. "My friends, something wonderful has happened. I knew the day would come, and at last it did."

"Tell us already," Angela said.

Fiasco's grin was as big as a keyboard. "My art has finally been recognized for its greatness."

Donny's eyes widened. Was Fiasco talking about what he *thought* Fiasco was talking about?

"The day you left Old San Juan," Fiasco began with a chuckle, "two special visitors came to my gallery." He strode back and forth and waved a finger dramatically. "They were being coy, but I knew who they really were. Obviously they were curators from some great museum, such as the Louvre or the Prado. Or perhaps the Metropolitan, now that I think about it. They were American women, and so astute in their appreciation that there can be no other explanation than an American museum."

Holy moley, Donny thought. He glanced at Angela, who wasn't completely buying what Fiasco was peddling.

"Very tricky of them, I must admit," Fiasco said. He scratched at the half inch of beard that had grown back. "Of course their plan was to acquire the art at a reasonable price, before my mastery became known to the world. I played along, because money means nothing to a true artist. Although," he added with another chuckle, "it must be said that I have bested the great Van Gogh in this regard, who barely sold any of his paintings while he lived, and died a pauper, miserable and somewhat depressed."

Donny figured he knew what had really happened, but

he had to be sure. "How many paintings did they buy?"

"A few small, and a few large," Fiasco said. "As many as they could carry. But I have a surprise for them when they return home. I cleverly coaxed an address from one of the women, and I packaged up all my works and sent them to her!"

"*All* of them?" Donny asked. He covered his mouth with his hand to hide his grin. Angela looked at him sideways. One of her elastic eyebrows arched high.

"Yes! Many hundreds! I imagine this museum will devote an entire wing to my works," Fiasco mused. He closed his eyes and rubbed his palms together.

"That's *completely* plausible," Angela said. "But, Fiasco, what will you do now?"

"Now that I have achieved my dream, I will vanish suddenly and leave behind nothing but an air of mystery! My disappearance will only enhance my fame," the big fellow said. Donny thought he heard a sigh of relief from Angela.

Fiasco clasped his hands behind his back. "And so you wonder, my friends, what comes next, now that I leave the brush and palette behind? What other form of human artistry shall I master? I must ponder this deeply. Poetry calls to my heart, and music beckons to my mind."

"I vote for poetry," Angela said. "Nobody can really tell if it's any good."

"I second that!" Cookie shouted from behind the counter.

Donny nodded. The horrible song still echoed in his mind.

Fiasco nodded sagely. "It will take some time to decide, of course. In the meantime, Angela Obscura, perhaps you could use a friend on the council?"

Angela's knowing grin expanded into a wide-open mouth. "Are you *serious*? Fiasco, I love you so!" She leaped into his embrace, and they laughed and hugged each other in a grip that would have crushed Donny like a bag of potato chips.

CHAPTER 52

I'm going to sleep for a day," Angela said as she shut the front door to her pillar home.

"Me too," Donny said. "I need a quick favor from you first, though." He held his hand out and showed his palm, where Angela's symbol was just a ghost of its former self. "Can you freshen this up for me?"

She stared at his hand, and then at Donny's eyes. "Of course I can." She held his wrist and pressed her ring against his palm, careful to position it over the same spot. There was the slightest tingle of pain, like a mild electrical charge. When she pulled the ring away, the symbol was crisp and white. Donny brought the hand to his face and inspected the fancy letter *O*. The curved shapes that extended from either side might have been the leathery wings of a bat or the feathery wings of an angel.

"In case I haven't said it already, I officially unrenounce you," she said.

Donny smiled and brushed his thumb over the symbol. "This mark . . . does it mean you own me?"

"It means I protect you," she answered. "You can leave anytime you want. I really mean that. But I hope you stay." She put her hands on both of his shoulders. "You mean the underworld to me."

"Thanks," he said. He knew his face was turning red, but he was fine with that. "You mean the underworld to me, too."

ABOUT THE AUTHOR

P. W. CATANESE is the author of ten fantasy-adventure novels. His books have been received with critical acclaim and have been translated into five foreign languages. His Books of Umber trilogy has been nominated for six regional book awards, including the Texas Bluebonnet Award, the Florida Sunshine State Young Readers Award, and the Pacific Northwest Library Association's Young Reader's Choice Award. He lives in Connecticut. When he's not writing books, Catanese draws cartoons, works for an advertising agency, and tries very hard to respond to every message from his readers. Meet him at pwcatanese.com, and on Facebook, Twitter, and Instagram.

"Oh no," the person said. And then the whole earth exploded into a zillion pieces, and everybody screamed and flew into space and died. Including all your favorite characters.

Ha! Just kidding. That was my little joke for you rascals who like to turn to the last page of a book before you read it.

Got you real good just now, didn't I?

All joking aside, this is your last warning, smarty-pants. Close this book immediately, open it from the proper end this time, and start reading. No fair peeking ahead to see how it turns out. And I'm certainly not going to tell you. If you ask me, there's a special place in Sulfur for people who spoil endings.

Gravely,

A. O.